Paths to

Stories of the joys and perils of old age

Craig Brown

RB
Rossendale Books

Published by Lulu Enterprises Inc.
3101 Hillsborough Street
Suite 210
Raleigh, NC 27607-5436
United States of America

Published in paperback 2013
Category: Fiction
Copyright Craig Brown © 2013

ISBN : 978-1-300-81052-0

Dedication

To Carole, Nick and Molly... caring friends

Acknowledgements

Firstly, my thanks to Valerie, who read everything and told me frankly what she liked and didn't. Some of my friends read extracts and I am grateful for their support, interest and encouragement. To Lorraine Chapman, Maria Davie, Liz Dibble, Tea Fisher, Sam Parsons, Rose Spratt and Carole Wood – my appreciation. Your being there helped make it worth doing.

.

Contents

Edward Grindle, For Example

Jacob's mother, Harriet, was the first to see the accident. Probably she was the only witness, as it was all over in a couple of seconds. Standing at the upstairs window, a slice of buttered toast held limply in her hand, she conducted her habitual early morning survey of the street, on this particular occasion vaguely interested to find how much of the weekend's snow had melted away overnight. Harriet noted that the road was clear, though the pavements wore ugly cancerous scabs of dull grey ice, impervious to the gradual increase in temperature.

She turned at the sound, craning her neck to peer up the street, where the ice patches were spread more thickly. The old man's cry was more a yelp of frustration or surprise than of pain, but damage had clearly been done, for he lay motionless on his side, one leg extended and the other drawn up under him, with a dark red jewel of blood already gleaming on the ground near his crushed ear.

Harriet chewed her toast and spoke with her mouth full. "It's Mr Grindle. He's gone down."

Jacob stood behind her, combing his hair in the mirror. "Gone down where?"

"I mean he's fallen over. Mr Grindle."

Jacob stared at her, still combing his hair. "Edward Grindle, for example."

"Quite. Only it's not funny."

Her son shrugged. Ever since his mother had discovered that Mr Grindle's initials were E.G., she had acquired the mildly irritating habit of announcing his appearance in the street with the declaration, "It's Edward Grindle, for example." Humour had never been her strong point.

Jacob joined her at the window. "He's not moving," he said.

"Looks like he's knocked out."

They stood gazing down at Edward Grindle, vicariously relishing a comfortable grandstand view of this small disaster. A

7

car came up the street, brake lights glinting briefly as it passed the inert body, and carried on.

"His wife," Harriet said. "Someone should fetch his wife."

"Sunday morning." Jacob sounded doubtful. "She'll be drunk, or sleeping it off. Routine."

"Even so. She ought to be told."

She slipped past him and into the next room. Jacob combed his hair in his reflection in the glass. Mr Grindle lay perfectly still, his head lolling over the kerb. The blob of blood had grown to a saucer-sized pool. Jacob exhaled anxiously, puffing out his cheeks.

Harriet was back at the window, nudging him to make room. "I've called the ambulance."

"Look!" Jacob pointed. "Little girl."

A small child in a denim skirt and a white anorak was standing astride a pink scooter, staring down at Mr Grindle. She seemed not to know what to make of him. Very slowly, she lowered the scooter to the ground and stepped into the road, pulling something from her pocket.

"What's she doing?" Harriet asked, more to herself than Jacob.

The girl tore at the object in her hand and prodded it at the old man's nose, leaving a visible brown smudge.

"It's a Mars bar." Jacob shook his head. "She's offering him a Mars bar."

"The last thing he needs," Harriet said quietly. "Jacob, go and get his wife. It's number sixty."

"She'll be out cold as he is," he protested.

"We don't know that. Anyway, someone should cover him up."

"He's not dead, is he?"

"I mean, to keep him warm. Hypothermia."

Jacob forced a laugh. "Mother, it's barely above freezing out there. I don't think a blanket'll make a scrap of difference."

They watched the little girl climb back on her scooter and ride off, chewing her chocolate bar, leaving Mr Grindle with a brown nose.

"One of them foil blankets," Harriet said. "Like they give you on the London to Brighton. That's what we need."

"What?"

"You know, silver foil."

"Oh, right. You mean, the London Marathon, Mum. The London to Brighton is a veteran car run."

"Is it? Whatever. I get them two mixed up."

He sighed. "Okay, so I'll just go to our airing cupboard and fetch a couple of foil blankets from our plentiful stock, shall I? Get real, Mum."

"Poor old man. Go on, Jacob, please. Mrs Grindle needs to know what's happened."

"I tell you, she'll be pissed."

"Do it, Jacob. It's only across the road."

Jacob went to find his coat. His mother made herself a fresh slice of toast and brought it to the window to watch him cross the street. She hoped he had wrapped himself warmly and wouldn't catch cold. You couldn't be too careful.

Some of the houses, including number sixty, had been converted into flats. Jacob reasoned that if he pressed the bell marked 'Grindle' and received no reply, someone else could probably be relied upon to let him into the hallway. He pressed the Grindles' button twice, but heard nothing. Stamping his feet to keep his blood circulating, he saw a movement in the downstairs window and waved his hand. A man with his coat on and a dog on a lead came to the door.

"Sorry. I wondered if Mrs Grindle was in."

The man snatched the dog towards him. "Huh. You can go up and try. Most prob'ly drunk."

"Yes. Thanks."

Jacob felt the door slam behind him as he slowly climbed the stairs. At number sixty he tapped on the door, then saw that it stood ajar. Old Grindle had probably gone out for cigarettes and not bothered with his key. So Jacob gingerly pushed the door open and crept inside.

"Hello. It's me, Jacob from forty-seven. Can you hear me?"

There was no answer. The place was in darkness. Waiting for his eyes to adjust to the gloom, he heard ragged, constricted breathing from the shadows ahead of him, and he moved forward to ease open a dark-painted door. A dim shape appeared on a bed, vaguely silhouetted against the pale wash from a curtained window.

"Mrs Grindle? Can you hear me? It's me, Jacob, from number forty-seven."

"Aaahmm."

"Mrs Grindle?"

He ran one hand over the wall, searching for a light switch. Then a yellowish glow from a naked bulb permeated the room.

"Mrs – oh my God!"

Edward Grindle's wife lay on her side facing him, her nightdress askew, one pendulous breast exposed.

"Are you asleep? I've come about Edward."

Mrs Grindle stirred and shifted, but did not open her eyes.

"Mrs Grindle, your husband – he's had an accident."

Jacob peered at the old woman, his nose and mouth wrinkling in distaste. Her left breast was splattered with vomit. A tawny porridge trailed over her arm and down the edge of the bed to the floor. On the bedside table, a capsized tumbler lay next to a half-empty bottle of Gordon's. The room smelled putrid.

"Can you wake up, Mrs Grindle? It's about Edward."

"Mmm?" She worked her lips, blowing a viscous bubble.

Jacob considered his position. He had done as his mother had asked, but his limited reserves of neighbourly concern did not extend to cleaning up old women covered in sick, nor even to touching them.

A blue light flashed through the curtains. Jacob switched the bedroom light off and went downstairs to the street. An ambulance was parked next to Mr Grindle's body. Two thin green-clad paramedics, splay-legged like stick insects, were attending to the old man's misshapen bulk.

Jacob walked quickly to the ambulance. Glancing up, he saw his mother watching from the window. "We dialled 999," he said to a ginger-haired paramedic. "He slipped on the ice."

"Okay. Do we know his name?"

"Yes, it's Edward Grindle, for example." He shook his head. "I'm sorry, I mean – he's Edward Grindle."

The other paramedic, fussing with his bag, barked in Mr Grindle's ear. "You in there, Ted? My name's Roy."

Jacob felt himself flinch at the familiarity, which seemed almost grotesquely inappropriate in the circumstances.

"No-one with him?" the ginger man enquired.

"His wife's at number sixty. I tried to get her, but she's pi- she's drunk."

Ginger man sniffed, thumbing his nose. "Well, he's half froze. What's that brown on his nose?"

"Chocolate," Jacob said.

"Eh? Why's he got chocolate on his nose?"

Jacob sighed. "Does it matter?"

The other stick insect was bald. Jacob thought his head must be very cold.

"Let's get him loaded," the bald man said. "Cracked his head, could be bad."

Standing back, Jacob watched them shove Mr Grindle unceremoniously into the ambulance. A pool of dark blood was already thickening to raspberry ice on the kerbstone.

The ambulance revved noisily and lurched away, blue light spinning.

"Bye, Mr Grindle," Jacob said.

They delivered Edward Grindle to the Emergency Department at St Joseph's. On a count of three he was hauled on to the hospital trolley and examined by a blonde nurse and a young Chinese doctor with a shock of black hair tufted into a duck's tail at the back. The nurse looked worried, but the doctor remained expressionless.

"This man is blue with cold," the nurse said.

The doctor stared impassively at Edward Grindle. He picked up the old man's wrist, blinked, and applied two fingers to the side of the scraggy neck.

"This man is dead," he said.

"He fell down in the street," said the nurse, superfluously.

Another doctor arrived. He had bleary eyes and designer stubble.

The Chinese doctor yanked off his stethoscope and stuffed it in his pocket. "You can take over," he said to his colleague. "I'm due for a break."

"I wonder what happened," the nurse said meekly.

"He got old," the Chinese man told her. "He fell down. End of."

The nurse carefully wiped the blood from the side of Mr Grindle's cheek. "Poor old man."

"Going for some nice buttered toast," the first doctor informed them.

The nurse nodded absently. She clasped Mr Grindle's ice-cold hand and warmed it with a smile.

Going Out With a Bang

On the side of the box it said 'Heinz Baked Beans – 57 Varieties'. Harry had been given the box by Maggie in the canteen. "To put all your bits in," she'd said, with a girlish giggle. Harry Mountjoy always thought of it as the canteen, but strictly speaking it was the staff restaurant, and Harry's terminology was simply a reflection of his advancing age. With some difficulty he had weaned himself away from calling the sofa the settee and the radio the wireless. Dear Marian, God rest her soul, had referred to the stereo as the gramophone and called ITV the Light Programme. Old habits die hard. Not that Harry wanted to forget the past; he merely needed to adjust to the present. The past was a friendly house to revisit occasionally, but you didn't want to get locked in.

Now Harry sat at his desk with his legs stretched out and wide apart, the Heinz box between his ankles. Slowly, for there was no need to hurry, he emptied his drawers into the waste bin or the box, according to a careful evaluation of the contents. It was the kind of task he liked: quiet, restful, personable, uncomplicated.

Someone came to the door, a middle-aged lady with immaculate blonde hair, a navy-blue suit and a pleasant, open face. Smiling, she tapped on the door with her knuckles, although she already stood in the room.

Harry looked up, drawing in his legs. "Hello, Ruby."

"Good morning, Harry. Bit of a sad job?"

"What? Oh no,no, not really. When you've got to go..."

Ruby nodded sympathetically. "Sixty-five at the weekend, is it?"

"Saturday. Long weekend coming up, you might say."

"I suppose." She sighed and, just for a few seconds, looked a little unhappy. "Harry, will you be in here tomorrow lunch-time?"

"Well, yes. I don't leave till tomorrow."

"But you aren't going out to lunch?"

"Oh. No, I thought I'd just - you know – bring a sandwich."

Ruby smiled and her blue eyes sparkled. "Oh, I think we can do better than that, Harry. You be here at twelve-thirty and – well, there's to be a little get-together for you in the Board Room. Your friends would like to say Goodbye to you, of course. And – and we've had a bit of a collection for you, and I dare say you can guess what we've got you."

Harry grinned broadly, swallowing to control his embarrassment. "Well, that's very nice. I shall look forward to it. You're very kind."

Ruby shook her head, gently refuting the allegation. "The least we can do. Twelve years with the company, Harry. These days that's a long time."

Harry lowered his gaze and nodded thoughtfully. He studied the box and wondered if it would be big enough. "So will you – er...?"

"Will I? Oh, will I be doing the presentation?"

"Yes."

"I'd like to, Harry, as you can imagine. But there's, you know, protocol and all that. Ann Minster is coming to say a few words and present you with your gift. I'll still be there, naturally."

Harry's head slumped towards his chest and his eyes seemed to go out of focus. "Why her?" he asked. "Bloody Ann Minster. You know she doesn't like me. Protocol!"

"I understand, Harry, but she is the Unit Manager. And, despite what you might think, she is deeply understanding of your contribution to the department over the years."

"Sod it, Ruby! Ann Minster nearly got me sacked!"

"That was all an unfortunate misunderstanding, Harry. You were completely absolved from blame."

"Ruby, my name was dragged through the mud for weeks. They said – Ann Minster said – I'd tried to falsify company records. Turned out it was somebody else who they should never have employed in the first place. And all Ann – "

14

"She apologised to you, Harry. She even put a paragraph in the journal."

"All Ann Minster did was cover herself by explaining why she thought it was me. Then she shook my hand. Call that an apology!"

Ruby shrugged awkwardly. "Water under the bridge, I think. A long time ago now."

"I might have forgiven, Ruby, but I've not forgotten. Worst days of my professional life. And all down to bloody Miss Monster."

"Yes, well, I don't think you should call her that, Harry. Let bygones be bygones, you know."

"Hmm. Can't you do the thing?"

"Love to, Harry. But it's all arranged. It'll be fine, you'll see."

Harry sat back in his chair, blowing out his cheeks and making a popping noise. He and Ruby Tatchell stared at each other. Ruby was the best office manager he had ever had. He would miss her, miss her calm fairness and gentle good humour. For now, there was nothing more to be said. He would go back to his box and then get himself a coffee. It was nearly lunch-time, but suddenly his appetite had gone.

At the hot drinks machine, he met Bert Stagg from Planning and Lucy Whittaker from Administration. Bert had a raddled face and ill-fitting clothes and looked older than his fifty years. Lucy was forty years Harry's junior. Harry stood close to her, inhaling her body.

"Nice scent," he told her.

She peered at him over her shoulder. "Perfume, Harry," she corrected him. "Scent's what you get off animals."

"Ah. That's me put in me place."

Lucy took her drink and moved aside. "Well, thank you, anyway. Is that right, you're leaving tomorrow?"

"Yes. Retiring. Sixty-five Saturday."

"Oh. I'll miss our little chats." She sipped her coffee and eyed him over the rim of her mug. "They having a do for you?"

"Apparently. Half past twelve, Board Room."

"I'll try to come down, see you off."

"Thanks, Lucy."

Waiting for the microwave to ping, Bert Stagg caught his eye, glanced at Lucy and winked lasciviously at Harry.

"Your pot noodle not cooked yet, Bert?" Harry generally found Bert's hulking presence intimidating.

The red-faced man studied the digital window. "Thirty-four seconds," he growled.

Harry wondered if Lucy would wait thirty-four seconds so he could be alone with her. They had always got on well, considering. Considering he was old enough to be her grandfather. She was attractive, but not exactly pretty. Her breasts were small, but rounded and held high. When she wore jeans, her bum was gorgeous, poetry in motion. In his fantasy world, Harry imagined Lucy Whittaker's naked bum with *Made in Heaven* stencilled across her buttocks. Perhaps he could ask her the name of her perfume, sort of showing an innocent interest. Then he might buy her some at Christmas; except, that could seem a bit forward, an old man trying too hard. Forget that. He like it when it rained, because then – not always, but sometimes – Lucy sat in the restaurant and had a pizza slice and didn't mind if he sat next to her. Once, he recalled, smiling to himself, she wore a mini-skirt and as they talked, her thigh rubbed his knee, and he dared to wonder if she'd done that deliberately. For a moment, Harry's hopes rose, and not only his hopes.

"Better go back," Lucy said. "Filing to do."

"What's that – filing yer nails?" Bert interjected.

Harry ignored him. Lucy rolled her eyes in mock contempt. She touched Harry's arm. "I'll see you tomorrow," she said.

"You don't need the microwave, then?" Bert asked her.

"Just getting a drink, Bert. Got a sandwich in the office."

Bert sniggered behind his hand. "Ah, active young girl like you. Should have more than that this cold weather. You need something nice and warm inside you."

"I shall ignore that remark," Lucy said, wearily.

Harry watched her back as she walked slowly up the corridor, holding her mug at shoulder height.

The microwave pinged and Bert rummaged about inside. "Reckon you could be in there," he said. "Hee, I bet you'd mount her with joy, eh, Mountjoy?"

Harry exhaled laboriously. Bert always had to reduce every relationship to its basest level, human interaction distilled to the lowest common denominator. He picked up his plate and his microwaveable cheeseburger and swaggered out.

For some reason he started thinking about Marian. Four years she'd been gone. God, he missed her, all day and all night. Of course, that was one of the reasons he'd chosen a Teasmade for his gift. Well, all right, you couldn't have it off with a Teasmade, but at least it would go a little way to making up for Marian's early morning kindness of bringing him a cup of wake-up tea. That was just one of the small gestures he remembered and missed. Dear Marian. So by the weekend he could wake up to a soft light and a clock and a pot of tea and even a radio playing his favourite music. It was a good choice. He hoped Marian would understand and wouldn't think he was replacing her with a machine.

Once, when Marian had met him at the office, she had seen him saying Goodnight to Lucy Whittaker. Bless her, Marian had greeted Lucy like a friend, though they had never previously met.

"Nice young lady," she said, when they got to the car.

"Just a work-friend, nothing much," Harry assured her.

"She had a nice smile for you."

"I suppose."

"Course, you know how it works, Harry."

"What?"

She shook her head, grinning through the windscreen. "Harry Mountjoy, aged twenty-five. Young girl sees him, thinks to herself, 'Hey! He's a looker, give him a smile, never know, I might get lucky.' Harry Mountjoy, aged sixty. Young girl sees him, thinks to herself, 'Hey! Poor old bugger, give him a smile, make his day.'

Harry shifted uncomfortably in his seat. "Right. And your point is?"

17

Marian fiddled with her hair in the rear view mirror, not looking at her husband. "My point is, Harry dear, it is imperative that in your fertile imagination, to avoid mortal disappointment, you do not allow the first scenario to become hopelessly entangled with the second."

"Hmm." Harry felt himself accommodated but not rebuked. "That what they call women's intuition?"

"Exactly. Drive us home, Harry, and just keep looking straight ahead."

On Friday morning Harry's cardboard box was full, and he closed the flaps and sealed them with Sellotape. He carried the box to his car and put it in the boot, taking care to leave space for his gift. Then he made a slow circuit of the building, chatting to colleagues and pausing occasionally to rehearse in his mind what he should say in reply to Ann Minster's presentation speech.

Just before twelve-thirty Ruby Tatchell appeared in the doorway. "We're ready for you, Harry," she said.

Harry straightened his tie and wiped his nose, in case there might be any excrescence about to emerge from it. In his childhood, his mother frequently warned him of this risk. "You've got a black man," she would say. In Weybridge in the 1950s, these were the only black men you ever saw.

Ruby's announcement made his heart thump. They were ready for him. It sounded as if his execution was imminent. Perhaps he should invent a last request. "Lead the way, Ruby," he said, and his voice seemed to falter.

The Board Room was crowded, the scene orchestrated by a low buzz of conversation, which abated to a virtual whisper as Ruby led Harry through the door. Red crepe paper had been spread over the table, and large plates of buffet food were still arriving from the kitchen. Wide-eyed, Harry licked his lips. They had gone to a lot of trouble. He felt proud. Someone tipped a salad bowl an inch too far, and a tomato rolled, bursting softly, on to the floor. Maggie from the restaurant hurried over with a cloth to wipe up the mess.

Just as he was enjoying the reassuring warmth of Ruby's arm on his shoulder, the sensation vanished as she stepped aside and, in the corner of his eye, he saw Ann Minster approaching with a pink envelope in her hand. Behind her, Bert Stagg entered, partially obscured by a large, colourful box cradled in his arms. Together, they manoeuvred the box carefully on to the end of the table.

An expectant hush fell over the room. Someone sneezed, precipitating a brief ripple of laughter. A man in workman's overalls coughed lustily, averting his face. Harry waited, wondering if somebody was going to fart, and hoping fervently that it wouldn't be him.

Ann Minster stepped forward, raising a hand to call for quiet. Harry turned aside, covering his mouth with his hand. "Nearly feeding time for the Monster," he murmured.

The Unit Manager, affecting ridiculous self-importance, timed her introduction by turning her head slowly to left and right, courting the full attention of the audience. Someone muttered "Get on with it," but to no avail. It appeared to those present, not least to Harry, that Miss Minster saw the occasion not as a mere celebration of Harry Mountjoy's achievements, but rather as an opportunity for her own self-aggrandizement. In a few seconds too fleeting to be noticed, Harry had become a tool in her personal weaponry, a shambling stooge who gazed forlornly at the floor and wished he could be somewhere else.

"I thank you all for coming," Ann Minster declared, at last.

"Is that it?" Harry hissed through his teeth. "Giss me present and I'll go."

"We are gathered here today…"

"Christ, she thinks it's a bleedin' wedding!"

"…to pay tribute to a man who has unstintingly given twelve years of his professional life to the service of this company." She paused to wave the envelope in the air. "This card bears the signatures and good wishes of more than one hundred people, an eloquent testimony to the respect and esteem in which Harry is held by so many of us, and a collective tribute to which

I, without reservation, would like to add my own message of appreciation."

Harry coughed, patted his lips and shuffled his feet as he struggled to remember what it was he had intended to say by way of reply.

"Of course, as some of you here may know, the long voyage has not been all plain sailing. At times Harry and I have not always seen eye to eye, but..."

"Ah, 'ere we go," Harry scowled.

"...but with the passage of time, our differences have been blessed with the mellowing light of resolution, and today I believe I can say with my hand on a heavy heart that in bidding a fond farewell to the ever-youthful Mr Mountjoy, we may all..."

Harry felt he had heard it all now. In so far as it was within his power to do so, he switched off his ears and decided to kill time by gazing around the room, waiting for the performance to be over. A few people, he noted, had already started eating the food, and there was also the faint clink of glasses and the soft fizz of Lambrusco from the far end of the table, sounds to which Ann Minster's unstoppable oration was to become but a droning counterpoint. The man in the overalls hitched up a sleeve to check his watch, prompting Harry surreptitiously to do the same. In the corner, Lucy beamed at him, waggling her fingers mischievously. By the open door, Ruby stood with arms folded, smiling pleasantly.

Perhaps, Harry mused, a study of the ceiling might prove an interesting diversion, and his eyes took off and soared above the room like toy helicopters. Over the window there was a yellowish stain, presumably from an old water leak. The patch suggested a map of Australia. Next to it, a tag of blue paper projected from the lintel, a stubborn remnant of last year's Christmas decorations. He noted how the candle bulbs in the chandelier had imprinted grey smudges on the white plaster. Then his eyes flew down and landed on the table, roaming among the cheese straws and sausages and sliced peppers and neat triangular sandwiches.

He jumped as something gripped his elbow. Ann Minster was seeking his attention, drawing Harry out of his reverie. With dabbing fingertips, he massaged the skin beneath his eye sockets like a man waking after sleep.

"And now, Harry, on behalf of all your friends and colleagues – that is, those present in this room and the many others who regrettably cannot be here today – it gives me great pleasure to present you with what we hope will be a long-lasting token of our grateful appreciation. I think you'll find it's exactly what you wanted, a most useful and practical gift by which you will be able to remember us each morning, as we all go off to work while you languish comfortably in your bed." She inclined her head towards Bert Stagg, poised at the opposite end of the table. "Mr Stagg, could you help me, please?"

Bert nodded and began to push the large gift-wrapped box along the polished surface towards her, but the plates of food were in the way, and soon he encountered the edge of the crepe cloth, whereupon he hoisted the box into his arms and offered it to Ann Minster. She stepped forward, accepted the burden and turned to face Harry once more. Harry waited. Ann Minster grimaced under the weight, smiled fleetingly in Harry's direction and, extending her left foot, planted her toe squarely upon the smeared residue of the dropped tomato. The rest of the scene was played out, apparently, in ghastly slow motion. Ann Minster's foot skidded sideways, driving her hip into the table, then she arched helplessly backwards so that the heavy box toppled away from her, while her scrabbling hands fought hopelessly to restrain it, salvaging only two ragged strips of ripped paper, flapping from crabbing fingers, as the entire cargo tumbled with a hideous crash to the wooden floor.

In a room crammed with people, silence sucked at the ears like a vacuum. Mouth hanging slackly agape, Harry stared in a kind of mortified wonderment at the wreckage strewn across the floor, shards of plastic scattered amid buckled cardboard. Ann Minster was crouching, almost on her knees, attempting to burrow into the broken box, her eyes gathering in the enormity of the damage, quite unable to meet Harry's disbelieving gaze.

Ruby Tatchell had not moved from the door, now standing with both hands pressed against her temples, as if to blinker the accident from view.

A single pulse throbbed in the room, a unified exhalation of dismay, as though even the walls themselves had been holding their breath. "Oh my God!" someone whispered.

Harry's feet seemed to have taken off without him. He had no awareness of how he reached the doorway, no physical sense of locomotion; but he found himself in the corridor and the walls and floor were lurching towards him, while ahead of him, if he could only get there before stumbling, the bright light of the exit gleamed, beckoned.

A voice rang out behind him. "Harry, wait – please!" Ruby stood with hands spread at her sides. "We – we can get you a voucher."

Harry ran with both arms outstretched, reaching for the door. "Don't bother!" he yelled, not turning round.

"At least take your card."

"Stick a stamp on it!"

"Harry, you've left your coat!"

He shouldered the door open, turning quickly to look at Ruby's anguished face. "Got coats at home, Rube."

"Harry, you're being ridiculous!"

The door slammed. Shivering in his shirtsleeves, Harry found his car, fumbled for the keys and dived inside. From where the car stood, by craning his neck, he could just make out the door he had come through. It was closed and in shadow, so Ruby must have gone back to the scene of the disaster. No-one else had followed her out. He was quite alone.

He started the engine and moved towards the exit barrier. His clutch leg was quivering on the pedal and his hands trembled on the wheel. When he got home, he would have a stiff drink, a Scotch, neat with no ice. Bearing left, he drove slowly down past the main entrance, immediately distracted by a red flash at the kerb. Someone was waving at him, a figure in a red jacket. Lucy. She stood precariously with one foot on the pavement, the other in the road. Harry's initial reaction was to keep on going, as though to stop now would be tantamount to a bungled attempt at closure; but he sensed the *whirr* and *click* of tumblers and ratchets in his brain, and knew that the innermost machine that moved him would not let him ignore her. Some things you just didn't do.

Powering down the passenger window, he pulled up and flicked the hazard switch. Lucy leaned in, forearms on the window ledge.

"Oh Harry! This is dreadful, just awful!"

"You're telling me," he said flatly.

"What'll you do?"

"Go home. Get pissed. Forget today ever happened."

Lucy nodded in evident approval. Her perfume wafted into the car.

Harry jerked his thumb across the windscreen. "Come round my side."

One hand trailing over the bonnet, she stepped into the busy road and pressed herself against the driver's door. "I'll get run over, Harry."

"I'm sorry about all this, Lucy," he said. "You're a good girl."

"Yeah, well. You – Harry, you will come back and see us – won't you?"

"Maybe. I suppose. Lucy - ?"

"What?"

"If I came back, would you come to lunch with me?"

"Love to, Harry. Ring Admin and ask for me."

For a moment he sat and processed this agreement. Go for it, Harry, he told himself. Faint heart, and all that. "Gotta go, Lucy. One more question."

"Go on."

"Can I have a kiss?"

She tossed her head, grinning broadly. "Course you can." And she angled her face through the window and kissed him softly, a little wetly, on the side of his mouth.

A van coming up behind hooted noisily. Frowning, Harry thrust two fingers out of the window and held them in the air.

"Harry, look, I – "

"It's okay, Lucy, you better go. Don't get into trouble."

With a final swift squeeze of his shoulder, she darted back to the pavement and up the office steps. The van eased slowly alongside, the driver mouthing something inaudible through his closed window. Harry smirked at him. He couldn't have cared less. His tongue slid out and licked the place where the girl had been. He tasted a damp stain of lipstick there. Lucy juice.

Moving off, he saw that the windscreen had started to mist up. Driving one-handed, he reached forward and drew in the fog with an extended finger: 'Welcome'. Then he turned the radio on, tweaking the volume to loud and louder. Pixie Lott joined him in the car, and he sang along with her. For the first time in hours, he smiled. Pixie was yelling in his ears. Harry was laughing, tears brimming in his eyes.

"Welcome, Harry-boy!" he yelped. "Welcome to the rest of your life!"

The Great Race

He had gone to the dentist. His son Roland had taken him in the car. They had only been out for an hour, so the delivery van must have arrived within minutes of them leaving the house. When they returned, it was there, standing in the hallway, brand-spanking new, and Martha was standing behind it, one suitably proprietorial hand resting on the back of the seat.

George smiled like the sun coming out and leaned heavily on his stick. He was panting from his walk up the front path and there was a thin track of dribble on his chin.

"Well, what d'you think?" Martha asked him.

Roland shut the door and seemed to hang back, somehow sensing that this moment was rather special for both his parents, their faces registering a childlike delight mingled with gentle pride.

"Isn't it beautiful?" Cautiously, so he would not overbalance, George stretched out a hand to stroke the tiller. "Did the man put it together?"

"Well, I certainly didn't do it, dear. He was very nice. I made him a cup of tea. He had a piece of carrot cake and he used the toilet."

George nodded, wondering idly if the last two statements were interconnected. Sometimes Martha's carrot cake was a touch indigestible. Her previous one had made him unusually loose.

"I'm glad I chose the silver," George said. "It looks a bit like a Mercedes-Benz."

Martha pulled a face. "I think that's a little fanciful, dear." She sighed. "I'm afraid we'll never be able to afford a Mercedes-Benz."

George appeared not to have heard her. His mouth hung slackly open, emitting a dangling cord of saliva. His eyes glittered with happiness.

25

"Come on, you two," Roland urged them. "Let me get by. I'll make us some coffee. Then you can carry on gloating."

The burgundy-coloured script on the side plate read *Pacesetter Rapide*. George ran the tip of his stick over it, wobbling slightly as he lost his support.

"How was the dentist?" Martha enquired.

"He was fine," George said, absently.

Martha shook her head and made a *tutting* sound. "Obviously I don't mean 'How was the dentist?' It hardly matters to me how the dentist was."

George slowly lifted his head and peered at her. "Well, you asked me that and I answered. You asked me how the dentist was, and I told you."

His wife blinked rapidly in exasperation. "What I meant was – how did you get on at the dentist? Did he say you had an abscess?"

"What?"

"George, just forget the scooter for a minute and tell me what the dentist said about your tooth."

Roland looked back from the kitchen. "Leave him, Mum. It's okay. Mr Davy gave him some antibiotics. He's filled the hole. Dad'll be right as rain."

"All right. I don't know why your dad couldn't have told me that."

"It'll do ten miles an hour, you know," George said, proudly.

"Yes, well you mind you don't run somebody over, dear, going that fast."

"I didn't say I was necessarily going to drive it ten miles an hour. I just meant that was its maximum speed."

"When the turbo cuts in," Roland added, and laughed.

"Hmm." Martha looked a shade doubtful. "I don't know why you couldn't have saved a few hundred pounds and gone for a more basic model, like mine."

George straightened up and stared her directly in the eye. "Martha, I am seventy years old. If I can afford the best, the shiniest, the most sophisticated, the fastest...then that's what I shall have. I mean, I could be dead next week."

"Yes, well, you probably will be if you go hurtling around the streets at ten miles an hour."

"Oh, don't worry, woman, I won't be hurtling anywhere. Safe driver, that's me. I passed my IAM test, remember."

"George, that was forty years ago. A lot's happened since then."

"What do you mean, a lot's happened? What's happened, exactly?"

"What's – well, you've done your leg in and started dribbling down your front and not being able to get out of your chair, just for starters."

George sniffed and looked hurt. Sometimes women went straight for the jugular. He had a good mind to point out Martha's moustache; that would silence her.

Next day dawned warm and sunny. George's tooth wasn't so painful. Roland had wheeled the new scooter into the shed alongside Martha's Pacesetter Junior. After a hurried breakfast, George limped down the path and sat quietly on his silver steed. Martha found him there, reading the owner's manual as though it were a gripping novel.

"Nice day. We could go out," he said.

"Go where?"

"You and me. We could go to the park on our scooters. What d'you think?"

She chuckled. "I doubt I'd keep up. Mine doesn't go ten miles an hour."

"How many more times? Ten miles an hour is the maximum speed. You don't have to go ten miles an hour. It's not a race." He averted his head, as if listening for something. "That's a thought," he murmured.

"What is?"

"Eh? Oh, doesn't matter. Just – come on, Martha. Fresh air'll do you good."

She grinned and nodded, touching his hand affectionately.

They cruised along the park walkway side by side. Martha's scooter was red with a big yellow basket on the front. It reminded George of Noddy's car. After a few minutes they saw

Mrs Pargeter from across the road approaching on her blue scooter, with her dog padding along beside her, his lead looped round the handlebars.

Mrs Pargeter waved and all three of them came to a halt together. The dog crouched on the grass verge and dropped a curly turd shaped like a Mister Whippy.

"Lovely day," declared Mrs Pargeter. She peered at the name on George's scooter. "I didn't know you had one of these," she said.

"He got it yesterday," Martha told her. "It goes ten miles an hour."

George sighed and shook his head.

Mrs Pargeter's eyebrows arched in apparent admiration. "Well, well. Mine only does six."

"Huh," George grunted.

"Tell you who else has got a new one," Mrs Pargeter said. "That spivvy-looking chap from The Laurels. Always wears a checked jacket and a cravat. Him with one leg shorter than the other." She fumbled in her pocket, frowning. "I thought I'd brought a poo bag."

"I think you mean Mr Hart-Dooley," Martha offered.

"That's him. Smokes a pipe. You don't see many pipe smokers nowadays. Myself, I like a pipe."

"What, you smoke a pipe?" George said, affecting surprise.

Martha nudged him with her elbow. "Don't be daft! She means she likes to see a man smoking a pipe."

Mrs Pargeter smiled gratefully. "His is called...er – it's a Lionheart."

"What, his pipe?" It was Martha's turn to be confused.

"She means the scooter," George said. He leaned back, looking impressed. "A Lionheart, eh? That's top of the range transport. Costs a pretty packet. Fast as mine, too."

"Yes." Mrs Pargeter produced a small plastic bag and rubbed it to find the opening. "His is green. He says it's British Racing Green."

"Hoo!" Martha sounded unexpectedly thrilled. "He'll be whizzing about like that Jackson Button!"

28

"The name is Jenson," George intoned, trying to defuse her enthusiasm. "Fancy. A Lionheart!"

As they turned for home, George drove with his head held high and his eyes lightly glazed with envy. Imagine. A Lionheart. Someone in the village had a Lionheart!

In the afternoon Roland took his mother into town to have her hair done. George waited until they had gone, then he found Mr Hart-Dooley's name in the phone book and rang the number.

"Hart-Dooley!" The barked response compelled George to stifle a snigger of laughter, for it sounded like some kind of mad chant. *Haart Dooooley!*

But once the introductions were over, Mr Hart-Dooley's tone mellowed and he warmed to the prospect of a rendezvous with a fellow enthusiast. George needed no second bidding, and he climbed aboard the Rapide and rode cheerfully round to The Laurels. Mr Hart-Dooley's flat was on the third floor, but he met George at the street door, the key to the Lionheart in his hand.

They quickly shook hands. "Good to meet," said Mr Hart-Dooley. "She's in the garage."

"Who is?" George asked.

"Me scooter." He cast a critical but appreciative eye over the Rapide. "Nice little motor. Like the rear view mirrors. Think I might get some meself."

To George's delight, he suggested they swap over and take each other's vehicles for a spin round the car park and grounds. George thought the Lionheart's acceleration was better than the Rapide's, but he preferred his own machine for its feeling of nimble manoeuvrability. For sure, the Lionheart was fast, very fast, but he wondered about controllability in confined spaces. At the end of the road test, he was impressed but a little less envious. The Rapide would suit him just fine.

"Care for a snifter?" his host enquired.

"Er...thanks. Did you like the ride?"

"Ah. Excellent little craft. Nippy little devil. Come on, have to wait for the lift. Walked down, can't walk up." He reached for George's hand again. "Name's Roger, by the way."

Mr Hart-Dooley's idea of a snifter was a rather large glass of twelve-year-old malt. George hoped he would be safe to drive back. Was it an offence to be drunk in charge of a mobility scooter? He swigged the Scotch, accepted another and decided to trust his luck.

It was a modern, sparsely furnished flat with a large flat-screen television fixed to one wall and an uncomfortable looking three-piece suite with wicker sides that ought surely to have belonged in a conservatory. Roger Hart-Dooley evidently eschewed creature comforts. Uncompromisingly confined by the rigid wicker arms and spartan cushion of his chair, George shifted awkwardly left and right, backwards and forwards, quite unable to relax. A low glass-topped coffee table in front of him carried an open local paper and two soft-porn magazines whose garish covers displayed naked girls with advertising labels perfunctorily censoring their breasts.

Roger noted the direction of George's gaze. "Sorry about the reading matter," he said. "You know how it is. On me own five years now." He coughed apologetically. "Got to exercise the old feller occasionally."

"Umm, why yes, of course." George took a deep slurp of Scotch and pushed the magazines under the newspaper.

Roger gesticulated at him with his glass. "On the phone, old chap...you said something about a race."

"Well, I – I sort of had this thought, talking to the wife. Never brought it up again. Probably just a daft notion, you know, only I quite – "

"No, no, not daft at all. Damned good idea." He proffered the bottle again. "Care for a replenishment?"

"Er – no thanks. She'll smell it on my breath, give me a roasting."

"Ah well. Another day. Yes, I like the idea, George. Time for British Racing Green to be seen in full flight about the village."

"Hotly pursued by Mercedes-Benz silver!" George added zealously.

"Yes, yes, of course. Need more than just the two of us, though. To make a proper race of it, I mean."

George's head was beginning to spin. He draped a hand over his eyes and took several deep breaths. "Could try to get four," he mumbled.

"Ye-es." Roger pensively rubbed a caressing thumb and forefinger over his salt-and-pepper moustache. "What about your – uh?"

"Eh?" George peered at him from beneath his hand. "Oh, you mean Martha."

"You said on the phone, she's got a little red job."

"Yes, a Pacesetter Junior. Loves it."

"Ah, right." He tugged at his cravat, as though to give his mottled neck some air. "I was thinking...what about that Betty Pargeter? Reckon she'd be a sport. Been round the block a few times, don'cha know."

"Has she now? Hmm. Actually, I was proposing something a tad more interesting than just round the block."

Roger sat back and stared at him. "What? Oh, I see, yes. Ha ha, yes. Very amusing."

"I thought perhaps a few laps of the park. Some tricky S-bends on the south side. Be more of a challenge." He burped and tasted unpleasant bile on his tongue. "But it'd be a good idea to have two men and two women. Sort of a more open event."

"Quite, quite. The way I see it, we invite the girls along and then we give 'em a damned good thrashing. Well, figuratively speaking, of course."

Despite his best efforts at concentration, George felt himself drifting away again. He imagined he and Roger Hart-Dooley administering a good thrashing to Betty Pargeter, only somehow once he had grasped the concept, it didn't bear thinking about.

"Look here!" Roger wagged a hairy-knuckled finger demonstratively in the air. "What we must have is a pre-race briefing. Have to set down some rules. Can't just go careering about like a bunch of lunatics. What d'ya say?"

31

"Actually "- George teetered to his feet and fumbled under the sofa for his stick – "I'd say it was time I was going. Could do with a bit of a lie-down."

"Here, you all right, old chap? Gotta be careful on that velocipede of yours."

"I'll be fine once I...um, I'll be fine."

Roger stomped lop-sidedly in front of him and opened the door. "Mind how you go. Here's looking forward to a great race, eh?"

Turning, George pivoted artfully about his stick and, with his other hand, clutched the door post for additional support. "Thanks Mr Ha- er...Roger. I shall speak to Martha directly. Maybe we can get you and – and Mrs Pargeter round to ours, make a few plans. Martha'll make some sandwiches, perhaps do a spot of baking." He tamped his stick on the floor enthusiastically. "She does a mean carrot cake."

Roger nodded. "Damned good show!"

Which indeed it was. A good show. Martha had baked herself to a frenzy. There was a cream sponge, a carrot cake and an apple shortcake. On a blue china plate at the table's centre were stacked a selection of neat triangular sandwiches, artfully arranged in overlapping tiers resembling the Sydney Opera House. Even George was impressed.

"Help yourselves," Martha urged them. "There's chicken salad, cheese and pickle or salmon and cucumber."

Roger Hart-Dooley, beaming, adjusted his scarlet cravat. "I say. You're spoiling us, dear lady."

"Oh you!" Martha flushed, tracing an anxiously tentative forefinger below her nostrils, where she had recently applied talcum powder in the hope of camouflaging her moustache.

Betty Pargeter leaned forward to load her plate with sandwiches. "Perhaps we should press ahead?"

"Quite so, quite so." Hart-Dooley's bad leg made a clicking noise and he winced. "Over to you, George, I think."

"Okay. Well, using the mileometer on my Rapide, I have planned a circular route around the park – well, it's a square, actually – measuring point four of a mile. I suggest three laps, hence one point two miles in total."

Martha rested a hand lightly on Hart-Dooley's arm. "Do try some carrot cake."

George grimaced at the interruption, lowering his gaze. "Best change into your brown trousers," he muttered under his breath.

"Yes, go on, go on," Roger enthused, reaching for a slice of cake.

"There's a rib of old bricks across the tarmac by those commemorative flower beds; you may have seen it. I thought we'd start from there, sort of take it as a start and finish line."

"Ah, got that feature at the Indianapolis Five Hundred," Roger said, approvingly.

"Indeed. Now my son Roland has a Union Jack left over from the Jubilee or some such, plus he has a chequered flag hanging in his garage. They'd be perfect, don't you think?"

"Hmm." Roger used his thumb and forefinger to wipe the crumbs from his mouth. "I suppose so. Course you know they don't use starting flags much these days."

George looked indignant and a little offended. "Of course I know. But what do you expect, Roger? An overhead gantry with five red lights and that Charlie Whiting with a computer?"

"No, no, please, I understand."

"You have some more carrot cake," Martha said. "Who's this Charlie Whiting? Is he in the race too?"

George sighed. "He's the official Formula One starter. I was merely being facetious, dear."

"Carry on, George," said Betty Pargeter.

"Right. Now we have to agree on the direction of travel. What do you think of anti-clockwise?"

"Certainly have to agree," Roger declared, waving his cake in the air. "Can't go thundering off in opposite directions. Be chaos, like the bloody dodgems."

"All right, we'll take that as agreed. Three laps, one point two miles anti-clockwise, Roland to flag the start and finish from the brick infill. Also he will wait at that point and call out the number of completed laps to each competitor as they pass, so no-one has to keep count."

"It seems to me," Martha said, "that the likely outcome will depend simply on which of you men with the fast scooters can get round first. Betty and I will be bound to follow up the rear."

"If you'd let me continue," said George, "I was just coming to that. The race must be completely fair."

"Carry on, old chap," Roger told him. "Delicious cake, my darling."

Martha blanched, unable to decide whether to be affronted or flattered by the familiarity.

"The thing is, we must be handicapped." George smiled triumphantly, considering this his revelatory moment.

Betty threw up her hands. "Of course we're blinkin' handicapped! That's why we've got scooters!"

"No, no, you don't – look here! I've worked it all out. You'll have to trust me. Two scooters can do six miles an hour, two others ten miles an hour. Right?"

Roger blinked obligingly. The ladies looked patiently baffled.

"Very well. So here it is. The only practical basis for calculation is to assume a constant. Thus, you ladies race at six miles an hour for the duration, taking twelve minutes flag to flag. That's one point two miles averaging six em-pee-aitch. Got it?"

"Damned fine work!" Roger growled.

"And the men average ten miles an hour, their race therefore lasting seven minutes twelve seconds. As I say, I've worked it out. Which means that we all four leave from the same point, but the ladies go first and the men follow at an interval of four minutes and forty-eight seconds. Roland will time the separation with his stopwatch. The pathway is hardly wide enough for four abreast, so the men will line up behind the women." He coughed, took a sandwich and gazed at it thoughtfully. "If my calculations are correct, we should all end up running together by the finish, hopefully for about the last hundred yards."

34

Roger Hart-Dooley slapped his thighs in satisfaction. "Jockeying for position, you might say!"

"Exactly," said George.

"Right on. Handicap race. Reminds me of the old Mille Miglia."

"Oh, do we have to wear crash helmets, like in a real race?" Betty Pargeter asked, sounding as if the possibility excited her.

"It is a real race," George replied sourly. "And no we don't, mainly because we don't want to draw attention to ourselves."

"I see. Right." Betty seemed disappointed.

"Prize!" Roger Hart-Dooley exclaimed, as though the idea had just occurred to him. "Think I'll just go for – "

George grabbed his hand as it reached for another slice of carrot cake. "Best not have any more."

"I – er...whyever not?"

"Could be certain consequences."

"Really?"

"Take my word for it," George said quietly. "Now about a prize."

"Yes. Can't have a competition with no reward."

Martha was busily rearranging the remaining sandwiches. The Sydney Opera House now languished in a state of terminal disrepair.

"I would suggest," George said, "we each put in a tenner, winner takes all."

"Very well," Roger said, still licking his lips. "Anything else?"

George tugged thoughtfully at his nose. "I don't know." He glanced at Martha. "I suppose there could be a victor's kiss. If I win, I get to kiss Betty."

"Hoo!" Betty giggled into her hand.

"And if I win?" Roger tweaked his moustache.

"You can kiss Martha."

"You can kiss my arse!" Martha declared defiantly.

"Ah, right." George massaged where his beard would have been if he had one. "Cancel that particular incentive."

"Think we're nearly there, old chap. Date and time of race?"

George nodded pensively. "How about Wednesday morning? Ten o'clock. Should be quiet then. Can't do it at the weekend, too many obstructions. Kids on bikes, women with pushchairs, you know the sort of thing." He shook his head disparagingly. "The park is an area for adult recreation, not a playground."

Betty hunched her shoulders and chuckled.

Martha stared unhappily at the untouched cream sponge.

George sat back in his chair, folded his hands in his lap and allowed himself a gentle, self-congratulatory smile.

"Wednesday it is." Roger Hart-Dooley clicked his leg and ran a finger round the inside of his cravat. "Should be a great race."

Wednesday dawned bright and dry. The competitors arrived at the starting line within minutes of one another, soon after a quarter to ten. Roland was already waiting for them, flags on the grass verge at his feet and a pair of binoculars strung round his neck together with a stopwatch on a tartan lanyard. Apart from a few isolated strollers, the park was deserted.

"Time for a formation lap?" Roger Hart-Dooley shunted his Lionheart eagerly backwards and forwards. "What time d'you make it, boy?"

Roland consulted his wristwatch. "Eight minutes to go."

"Need to get everything warmed up."

They made one circuit at modest speed before Roland called them in. He directed Martha and Betty to the front, side by side, with the gentlemen in alignment behind them. It was nine fifty-seven.

Roger flexed his hands on the tiller like a motorcyclist. He was wearing perforated driving gloves in thin blue calfskin. Both ladies had discarded their front baskets. George speculated that this was in the interests of aerodynamic efficiency, but Martha had simply reasoned that they would not be doing any shopping.

At nine fifty-nine Roland picked up the Union Jack. Betty grinned impishly and gave him a thumbs-up. Roland nodded and raised the flag above his head. Upon a swift flick of the wrist to check the hour, he dropped the flag and the two ladies swept away, gleefully maintaining parallel station. Roland stood with left hand outstretched, palm down, holding the men in handicap position, while with the Union Jack tucked under his arm, he operated the stopwatch.

"Feels like a damned long time," Roger grumbled.

When the time interval which George had calculated had elapsed, the women were already rounding the final curve towards the start line. With seconds to spare, Roland released Roger and George, who now had almost a lap to make up.

Roger punched the air as he accelerated away. "Hell for leather!" he cried.

Roland relaxed, studying the group through his binoculars. Martha and Betty rode in stately fashion, upright, staring straight ahead, while George and Roger were hunched menacingly over their tillers, mindful of the benefits of drag reduction.

At the halfway stage Betty Pargeter held a slender lead over Martha, Roger and George. Roger was leaning precariously inwards on the bends, and Roland hoped he would not lose his balance. He was surely the more aggressive of the two men.

Lowering the binoculars, Roland lifted a hand to shield his eyes against the sun's early glare. "I can see Betty winning this," he said to himself.

They completed lap two with only sixty-five seconds separating first and fourth. On the long straights the superior speed of the Rapide and the Lionheart was telling, as was Hart-Dooley's determined cornering. At each apex of the last two bends, he regularly cranked the inside front wheel off the ground, yelping with delight as his machine squatted back to the tarmac and lunged ahead.

"Banzai!" His battle cry carried on the wind.

Approaching the corner by the war memorial, the Rapide was nudging the Lionheart's rear wheels and George scented an opportunity to squeeze past Roger on the inside and spurt to challenge the ladies for the lead. Then he saw the black iron hoops embedded in the turf to protect the flower beds and was forced to abandon the attempt for lack of space. Roger, however, feared an attack and swung left to block the action, running with two wheels on the grass. To his horror, George watched in hypnotic disbelief as the Lionheart's left front wheel speared into a hoop at unabated speed, spinning the scooter round in a green blur and catapulting the driver from his seat on to the unforgiving flagstones. The rush of air in his ears could not obliterate from George's stunned awareness the crunching snap of Roger's neck as his flailing body smacked the stone pedestal and rolled over.

Roland saw the accident through his glasses. "Should have brought a red flag," he cursed.

Martha and Betty slowed and circled round to meet George by the upturned Lionheart. The seat had skidded away into some bushes and the tiller and base were mangled like a huge dead insect. For almost a minute nobody spoke. Roger's inert body lay crumpled on its side, one shoe on, the other in the flower bed. After a while Betty dismounted and stepped gingerly over the victim's legs.

"Don't touch him," Martha warned.

Betty stooped to peer into Roger's face. It was deathly pale. "His eyes are open," she said.

"Not a good sign," Martha advised.

Betty chewed the side of her finger. "Do you think he's – "

"We don't know," George said. "We ought to get help."

Roland arrived, panting. "Dammit, I forgot my phone."

They lined their scooters up neatly at the kerbside and switched off. They were still staring at Roger Hart-Dooley when the park keeper reached them.

"What's happened?" he enquired.

"He fell off," Betty told him, needlessly. "We were having a race."

The park keeper sucked in his breath, shaking his head. "Daft old buggers," he muttered.

"Perhaps we should try to keep him warm," George suggested.

"Best just wait," the keeper said. "I've rung for an ambulance."

"Oh dear," Betty moaned tearfully.

Some small children on bikes appeared behind them, gawping. Martha told them to go away. George, Martha and Betty sat on their scooter seats while the park keeper stood with his hands in his pockets, head lowered respectfully.

"He was such a nice man," Betty said.

"He loved that scooter," said George.

"He loved my carrot cake," Martha added.

"I can hear bells." Betty raised a forefinger and tipped her head to one side. "Must be the ambulance."

"That's an ice-cream van," Martha told her.

George crossed to the bushes and retrieved Roger's broken seat. He heaved at the inverted Lionheart and brought it the right way up.

"Maybe you should ring them again," said Betty.

"No need," the man said. "Look!"

They all followed his pointing finger towards the distant trees. Through the green lacework of the foliage a sparkling necklace of blue lights shimmered. Martha got up, went to Roger's side and put one arm around his shoulders. "There, there," she murmured.

Betty looked up at the gathering clouds. "You know," she said, "I think we're in for a spot of rain."

Not All It's Cracked Up To Be

When Percy came sleepily downstairs, wrapped securely in his tartan dressing gown over paisley pyjamas, Dot was already up and dressed, perched primly in her favourite lounge armchair with a tray of tea and toast balanced on her lap. Percy settled himself in the other armchair and smiled thinly at his wife, who peered critically at him over the rim of her teacup.

"You've got up then," Dot said.

"You're up early," said Percy.

"Eight-thirty. That's not early. It's you that's late."

"What time is it now?"

"It's nearly ten."

"I must have been tired."

"Huh. You must have been lazy."

"First Monday," Percy reminded her. "First week of my retirement. Think I'm entitled."

"Entitled to what? To lie in bed all morning? To sit in that chair all day?" She chewed the corner off a triangle of toast and stared at him levelly. "You can think again."

"I wasn't planning to do either of those things. I'm just up a bit later than you are. I've committed no offence. I'm not on trial."

"You'll be a trial if you don't have a plan. If you just sit in that chair all day."

"I can do what I like," Percy said testily. "I'm retired."

"What, from work or from life?"

"From work. I'm sixty-six."

"I'm sixty-seven," Dot said. "You won't catch me sat in a chair all day."

"I never said I was going to sit here all day. Anyway, you stopped work twenty years ago – twenty years when I was working to keep you."

"Pardon? I had the opportunity to leave, and I rather think I came home to look after you, to cook your meals, make your bed, tidy the house, do the garden, wash your clothes. I don't recall anything about stopping work. You've been my work ever since we were married."

Percy pursed his lips crossly, nodding his head. "I get it. So what is it you want me to do?"

"Well, you could get dressed for a start."

"I will when I've had my breakfast. Thought I might have an egg."

"Up to you. Just don't expect me to cook it for you. Retired now, time on your hands."

"I could make you some more toast. As you're sixty-seven."

"Don't patronise me."

"I wasn't. I just thought I'd be doing something useful."

"Hmm. If you want to be useful, you could get dressed and take my library books back, get me some new ones."

Percy smiled, perceiving a subtle shift in Dot's mood from destructive to constructive. At least, for the present, he suspected this was as good as it would get.

"Find me some Harlan Coben or John Grisham," Dot continued. "And get yourself something to read as well. You'll need a book if you're sat in that chair all day."

Percy boiled himself an egg, then he shaved and showered and put on a clean shirt, his sharply-pressed cavalry twills and a pair of two-tone deck shoes. He paused by the hall mirror and admired his sartorial elegance. Not bad for sixty-six, he thought. As the sun was breaking through early cloud, he decided upon a bracing walk to the library, about a mile away. From the hallstand he took a shopping bag and loaded it with Dot's books and a moleskin cap in case of an unexpected breeze.

Dot watched as he walked to the front door. "You could get yourself some lunch," she said.

"They don't do food in the library," Percy retorted, with his back to her.

"I mean, while you're out. Go to the pub. Act like a normal bloke." She wrinkled her nose. "What's that pong?"

41

He beamed at her from the open doorway. "Calvin Klein, *Eternity.*"

Dot rolled her eyes disparagingly. "Sounds appropriate. For a romantic assignation, you'll wait an eternity. You're forty years too late."

Outside, in the crisp sunshine and bracing air, Percy swung his bag as he walked, beyond discouragement. He noted how the sun highlighted the pastel panels on his deck shoes and defined the razor-sharp creases in his cavalry twills. There was lightness and freedom in his step, but his easy stride was not without a sense of purpose, nor did he deny himself the pervasive warmth of a carefully constructed self-awareness. At sixty-six, he was marching bravely into a new realm, embarking upon a new chapter in the story of his life.

The library was well-stocked with books but sparsely populated with readers. After handing in Dot's returns at the desk, he sat down at a table by the window, took a *Times* from the shelf and, stretching out his legs until his feet pivoted on the heels, slowly and methodically pored over each page in the manner of one who would confront anew the manifold complexities of the world.

A wooden trolley creaked into his sight, pushed by a young girl in a white blouse and pleated black skirt. Her name badge read 'Rebecca'. Percy looked up from the paper and smiled. Rebecca, busy with her books, paid him no attention. She had a pretty face, Percy thought, but her knees were a touch on the thick side. As she grew older, she would have trouble with those knees. As a major weight-bearing joint, knees were not to be trifled with, or they would surely wreak havoc in later life. Knees, in both the orthopaedic and the metaphysical sense, could be your downfall.

"Good morning, Becky," he ventured brightly.

She peered over her shoulder, brandishing a book in the air. "Actually, I like to be called Rebecca."

"Ah. Right. That's me told, eh?"

"If you don't mind."

"No, of course."

He turned over a page and found some interesting obituaries. God, three of these unfortunate characters were younger than him! Some people just didn't look after themselves. Like walking blindly through the wrong door and falling into space. Percy didn't have much truck with dying, suspecting that it frequently resulted from carelessness. His father had lived to be ninety-five, leaving his mother a scornful widow. At sixty-six, Percy considered himself a mature youth, born again with all his clothes on.

"Excuse me, Rebecca."

"Yes?" Rebecca probably possessed an engaging smile, but she was not about to switch it on.

"I – uh – I wondered if that pub up the road..."

"The Three Horeshoes?"

"I think so. I wondered if you'd been in there – if the food was any good."

"Umm. Once or twice. The chicken salad sandwiches are quite good, very filling."

"Is that so? In that case..." He coughed, let the newspaper drop and shuffled his seat conspiratorially towards her. "Would - er – would you perhaps care to pop in there later for a spot of lunch with me? Rebecca?"

Rebecca stared at him, a hefty volume of *War and Peace* held somewhat menacingly aloft above his head. "Actually, I don't think so. Rather busy, you see. Only get half an hour break."

"Really?"

"Yes. Sorry." She shoved the book into a gap on the shelf. "Must get on."

She bent down to grab another handful of books, and Percy studied the flexion in her knees. This young lady'll be heading for trouble, he thought. Could affect her in other ways. A man likes a good, strong pair of legs. Those knees, they'll swell up like vintage cheeses, give them twenty years. She'll not be marriageable material.

He folded the paper into a neat rectangle on the table before moving along the shelves, where he selected a Coben and two Grishams for Dot and a couple of biographies for himself. Leaving the desk, he layered the books carefully in the bag according to size and stepped out towards The Three Horseshoes. The gloomy bar was as quiet as the library and he felt oddly conspicuous as he approached the hovering barman, whose raddled face glowered at him through coal-black eyes.

"Pint of best bitter, please. And could you do me a chicken salad sandwich?"

The barman straightened a soaked beermat and shook his head grimly. "Don't do food on a Monday lunch-time. Start at five o'clock."

"I see." Percy, watching the man pour his beer, considered his options, which appeared almost entirely absent. "Packet of nuts, perhaps?"

"Peanuts, cashews, salted, dry roast, large, small." He pushed a pint glass across the bar and straightened the beermat again. "Full menu five o'clock."

Percy took a seat by the grimy window, manoeuvred his bag of books under the table and picked listlessly at a small packet of cashews. A middle-aged couple with backpacks came in and asked for a Ploughman's, eliciting only a dark stare as the barman mopped the woodwork. You'll be lucky, Percy thought. The couple settled disconsolately for two halves of lager and shambled past him to the back of the saloon.

Halfway through his beer, he glanced up at a tapping on the window and saw that the clouds had massed overhead and fat raindrops were beginning to splatter the glass. Percy had no coat and his smart clothing would surely be ruined if he had to walk a mile home in the rain. His free bus card was his passport to salvation, but he knew that the only bus route passing close to the house ran as an hourly service whose exact times were a mystery to him. Stuffing the nuts in his pocket, he reached for a final slurp of bitter and strode anxiously to the porch and a clear view of the road. The rain was falling harder and the darkening sky had relinquished its last tiny patch of blue to a vast baggage of iron-grey cloud. Then, as an infusion of hope and relief to his sinking heart, he saw it on the horizon: the yellow blob of a number twelve, threading its way between railings and parked cars, headlights glowing in the premature gloom.

Percy waved the bus down and jumped on at the stop opposite the pub car park. There were few passengers: an elderly woman with a wheeled shopping basket, a young girl with a ponytail, chattering on her phone, and two youths in tracksuits sitting at the front, laughing and slapping each other. Percy sat by the gangway and inspected his trousers, dappled with rain spots which he felt sure would disappear once the fabric had dried on a hanger at home. He gazed through the windows at the slanting rain, feeling the driver dab the brakes as the youths scrambled from the forward seat and rang the bell. They lunged towards the exit, still childishly punching each other, and as the bus shuddered under braking for their stop, the nearer boy overbalanced and fell roughly against Percy's shoulder, wailing some unintelligible apology as the pair stumbled away and leapt to the pavement.

"Bloody hooligans," Percy muttered under his breath.

He had to walk the last two hundred yards to his front door, marching rapidly with his head down as he fumbled for his keys. As he stood in the hallway, he was panting from exertion, a light sweat glazing his brow. He could hear Dot clattering cups in the kitchen and realised how much he was looking forward to a hot drink.

She peered from the doorway with a mug in her hand. "You want coffee? Or there's chocolate."

"Hi. I think – coffee, please."

Dot returned to boiling the kettle. "Get any lunch?"

"Er – no. Slight problem."

"You can do toast. Any good books?"

Percy's mouth quickly flooded with a searing acid of dismay. "Bugger it!"

Dot seemed to freeze, holding the milk in mid-air. "Now what?"

"I – oh Christ!"

"What's wrong?"

"The bag of books. My hat."

"What about them?"

"I must've left them in the pub. I put them under the table."

Dot leaned against the door jamb and closed her eyes. She sipped her drink, clutching her mug in both hands. "Are you drunk, Percy?"

"What? No, of course I'm not drunk."

"Well, if you're sober, you must be stupid. That was a new hat. I bought it for your birthday."

"I know. I'm – oh this is ridiculous!"

"Got it in one," Dot said. "Now I've got nothing to read."

"Forget the coffee. I'll go back. I'll get my coat and catch the nineteen, there's more of them. Then I can just walk from the supermarket."

Dot shook her head, sighing elaborately. "What's the matter with you?"

"I don't know," Percy said miserably.

"Jesus!" Dot gazed hopelessly at the floor. "I could have twenty years of this!"

"All right, I'm going!"

He went slowly upstairs to fetch his coat and an umbrella. He thought briefly of changing into some older trousers and a pair of waterproof shoes, but he wanted to get back to the pub as soon as possible, before the forgotten bag vanished. He was rather fond of that cap. He knew that Dot had paid quite a lot for it, for she had taken the precaution of telling him so.

Without so much as a goodbye, he swept through the door into a steady rain. At least he had his umbrella. He walked quickly towards the bus stop, ferreting with his free hand in his inside pocket for his wallet and bus pass. But something was wrong, something else. Halfway to the bus stop, he came to a halt. Caring nothing for the rain, he slackened the umbrella and hung it over one arm. Again, he searched his pocket, then all his other pockets, but they were flat and empty. Despair, solid as a lump of rock, balled in his stomach. One final, desperate fleecing of his pockets confirmed his worst fears. There was no wallet.

Raindrops trickled down his face. They might have been tears of frustration. "On the bus, those lads. They nicked my wallet!"

Percy's instinctive reaction was to beat a hasty retreat for home, lest his mere appearance on the street should invite a fresh wave of disaster to be visited upon him; but he reasoned that by his immediate return he would instantly expose himself to Dot's vituperation, compounding his misery. A modicum of breathing space would not come amiss.

"Police," he growled, through gritted teeth. "Doubt they'll do much, but I ought to report it."

He crossed the road and walked down a side alley to the police station. Water was squelching in his shoes, but he didn't care. Rain blew under his umbrella, an icy punishment flung contemptuously in his face. He reflected morbidly upon the elemental crime of rising from his bed, of going out, of being there, daring to confront an uncontainable world.

A grey-haired duty sergeant, making entries in a ledger, glanced up at him.

Percy tossed his umbrella on to a chair and thrust both hands out in front of him, fingers interlocked. "Cuff me! I've come to confess a crime."

The sergeant regarded him blearily, pen poised. "I see. What crime would that be?"

"The crime of recklessly walking the streets without due care and attention. Will that do for a start?"

The policeman put down his pen and used a thumb and forefinger to rub his nose, gazing solemnly at the unlikely offender. "Tell me exactly what you've done. Then we can decide on the appropriate action."

Percy felt tears welling up in his eyes. He produced a handkerchief from his trouser pocket and blew his nose extravagantly. "I've just retired," he said. "I've given it all up, everything."

"Good for you," the sergeant said, encouragingly.

"That's what you think." He proffered his wrists again. "Arrest me. Put me in a cell. I claim immunity from nefarious circumstance."

"Would you like a chair?" The sergeant lifted a flap in the counter, preparatory to coming out.

"Preferably an electric one," Percy said.

"I'm Sergeant Wilmot." He led Percy to a battered leather armchair and made him sit down. Bending over, he studied Percy's rain-flecked face and almost managed a smile. "Now make yourself comfortable and tell me what this is all about."

Percy peered up at him. "How old are you?" he enquired.

"Me? I'm sixty. Retiring myself soon."

"Really? A word of advice. The first day, stay in bed. Pray the ceiling doesn't fall in."

Sergeant Wilmot nodded earnestly. Then he scratched the back of his neck and examined his finger. "We don't get many like you in here."

"You see, it's not all it's cracked up to be," Percy warned him.

"I can see you're in a bad way. Can I get you a drink? Something to eat, perhaps?" He spread his arms submissively. "There's nothing going on today."

"Cup of coffee would be nice," Percy said. "You're a very nice policeman. Couldn't manage a chicken salad sandwich, I suppose? Or don't you do them Mondays?"

The sergeant stood up, chuckling. "The wife's out the back. She does lunches three days a week." He winked, patting Percy's knee. "I'll have a word, see what I can do."

Percy smiled, settling back in the squashy old chair, until he felt his eyes closing. After a minute, he decided not to fight it, not to struggle. He'd been struggling since ten o'clock. The clock on the wall said two-thirty. Time for an afternoon nap. Time to ride a dreamy magic carpet to impossible places, idyllic hamlets where no-one hectored you or tried to run the vacuum over your feet or told you how to behave.

He heard the chink of china, and from one smeary eye he saw a woman in a pinafore place a tray next to the magazines

48

on a table beside him. He sighed gratefully and smiled a warm, woozy, self-satisfied smile. Retirement had challenged him, and he had squared up to it, called its bluff. Today the dark forces had nearly won, but in doing so they had shown their colours, and tomorrow he would be wiser, he would be ready for them. Tomorrow he would hold them to a stand-off. He had the knowledge. Hallelujah!

Water Music

I t was a long time since those old bedroom curtains had met
properly in the middle, but Jeff had always resisted paying
for new ones, bless him, even though he thought nothing of
buying another CD every few days, a different performance of
the same concerto or symphony he already owned in numerous
versions, presumably because he regarded music as something
spiritual and life-affirming and therefore immeasurably more
important than whether your curtains looked right, and so
Thelma just put up with what was, after all, a minor irritation,
bearing in mind the imperfection only showed when the
curtains were pulled together and that was at night when she
was asleep and couldn't see them, and during the day if she was
in the room the curtains would be drawn back and,
as Jeff was quick to point out, then you wouldn't even notice
that they weren't quite wide enough, so really there was no
problem, nothing to worry about.

Now, perversely, Thelma felt some small gratitude for the
unsightly gap, as she woke to find the sun shining through it,
spilling a bar of buttery light on to the carpet and the edge of
the bed. On first opening her eyes, she could scarcely have
believed the sudden brightness, for it signalled the end of day
after gloomy day of cloud-laden skies, wretched nimbus
panoramas of dirty laundry hanging over monochrome streets,
suppurating a cold, desultory rain that greased the landscape to
a grey, sodden ruination.

Easing on her dressing gown, she drew the curtains back
and peered down into the leafy park. There, starkly defined in a
shaft of sunlight slanting between overhanging branches, stood
the bench where Jeff used to sit to read his paper. Something
yellow lay at one end of the wooden slats, flapping in the
breeze — a discarded takeaway chicken box, perhaps held
precariously in place by the weight of some uneaten contents. A
girl in blue lycra, dark ponytail rhythmically swinging, ran past

with headphones clamped on her head, raised fists pumping the air, thin legs high-stepping like a cantering foal. Thelma followed the girl with her eyes until she disappeared into a screen of bushes. She stood back and smiled. How Jeff had loved the park, had surely agreed to buy the house primarily because of its proximity to that calm green oasis where each fine day he had strolled from bench to bench, seeking a sun-dappled seclusion in which to read his newspaper or library book or sometimes to eat a lunch-time sandwich or talk lazily to a passing neighbour. On many a sunny day, she reflected, Jeff would get up in the house and go to bed in the house, but spend the intervening hours in the fragrant quiet of the park, immersing himself in the softly elemental tranquillity of his earth-scented sanctuary beneath the trees.

Poor Jeff, she thought, stepping back to perch on the edge of the bed. No, not poor Jeff. All that was done now, dear Jeff released from the unremitting pain of his cancer, mercifully freed from the obscene bondage imposed upon him by that awful disease. Hers now the pain, relieved only by the slow, inexorable salve of tears and the brief anaesthesia of fitful sleep. Dear Jeff. In those dark, aching days when hope was gone and time itself was poisoned by a knowledge too terrible to face, she wandered in the quiet house while her wasting husband slept, and picked and poked at his neatly ordered possessions, the poignant remnants of a life, and asked of herself how she would live among these small parts of him when they were all she had of that good man.

Thelma showered, dressed, moved silently about the kitchen, wept a little as she thought anew about the sunshine in the park, Jeff's park, and finally settled to make herself some breakfast and a pot of tea and turn on the radio for some undemanding human company. When she tired of the presenter's aimless prattle, she switched to a music station, smiling inwardly at her easy satisfaction with a chart song or a folk ballad, a few minutes' cheerful trivia of a kind Jeff had always responded to with a seething irritation.

She admonished him once: "We can't start the day with toast and marmalade and thundering Wagner. Be reasonable."

"Hmm. Perhaps a little Mozart?" he replied, and they both laughed and the room was filled with lightness and harmony as he kissed her, leaving crumbs on her mouth. Dear, funny, serious, gentle Jeff.

The letterbox clattered and a cascade of envelopes littered the doormat. Thelma scooped them up and carried them into the kitchen, confident that much of the mail would instantly find its place in the bin. She smiled a little sadly as she unsealed an air mail envelope from the United States, one more late card of commiseration from distant friends who had only recently learned of Jeff's death, a month after that fateful day. By now all the bereavement cards had been removed from the mantelpiece, but she displayed the American one anyway, on its own next to the carriage clock.

While she was opening the other mail, the doorbell rang, and from the hallway she saw a man's figure through the frosted glass. She opened the door and stood back in quiet, appreciative surprise, recognizing Jeff's friend John from the bowls club.

"You're an early bird, John." She held the door open wider.

"I'm sorry. It's just, well you see – "

"It's all right, John, really. Come in."

John stepped inside, wiping his feet on the mat and removing his trilby. He wore a black corduroy jacket and carried a folded shopping bag. He was a gentleman and had been a good friend to Jeff for ten years. Thelma fondly recalled how he had held her arm at the funeral.

"I didn't want to come before," he said. "I mean, you'll understand. It's just that – Jeff spoke to me when he was in hospital."

"Of course." Thelma indicated with a motion of her hand that he should go into the kitchen and sit down. "Please. I could make you some tea or coffee."

"Thanks. Coffee would be nice." He put the folded bag on the table, his hat on top of it. "As I was saying. When I saw him

– you know, before – he asked me if I would like to have some of his CDs. Some of our musical tastes coincided, you see."

"I know. You'd be most welcome. I hate having to throw his things away."

"I'm sure. So perhaps, when I've had my coffee, I could have a look on the shelves. I believe he had quite a collection."

Thelma pulled out a chair and sat down facing him. "There's about nine hundred CDs in there. Most of them are orchestral. You just help yourself, it's what Jeff would have wanted." She let out a short, brittle laugh. "Take all the Scriabin, for God's sake!"

He responded with a nervous smile. "Ah, right. Scriabin's a bit worrying, I always think. A bit, you know, unnerving."

Thelma nodded and patted his arm. "I'll get your coffee," she said.

John passed a contented hour browsing along the multi-coloured rows of CD cases, pausing at intervals to drop a chosen recording into his bag. Thelma was generally inclined to leave him in peace, but from time to time she came quietly into the room and stood behind him, finding an unexpected pleasure in seeing someone she liked evincing a respectful appreciation of Jeff's treasured library, handling the discs as Jeff himself would have done, opening the cases, reading the notes, clicking them shut again and allowing himself a sigh or grunt of mellow satisfaction with each carefully considered selection.

"Looks like I'm taking quite a few," he said, over his shoulder, a note of apprehension in his voice.

"No, please. Take all you want, John. If Jeff were here – "

"I know, you're right, of course." He pointed to a separate stack of discs on the sideboard. "Those are quite special. I mean, if you love the sea."

"He did, yes. Funny, he never learnt to swim, but he loved the sea, loved everything about it. He said its power transfixed him."

John picked up the pile and shuffled the pieces in his hands. "Some favourites of mine here. Bax, *Tintagel*. Vaughan Williams, *A Sea Symphony*. Then there's *La Mer*, of course, two recordings of that. Think I'll take the Boulez. Got *Sea Drift* as well, Delius. Oh, and, look, Frank Bridge, *The Sea*."

"You have all you want," Thelma told him, moulding her hands as tears swarmed in her eyes. "This is lovely."

"What?"

"That you're looking after something of his, something that won't be thrown away or left to gather dust. Bless you, John."

He put the sea music in his bag and turned to face her. "One line of thought leads to another."

"Oh?"

"Yes. I wondered if..." He shook his head and looked a little sad for a moment.

"What is it, John?"

"I thought this afternoon, now the sun's come out, I might take a stroll on the pier, look at the waves, maybe take some pictures." Turning away, he tugged awkwardly at one ear lobe. "The thing is – well, would you like to come with me? You know, just for an hour or so."

"Come with you?"

"I'd be glad of the company."

Thelma thought for a second or two and smiled, lowering her eyes. "You're very kind," she said, shyly.

"Hardly." He grinned. "All I'm offering you is a breath of sea air. Maybe an ice-cream. Stick of rock."

"Thank you. I think – yes, I'd like that. Perhaps it would do me good."

"Get you out of the house."

"Yes."

"That's settled then." He picked up his bag and turned towards the door. "I shall call for you at three o'clock. I've got the car, it's a long walk."

"I'll look forward to it, John. I'll bring a flask of tea for us." Tears were stinging her eyes again and she turned aside, blinking them back.

John pretended not to notice, but he touched her shoulder to let her know he understood. "Thanks for the CDs." He smiled quickly, uncertainly. "Say thanks to Jeff for me."

"I will."

Thelma was ready by half past two and John was there at ten to three. He was so like Jeff, she thought, always punctual, always disciplined, polite and reliable. Small wonder they had been such good friends. In a way, it was as if Jeff had bequeathed him to her, and for that she was grateful. It seemed right, somehow.

John parked the car in a side street opposite the pier and took her arm as they crossed the busy road. The long-awaited sunshine had brought out the crowds and there were more people milling about than Thelma had encountered in the weeks since Jeff had passed away. Their careless proximity made her nervous and she kept close to John's side as they walked to the turnstiles, her companion fumbling in his pocket for some coins. She carried a canvas bag containing a flask and cups, some foil-wrapped sandwiches and her handbag. John wore a cable-knit sweater and had a camera strung round his neck. Thelma felt sad and happy at the same time and hoped that this outing would not be a mistake. She reassured herself with the confidence that Jeff, if he could see them now, would look happily upon the acquaintance.

John guided her to a seat on a plinth where they would sit with their backs to the sea. Thelma hesitated. "Do you mind if we walk on?" she said.

He shrugged. "No, of course."

She led him past the seat, and the next one, to a smaller bench in an alcove, facing out over the water. "We'll sit here," she said.

"Don't tell me. This is your favourite spot."

"Something like that."

"Hmm?"

She shuffled up close to him and put the bag between her feet. "Jeff and I walked on the pier a few weeks after we met. We sat here, on this seat, and we talked for ages and ages. Then he asked me to marry him."

"Oh Thelma!"

"Three weeks I'd known him." She laughed shortly, shaking her head. "I don't know, I suppose you'd call it love at first sight. You see, I thought he was the most lovely man in all the world."

"Perhaps he really was," John said.

She gazed out to sea and the breeze drew tears into her eyes, and this time she didn't care any more, just let them trickle down her cheeks until the wind dried them and the sea was a blue-green blur, shifting beneath a pale horizon. A seagull appeared from nowhere to perch on the rail in front of them, cocking its head and appraising her out of a twitching yellow eye. John surreptitiously raised his camera, but before he could focus, the bird had gone, swooping down over the waves and up again, suddenly black against the sky. Then she felt his hand on her shoulder, gently kneading the muscle, drawing her back to the moment, bringing her nearer.

"It's all right, Thelma," he said, "I do understand. You mustn't fight it, there's no need."

She shook her head, not in disagreement, but as if to clear an obstruction. "Isn't there? I have to get out of all this somehow, that's the thing." She turned to look at him. "But it's so difficult. Oh, the illness was bad enough, God knows, but then at least I knew the pain, his pain, would come to an end and it would soon be over. Now this is different. I don't know when this pain will be over, or if it ever will be. Can you imagine that, John? A searing ache that just goes on and on for ever. I don't even know if I can take that, don't know if I have the strength. Perhaps it's just too much."

"Losing someone you love is always too much." He fiddled with the camera lens, twisting it round and back again, not meeting Thelma's gaze. "It's a burden we're not made for. Well, I suppose some people manage it better than others, that's what I'm saying."

"Yes, probably. I reckon I must be one of the others. Or perhaps I just want to torture myself into some kind of terrible submission."

"But that wouldn't be doing much of a service to Jeff's memory. He would be horrified – don't you think?"

She nodded, making no reply. An errant gust of wind buffeted the alcove, ruffling her hair, and she remembered how Jeff had sat facing her where John was sitting now, and had tousled her hair, twisting the strands tightly around his forefinger, tugging gently but insistently, until she winced and playfully slapped his hand away. Dear Jeff, he had that way with him, always knowing what to do, what she would like, how to please her and make her smile and feel cared for.

The canvas bag toppled on to her ankles, and she hoisted it up and balanced it on her lap. "Could be time for tea, John — yes?"

He held the flask while she took out the cups and sandwiches. She saw the puzzled look on his face as she produced three cups, placing them carefully on the seat slats between them. "Let's get them filled before the wind blows them away," she said. "Do you take sugar, only there's none in?"

He told her he didn't, then watched and waited. Thelma filled two cups and poured a third half-cup. She offered John a sandwich. "Ham and pickle, I hope that's all right."

"Perfect." He was staring solemnly at the extra cup.

She replaced the bag on the ground and sat back to sip her tea. "Oh, I know what you're thinking," she said, reflectively.

"Do you?"

"Obviously. It's just — well, the third one is for Jeff. I still tend to lay two places at meal-times, you see. I mean, I'm not mad, I don't cook him a dinner, but it's my way of coping." She paused to brush away a tear with her knuckle. "Oh, you probably think I'm a daft old woman, unhinged by bereavement." Clasping her cup in both hands, as though seeking pleasure in its warmth, she squinted into the actinic light, watching the waves as they creamed on to the shore. "Go on, John, tell me I'm silly. Tell me I have to start living again."

Bracing himself slightly for rejection, for it could have been the wrong thing to do, he rested one hand lightly on her stockinged knee and turned towards her. "As a matter of fact," he said, "I think you're wonderful. You're thoughtful and sincere and brave." A shiver seemed to run through him. "God, I hope I never lose Sally. But if I do, I hope I can be at least a little like you, just strong enough to do her some kind of justice."

"All right. Thank you." She pointed along the beach. "Don't let's talk about death any more. Look at the waves breaking on those rocks."

He gazed beyond her fingertip. "Ah yes. That reminds me."

"Of what?"

"When I got home this morning I sat and listened to one of Jeff's CDs, *Tintagel.* When I look at the sea crashing over those rocks, I can hear Bax again, that glorious opening breath, that flute like a clarion call, the craggy splendour of it all as the orchestra comes in."

Thelma wanted to tell him again how much she appreciated his interest in Jeff's music, his respect for the collection, but she thought that to mention this now would seem like a return to the subject of her loss, and they could surely enjoy the sea air and sunshine and talk of other things or perhaps allow themselves the lazy comfort of trivia.

"How long do I have to wait for my ice-cream?" she asked chirpily.

John smiled broadly. "That's better. You almost sounded cheeky."

"I'm working on it. You can get me a big vanilla cornet, one of those whippy ones."

"Right you are. With a flake?"

"No flake."

"I'll be right back." He stood up, brushed some crumbs from his front and stretched out a hand to her. "Don't go away."

Surprising herself, she reached for his hand and felt him squeeze it briefly before he walked away. "It's all right, Jeff," she murmured, "I'm just being friendly. Oh, I've made you some tea, just how you like it, strong and dark." She sipped from Jeff's cup, eyes closed. "I hope you don't mind, I've drunk it for you."

To the right, lining the rails on the open reaches of the pier, anglers in jeans and anoraks, singly or in small knots, stood surrounded by rucksacks and scuffed plastic pots, gazing noncommittally down at the churning water. At infrequent intervals a flapping silver fish would be hauled on to the deck, to be peered at by a handful of linesmen with an air of uncomprehending detachment not far removed from mystification, as though they wondered where it could have come from. Strolling along the pier with Jeff, she had glanced occasionally into the anglers' tubs, only to be repelled by mounds of writhing maggots, like infested basmati rice.

From this brief distraction, she turned at a movement over her shoulder, and there stood John with the white torch of a glistening cornet in each upraised fist, a slime of melting ice-cream already oozing on to his knuckles.

"Mind you don't get ice-cream on your camera," she said, taking her cone. "You could have left it with me."

"It's fine. I took some photos. I took one of you from behind. You looked – serene."

"Really? Inside, I'm not serene."

He sat down and they were quiet for a while, licking their ice-creams, avoiding eye contact. The pier was busier now, though beyond the fishermen there was still space on the boards and some empty seats. Thelma thought it would be good to walk to the far end and look down, like being on the prow of a ship.

John was adjusting his camera again, cradling it lovingly in his hands.

"Looks like an old friend, your camera," Thelma said. "It's not new?"

"This? No." He laughed. "It's a very old Minolta. Nice lens. I think it's time I went in for a new one, move to digital."

"That's film?"

"Yes. Maybe I'll treat myself, eh? New Nikon DSLR coming out. You can get a dark red one, D3200."

"Then why don't you? You deserve it."

"Mmm. Over six hundred quid. But I think I might splash out."

"I see. A lot of money, John."

He sucked his teeth thoughtfully. "Is it? Cost you that for a night in a London hotel. *Boom*, and it's gone. Good camera's yours for life."

She nodded, and John took this as mute approval. How sensible he was, she thought, exactly like Jeff had always been.

One of the anglers shouted as he brought in a large fish, flailing wildly as he unhooked it.

"Ever been a fisherman, John?" she asked him.

"Same chaps there most days," he said. "No, it's never appealed to me. Sort of can't see the point of it."

"No, Jeff neither. He said – he said there was no intensity."

"Maybe if you land a ruddy great shark."

She leaned back, closing her eyes, and imagined the sea. Over the hiss and slap of the waves she could almost hear music, the torrents of *Tintagel* carried on the wind, could smell the seaweed tang rising up from the rusting ironwork and, in a tiny corner of her memory, the sweet whiff of Jeff's aftershave as he nestled close to her that day. That day. This seat. That day. That distant day. That gone forever day. That blown away on the wind day.

John was peering at her anxiously, leaning into her face. "Thelma, are you all right?"

"What? No, of course I'm not all right."

"I'm sorry. It was an unnecessary question. A stupid one."

Unhappily, she patted his knee. "No it wasn't. Forgive me." She grabbed her handbag and unclipped it, rummaging inside. The sun was in her eyes, and she looked up once more, straining ahead at the dark rocks and the soft explosions of foam. "Tell me," she said.

"Tell you what?"

"When you look at a vista of the sea, it's blue. But when you're here on the pier it's always green. Why is it green? The sky's not green."

"Maybe that's not for mortal men to know," he said gravely. He pointed at her open bag. "Lost something?"

"What? Yes, I thought I had some tissues. Damn."

"Eyes watering?"

60

"Oh, just me being silly. I don't know, maybe sitting on this seat wasn't such a good idea."

John shook his head slowly, studying the planks between his feet. "I'm sorry, Thelma. This was my idea – coming out, I mean. Perhaps it's a bit too early for you. Perhaps it's asking too much. If you think I – "

"John, please."

"Eh?"

"Just shut up about it." She ground her teeth together, trying in vain to stem the tears. He was such a good man. Sally was lucky to have him. Perhaps if they didn't talk at all now. She didn't want to hurt him. "You can do something useful for me."

"Of course. Anything."

"Walk back to that little shop by the entrance. Get me a pack of tissues. I thought I had some."

He stood up. He touched her shoulder. "I won't be long."

Thelma waited until she lost sight of him among the crowd, then she picked up her handbag and walked quickly along the pier, past the anglers, past a locked and deserted workmen's hut, out as far as the bend in the railings where the structure narrowed towards the end and there was nobody sitting or walking, just cloud shadows on the woodwork and the faltering breath of the breeze.

The workmen had gone now, finished early in anticipation of the weekend, and only a forgotten coil of wire and a strip of yellow tape warning of a break in the railings marked their abandoned site. Thelma stopped and cast a calculating eye over the broken rail and the rippling tape. Furtively, she glanced behind her, seeing only a lone man with a bike, crouching over his saddlebag as he prepared to push back to civilisation. The gap before her was scarcely a foot wide, but Thelma had always been short and slight – 'delicately framed', Jeff had called her – and she knew it would be an easy move to make. She dropped her handbag on the decking, for it was only right that they should know who she was and where she might be found. There was no need for anonymity. With one final backward peek, she eased her hips through the space and stood on a pitted,

61

weather-scarred wooden beam directly above the heaving water. On this exposed precipice, the wind whipped her face until fresh tears blinded her. The salt on her lips could have come from her brimming eyes or from the sea-spume. She licked the salt away with a rolling motion of her tongue, and looked down. How green the sea was. Sunlight slanted through the barnacled pilings, throwing bright skeins of spangling iridescence into the wave troughs, as though unseen aquatic spiders had woven golden webs across the water. How beautiful the gold was. A playful wave burst over a concrete stanchion, showering froth in silver sparks over the green swell. How perfect the silver sunbursts, how wildly incandescent.

Thelma knew her words would be lost on the wind, but she felt sure Jeff was close enough to hear her. "I won't wait longer," she told him. "Someone may see me and try to drag me back. Imagine, dear, a lifetime's embarrassment. This way, my way, I shall have nothing to fear, nothing to regret."

She gasped as her foot slipped on a patch of bird-lime. She held her balance. "You'll think me crazy, Jeff, or perhaps a coward. Oh well. You see, you turned the light off when you went and I'm afraid to be alone in that darkened room. So I need to be close to you again. Now, you hear me, put your arms out. Catch me. Hold me."

Silently, with no cry and no breath, she pitched forward with her eyes closed. The shock of the cold water smacking her face stunned her with its violence, as if someone's icy hand had smashed across her cheeks. Her legs spun downwards, dragging her under the surface, but she drove up into the light at enormous speed, glimpsing the dark trelliswork beneath the pier before her eyes filled with rushing foam. With superhuman strength, she brought up her arms and clawed the brine from her vision, and the green swamp of the sea swooped and sucked at her, bending her backwards so she saw the sky. How blue was the sky. How green was the surging sea.

"Jeffjeffjeffjeff..."

Water cannoned into her gaping mouth. Something roared in her brain like a great train coming. Her head bulged with exploding blood. The train crashed in a debris of bubbles, leaving another noise in her screaming ears. Music. The nearness of him. Music. Deafening music. Green music.

She tipped over, face down. How green was the sea. How green.

Green.

So green.

Black.

Black.

"**S**eems to me hospitals don't smell medicinal any more," Roy said. It was hard to tell if he was talking to his sister or to himself.

They walked on down the cream and grey corridor. A nurse passed them carrying an armful of pink folders. Roy smiled at her but received no response.

Jessica sniffed the posy of freesias she had bought that morning and adjusted the strap of her bag on her shoulder. "Is that good or bad?"

"I prefer it. In the old days it was sort of unsettling."

Jessica pulled a face, curling her lower lip. "Hospitals are always unsettling."

"Even worse if you're the patient," Roy said.

They stopped at the double doors to Ramsay Ward and squeezed pink gel over their hands from a container on the wall. At the nurse station a black charge nurse was sifting papers and a Chinese staff nurse was on the phone. They waited, gazing vacantly at the posters and the cards from previous patients. If the hospital smell was no longer unsettling, Roy considered, the poster display most certainly made up for it. The multi-coloured warning notices told him that if he dared to enjoy almost anything – a cigarette, a few beers, fornication, a good fry-up, a leisurely lie-in, a spot of sunbathing – the inevitable result would be imminent death.

The charge nurse tamped the stack of papers upright on the desk and dropped them in a plastic tray. "Can I help you?"

"We've come to see our aunt – Beryl Masterson," Roy said.

"Oh yes." He pointed to one side. "We've moved her into that room."

"And we can go in?" Jessica asked.

The man glanced sternly at the flowers. "Yes. It's not visiting time, but in the circumstances..."

Roy, pushing open the door for Jessica to go in first, pondered the vaguely sinister implication of these 'circumstances', resonating as they did with the probability of something irreversibly finite.

Aunt Beryl was propped upright in bed against a bank of pillows. A thin tube extended from her nostrils, another thicker one from somewhere under the blanket. Equipment parked by the wall flashed and beeped, hummed and clicked. Her eyes were closed, but as the door clunked shut they sprang open and darted from side to side, finally locking on to her visitors. Jessica had found a chair by the window and sat on it, while her brother stood awkwardly behind her.

"Oh. Wasn't expecting you," the old lady droned, blinking.

"We spoke to the staff nurse yesterday," Jessica said quietly. "She said to come in."

"Is it visiting already? I've been asleep."

"We're a bit early." Roy was about to add that the nurse's recommendation had sounded urgent, but he omitted this detail when he saw Jessica regarding him warily. "We thought they wouldn't mind, see."

"Up to you," Beryl said, off-handedly.

"Nice bright room," Jessica observed, glancing about at nothing in particular.

"Them flowers," said Beryl, nodding at the freesias still clutched in her niece's hand. "They for me or are you going to pin them on your blouse?"

"Oh, sorry." Jessica smiled and stood up. "Freesias. I thought they'd make the place smell nice. Specially when you wake up."

"Ah, I don't know how much more waking up I'm going to be doing."

Jessica shook her head, still offering the residue of a smile. "Now don't be saying things like that, Aunt Beryl." She turned to Roy, brandishing the posy. "Can you take these and put them in a glass or something. Fill it from the sink tap."

Roy bumbled about, poking into cupboards and drawers until he found a tumbler.

"Not supposed to have flowers," Beryl said. "Unhealthy."

Roy displayed the freesias unconvincingly on the window ledge. A small nurse came in with a plastic cup of water and a pill in a paper pot. Beryl swallowed the pill mechanically without saying anything or looking at the nurse.

"Should have asked her for another seat," Beryl said, when the nurse had gone.

"I'm all right here." Roy held on to the back of Jessica's chair. "Been sitting in the car for an hour."

Beryl's eyes were shut again. "Don't mind me," she said. "I'm still listening."

"So." Roy peered down at the crown of his seated sister's head for inspiration. "How's things, Aunt Beryl?"

Beryl sniffed. "Things? What things?"

"Well, I – uh – "

"What you mean is – how am I? Only you don't wanna ask explicitly for fear of receiving a discouraging reply. Am I right?"

"Well, I mean I – uh –"

Jessica perceived the appropriateness of rescue. "We just wondered how you felt in general. You're not comfortable, of course, but I'm sure they're doing all they can for you and having your own room must be a blessing."

Roy nodded, smiling gratefully at the floor.

"Had a bad night," Beryl sighed. She opened her eyes and closed them again.

Jessica leaned forward. "Couldn't sleep?"

"Had to press me button. Two o'clock, it were. They had to change me bed."

"Oh dear," Roy said, a sympathetic inflection in his voice which he hoped did not sound too contrived.

"It were everywhere," Beryl continued. "Even on t' floor. Stank to 'igh 'eaven."

"Information sufficient," Roy murmured.

"Well, don't you worry," Jessica told her brightly. "They're used to that."

Beryl opened her eyes wide and stared at her reproachfully. "I'm not used to that. For me it's a disgrace and an indignity."

66

She tried to shake her head, but only her chin moved. "Grown woman, pooin' everywhere!"

Jessica nodded solemnly, eyes downcast.

"They stuck me in this nappy thingy. Feels like I'm strapped in a beanbag."

There was a tap at the door and a doctor came in, unfurling his stethoscope. Roy patted his sister on the shoulder.

"We're just going for a quick coffee," Jessica called. "Let the doctor have a look at you. We'll be right back."

They went out and paused at the nurse station. The charge nurse was studying a set of notes which he held in both hands, a Mars bar protruding from his mouth.

"Beryl Masterson's niece and nephew," Roy said. "We're just going down for a coffee. She's with the doctor."

"That's right," the charge nurse said, the Mars bar waggling absurdly as he spoke.

Jessica took hold of her brother's arm. "We'll – can you ring us if there's a problem? Roy's mobile number's in the notes."

"A problem?"

"Only she really doesn't look very well."

The nurse removed his snack and placed it carefully on the desk. "Mrs Masterson is very ill. Staff Nurse Ohlsson told you yesterday."

"That's why we're here," Roy explained.

"Yes. Go to the visitors' restaurant, first floor. I can call you if necessary."

"She asked last time about coming home," Jessica ventured. "I suppose that's not advisable."

The man regarded her gravely, his elbow on the desk and one finger against his temple. "Mrs – "

"Miss Jarman," she supplied.

"Miss Jarman, your aunt is terminally ill. The cancer is spreading. She needs constant medical attention. She won't be going anywhere."

"Thank you for your frankness," Jessica said, turning away.

In the restaurant they found a space in the shadow of a potted palm and sat for a while without speaking. Roy smiled sadly at his sister and reached across to touch her hand, then she responded by placing her other hand over his, making a soft pile of fingers on the table, and they stayed like that for a minute or two, just quietly gazing around them at the other people moving to and fro and wondering if, for these ordinary strangers, the time and the place held the same unalterable meaning, the same sense of a critical corner about to be turned.

"I'll get cappuccinos," he said.

She nodded, not looking up.

He brought back the coffees with two sausage rolls and a bowl of mixed salad. They ate with their fingers and finished by spooning the froth from their cups as if it were warm ice-cream.

"I wish there was something we could do," he said.

Jessica worked her lips thoughtfully. "We're here," she said. Roy put out a hand and brushed some flakes of pastry from her chin. "Thank you," she whispered.

Roy's phone rang. It was the charge nurse, asking if the relatives' accommodation which the staff nurse had mentioned the previous day would be needed. Roy held the phone aside and spoke to his sister. She listened, eyes lowered, and just kept nodding her head.

"I think we should stay the night," he told the nurse.

Jessica squeezed his wrist, turning it over to see the time on his watch. "We can stay," she said. "Sunday tomorrow so there's no work."

"Of course. You know, ever since Jack died, she's not been the same. Not well, I mean."

"You can't blame Jack for giving her cancer."

"I'm not saying that. I just mean, she's gone downhill, become more – susceptible."

"I don't know. Maybe."

Roy studied Jessica's face. She looked almost as pale as her aunt, he thought. Why did she never wear any make-up? With her habitual taste in pastel-coloured clothes, her blonde hair slowly, inexorably edging towards grey, she put him in mind of someone in a fading photograph whose colours had leached away from exposure to sunlight. Under the taut fabric of her grey roll-neck sweater, her breasts remained rounded and firm, and he could not help but wonder if a man had ever seen or touched them, for try as he might he could not recall a single boyfriend featuring in Jessica's adult life. She was, at forty-seven, an attractive woman, but she appeared to have quietly, submissively despaired of making of herself something warm and appealing which would perhaps have rendered her years more intimately complete. As brother and sister, they were close, and would always remain so. Sometimes they had even taken holidays together, bringing Jessica's dog Polly along with them. This meant, obviously, that foreign travel was not possible, but in the aftermath of the American air crash which had claimed both their parents, neither of them had retained much appetite for flying. They were best friends, emotionally together if not inseparable.

"I think we should get back," she said, reaching for her bag.

"If you like."

Returning to Aunt Beryl's room, they met the nurse who had earlier brought the medication, just leaving with a bowl draped with a cloth. The nurse looked at Roy and slowly, wordlessly shook her head.

"We're back, Aunt Beryl," Jessica said.

Beryl's face was ashen-grey and her lips were wet. "Been sick," she groaned.

They nodded and looked at each other, uncertain what to say.

"We went for coffee." Jessica leaned close to her aunt and smelled the taint of vomit on the old lady's breath. "There's quite a nice little shop next to the restaurant. I wondered if we could get you anything – if there's anything you'd like."

Beryl seemed to go rigid and her eyes were suddenly wide open, cold and accusing. "You what?"

"If you wanted anything we could get you," Roy added superfluously.

"If – I – wanted – anything," Beryl repeated with slow, rather menacing deliberation, fixing her nephew with a brittle stare.

Roy and Jessica waited, hovering at her side, smiling vacuously.

Beryl shifted in the bed as though trying to sit up, then sank back into the pillows, breathing heavily. "Listen up," she gasped. "I'll tell you how it is. What I want."

Jessica seemed alarmed. "Aunt Beryl, can I help you? Are you not - ?"

"Shut up! You're proper daft, the pair of you!"

Jessica sat down, resting one hand on the bedclothes.

"What Beryl Masterson wants." Aunt Beryl moved her head slowly from side to side and gazed briefly at the ceiling before continuing in a husky voice. "Well, I want not to have cancer, for a start. I want to go home. I want to sit in me garden and hear the birds singing and have someone bring me a bucket of ice with a bottle of Moet in so I can get boss-eyed and maybe do a jig on the lawn and then go in for a nice hot bath with plenty bubbles, and after that I shall be tired and go up for a lie-down and most likely snuggle up warm next to Daniel Craig with me nightie tucked up under me armpits. There, that's what I want!" A sardonic smile creased her face and was quickly gone. "Now then. I've answered your silly question. So if you can tell me you can get all that from that 'nice little shop' of yours, well, thank you, I'd be very much obliged."

The buzzing and whirring of machines seemed louder now, in a room where speech, and even thought itself, had been suspended. The rattling and occasional laughter in the corridor was suddenly amplified to a level of obscene intrusion, a ghastly aural wallpaper.

Jessica sniffed, fumbling in her sleeve for a tissue.

Cued by this sound, Beryl narrowed her eyes to glare at her niece. "Hey, you with the pink eyes! Don't you dare weep in 'ere! I've had no-one cry since I've been in, either in the ward or in me room. Too much like selfishness."

Roy frowned. "How d'you work that out, Aunt Beryl?"

"Cos that's what it is, grieving in bereavement. Pure selfishness. 'Oh don't leave me, Beryl, it'll hurt me so much, I want you to stay with me whatever it costs you, or I'll feel like

70

I've been robbed. I can't stop the pain, Beryl, but you just go on smiling through, it makes me feel right good.'"

Jessica blew her nose and wiped her reddened eyes. Roy sighed, resting both hands on his sister's shoulders.

"You!"

Roy met his aunt's gaze, bravely managing not to flinch.

"Aunt Beryl?"

"I shall draw you a picture. You ready?"

"Aunt Beryl?"

"You got a mortgage, right?"

"Course."

"Mortgage and not a lot left in the bank. Car to run, bills to pay. Job to go to, but no security. Debts mountin' and problems lurkin' round every bend, too many to count. Sleepless nights, I'll be bound. And every day the same."

Roy nodded and allowed himself a gentle cough.

"All right. Well, there's none of us any different. But one day – hooee! – there's a man comes up the path with a ruddy great box and he knocks on the door and when you open up he says he's come to rescue you, and – you know what? – that man, he goes through yer 'ouse, through yer life, like a dose of salts, and in next to no time he's loaded every last bit of yer baggage into that box, and it's so 'eavy he has to hump it on to his shoulder, and God bless him, he carries it all away and you never see him or the box of troubles again. Well, imagine! You'd jump for joy! That man, he's Mister Freedom." She squinted sideways, tilting her head towards Jessica. "Can you pull that blind, it's shining in me eyes."

"I'll do it," Roy said.

"Okay, me dears. Now p'raps you see why I don't want no tears. I don't consider them appropriate. They are, if you like, ill-timed. So keep yer eyes peeled for a man with a box, cos that's what I'm doin', and I don't mean the one they'll drop me in."

Aunt Beryl settled deeply into the pillows and closed her eyes. Her chest rose and fell like a bellows.

"You must be tired, Aunt Beryl," Jessica said. She reached up and Roy squeezed her hand and held it for a moment.

"Right. Think I've wore meself out."

"Perhaps we should let you rest," Roy offered.

"Yeah, maybe. Go on, the pair of you. Come back in the morning and see if I'm still 'ere."

"No doubt about it, Aunt Beryl." Roy tapped Jessica on the arm and moved back to let her stand. "We'll not be far away."

His sister leaned over and kissed her aunt softly on the cheek.

"Oh, don't get soppy!" Beryl chided her.

Roy waggled his fingers at the bed as he followed Jessica to the door. They walked slowly along anonymous corridors to the accommodation block adjoining the car park. He let Jessica into the room and went to the car for their overnight bag. It seemed odd how little it weighed. This was hardly a holiday.

"This room will make me seasick." Jessica shuddered, glancing around at the turquoise duvet covers on the twin beds, the turquoise carpet, the drab grey-green curtains and the pale avocado walls. "It's not remotely cheerful."

"It's only one night," Roy pointed out.

"We hope."

"Should we get some food?"

She sat on a bed with her hands in her lap. "I'm not really hungry."

"There's a hospitality tray, look. Tea and biscuits?"

"That'll do. I'm tired. Ten minutes telly and then bed, I think."

They watched the news and checked the view from the window as the light went down. A rectangle of unkempt grass, a meander of rough flagstones, a hawthorn hedge and an abandoned wheelbarrow half full of old bricks. A ginger cat scurried past, chasing an escaping meal.

Roy switched off the TV as Jessica emerged from the bathroom wearing ankle socks and a knee-length pink T-shirt. To save space in the small bag, he had packed pyjama trousers but no top. Jessica slid into the bed nearest the window while Roy undressed in the bathroom, padded out on bare feet and climbed into the other bed.

"Are we going to read," he asked her, "or have we done with the lights?"

"I didn't bring anything."

"Goodnight then."

They were asleep before ten, but later, under the window, the squawk and yowl of fighting cats jarred them both awake. In the shadowy, unfamiliar dark, they lay on their backs, eyes roaming uselessly over the ceiling.

"You asleep, Roy?"

"Cats woke me up."

"I know. It's cold in here."

"What?"

"Cold. In the room. In the bed."

"Oh. There's an electric fire I could – "

"No, it doesn't matter." She sighed, tugging at the duvet.

"You all right?"

"I just feel...I don't know."

"You're worried, Jess."

"Hmm. You don't usually call me that."

"Dad used to call you Jess."

"Don't."

"Sorry. Would you like a hot drink?"

"No. But thank you. Roy?"

"What is it?"

"You could come in here. Keep me warm."

"It's a single bed, Jessica."

"We're single people."

He sat up and turned on the bedside light. "Jessica, you're my sister."

"Well, I know that."

"So what is it you want?"

"I just thought it'd be nice. Like when we were little."

"I think you'll find we're grown up now, Jessica."

"What's that got to do with anything?"

"Maybe it's just not a good idea. Us being brother and sister, I mean."

"A minor inconvenience," she snorted.

73

Roy rolled on to his side and looked at her. She was still staring at the ceiling. "Are you very cold?" he asked her.

"Cold enough."

A funny taste had risen into his mouth. Something fluttered in his stomach like a small bird. He clicked the lamp off, slipped out of his bed and eased himself in next to Jessica.

"Just enough room," she murmured. "Think we'll soon be warm."

He tried to lie comfortably without touching her. "Jess?"

"Mmm?"

"Have you - ?"

"Have I what?"

"Have you ever slept with a man?"

"What kind of a question is that?"

"Well, have you?"

She hesitated. "Yes."

"When?"

"Tonight. You're a man."

"That's not what I meant."

She moved towards him and groaned. "I know what you meant." She felt for his hand and held it lightly.

"Jessica?"

"Shut up, Roy! Go to sleep."

His mobile woke them at six. Staff Nurse Ohlsson sounded calm but serious. "Mr Jarman, if you could come to Ramsay straight away, I think your aunt is failing fast."

"Okay," was all he said.

There was an unclean smell in the room and wet patches on the floor to suggest that it had very recently been mopped. Aunt Beryl lay, or almost sat, propped against four pillows, her eyes closed and lips hanging slack and grey, worm-coloured. A red-haired nurse finished checking the monitoring equipment and stood back to let the visitors enter. Roy caught her eye and read her lips as she silently mouthed "Not long now" and shook her head.

A second chair had been provided so they were able to sit at opposite sides of the bed. Jessica whispered Beryl's name, and her aunt's eyes flickered open and tried to focus, the once-blue irises faded to the bluish grey of washed pebbles.

"Just in time," Beryl wheezed.

"Not had a good night?" Jessica asked timorously.

"Long sleep coming up."

They each reached for one of Aunt Beryl's hands, the old lady's skin now a waxy yellow and thinly translucent as tissue paper.

"Going backwards," Aunt Beryl said, closing her eyes again.

"What?" Roy leaned closer.

"Changing me nappy, feeding me with a spoon like a baby. And the dreams."

"Dreams?" Roy repeated.

"You know what dreams are."

"Sure."

"Keep having these ch- childhood dreams. Like when we were all by the seaside. Minehead, I think it was. See, it's like me whole life's gone into reverse, nothing but baby things."

"Minehead," Roy said sadly.

"Wanna ask you something, both of you."

Independently, instinctively, they squeezed her hands.

"When I close me eyes for proper, you just hang on to me. And you just keep right on talking to me, only they do say your hearin's the last sense as goes. Prob'ly you can be dead an' still hear." She jerked her head as if in a soundless sneeze. "Will you do that for me?"

Jessica nodded, moulding Aunt Beryl's wrist in both hands. "Course we will. We'll be here for you."

The old lady fell silent and a thin trickle of saliva spilled from her lips and ran down her chin. Her mouth hung open, distorted like a wilted flower. Jessica looked at Roy and inclined her head.

Roy understood. He kneaded Aunt Beryl's hand, blinking back tears. "Can you hear what I hear, Aunt Beryl? Seagulls, I can hear seagulls. They're all over the beach. But you can still hear the waves crashing, Aunt Beryl, hissing and clawing at the pebbles, scrabbling on the sand, making the crabs scamper this way and that. Do you remember when Jack dug that big hole in the soft sand and sat in it to read his paper and a huge crab came scuttling in and grabbed his toe and how we all fell about laughing and Jack, he came stumbling out on to the beach, hopping on one leg and swearing and the more he jumped about – "

Jessica was waving at him to stop.

"What's the matter, Jess?"

She shook her head, eyes brimming. "I've got her wrist, but I can't feel a pulse."

Roy leaned over and delicately prised open his aunt's left eye with his thumb and forefinger. Just a stone, no mistaking.

He got up and moved round to where his sister sat and placed both hands very gently on her trembling shoulders.

"That's it," he said. "Aunt Beryl can hear that man's footsteps on the path, the man with the box. "She's on the freedom trail."

The Reunion

When he had sat down after breakfast to study the initial invitation, the reaction that came over him had been one of mild surprise; surprise not so much that he had been approached in this way, but rather that he found himself inclined to accept. For a brief moment he wondered how well he really knew himself, for surely there was little in his past, and still less in his present, to encourage him to seek renewed contact with Downey Hill County Grammar. Perhaps he should attribute his vague but quite measurable interest to nothing more than open-minded curiosity. Perhaps.

"What was in your pink envelope?" his wife enquired, carelessly wiping her hands on a teacloth.

"What? Oh, this." He glanced again at the second page of the letter, stapled to the first, and read the various options set out for applicants. "Actually, it's from Downey Hill."

"Wasn't that your old school?"

"Yes."

Margaret smirked at him as she folded the teacloth. "Don't tell me – they want you to go back and be caned again."

"What? No, they're inviting me to become one of the old boys. Well, to be precise, to join the Friends of Downey Hill."

Margaret pulled a face, frowning. "Really? Are you a friend of theirs? You were hardly an academic. Two O-levels and a smacked bottom. Not to mention that bloody nose on the last day."

"Hmm. Don't remind me." Duncan Lumsden peered over his glasses at the details on page two. "It's quite cheap. Ten quid for a year."

His wife sighed dismissively. "Oh well. Up to you."

So it was that Duncan, marginally against his better judgment, became a Friend of his old school, three years before he retired from the bank in 2010. There followed three annual subscription payments, the amounts inconsequential despite a fee increase in the third year to keep the Society abreast of inflation; six copies of the twice yearly news bulletin, adorned with fuzzy black and white photographs in none of which did he ever see anyone he remembered; and a single invitation to a summer ball, which he declined as Margaret declared herself unwell at the mere thought of it.

It was soon after his retirement at age 66 that a pink envelope exactly like the first one landed on the doormat. Margaret brought it in with the rest of the post and waved it in front of his face.

"Looks like your old school again. Surprised they haven't run out of pink stationery by now."

Duncan took the envelope, fingered it open and read the letter without enthusiasm. "Hmm. Well I never."

"What do they want?"

"This summer is their seventy-fifth anniversary. They're planning a reunion, asking if I want to go."

"I see. And do you?" She sounded seriously unimpressed. "I mean, who would you be reuniting with?"

He scanned the letter again, eyebrows knitting together in a slow frown. "It says – it'll be fifteen quid for a buffet lunch and a wine bar. Umm...no beer. Get together and sing the school song. Walk the grounds if it's dry."

"So you don't know who's going?"

"What? No, they'll send a list later to everyone who signs up."

"Right. Nearly fifty years ago, Duncan. Some of them'll be dead."

"Not necessarily. I'm not dead." He turned the letter over and studied the back. "Seems there are major changes in the wind. Downey Hill is to become an academy."

"Really? Never sure what that implies."

Duncan sighed and dropped the letter in his lap. "Unfortunately, Margaret, it means that in education, as in pretty well every other sphere, we are entering an age of declining standards." He stood up, the better to emphasize his point, brandishing the pink paper in the air. "When I was at

Downey Hill, the teachers knew more than the pupils and walked about in suits and gowns, exuding authority. If you go back there now, likelihood is, the Downey tradition has carried the pupils with it, and they have ambitions and aspirations which it is beyond the capacity of the staff to bring to fruition, not least because most teachers turn up for work in greasy trainers and jeans and are unable to spell or frame a sentence in the Queen's English. Call it role reversal, if you like. I suppose it's a bit like something from a Harold Pinter play, where everyone ends up in the wrong place."

"But you don't know that, Duncan." Margaret peered sternly at him over folded arms. "If you're so disparaging about contemporary education, I wonder you want to go back."

"I never said I did."

"I sense a curiosity; a willingness, maybe."

"Hmm. Hard to say." He chewed a corner of the envelope, gazing glassy-eyed at the floor. "So if I said I'd go – would you come with me?"

She puffed out her cheeks, rocking her head thoughtfully from side to side. "If that's what you want," she said.

"It's just – going on my own, I think I'd feel vulnerable."

"Vulnerable to what? To temptation?"

Duncan kept his head down, briefly silenced by the pointless malignancy of this remark. There was something childishly insulting about Margaret's implication, if such it was, that he was not adult enough to behave himself in mixed company. In a fleeting retaliatory moment, he swiftly reviewed the wisdom of taking her with him. If she spoke of temptation, presumably she meant weakness, inadequacy, lack of self-control. In a relationship underpinned by trust and mutual respect, any suggestion of emotional infidelity churned inside him like vitriol, an acid he must either swallow or regurgitate.

Before he could counter the sideswipe, Margaret moved to prod the tender area again. "Perhaps that girl'll be there. What was her name – the one you told me about?"

"Who are you talking about?"

"You know. Linda something, wasn't it? Undid your trousers round the back of the gym."

Duncan had not forgotten Linda, but he was peeved and disappointed at the spontaneity of his wife's recall. A juvenile memory vouchsafed as a nugget of harmless reminiscence was being used to belittle him, a spiteful whack from a blunt instrument.

"I don't remember her name," he said, at once regretting that Margaret had manipulated him into telling a lie.

"You told me it was Linda...Linda..."

"Draycott," he said, resignedly.

Margaret nodded and smiled, as if she had scored a point, perhaps a small victory.

"Well, I'd hardly recognise her now. And no doubt she'd be married," he added.

"Oh, I'm sure they'll give out girl pupils' single names. I wonder if she'd remember you. You never know, she might instantly relive – "

"Margaret, please! Just leave it!"

"Ooh, sensitive!"

"That would absolutely not be my reason for going." He turned and balanced the letter against the toaster. "Any more coffee in that pot?"

"Why don't you sit down and stop fretting? I'll see to it and make you another cup."

They sat facing each other, drinking fresh coffee and gazing abstractedly at the table-top. Duncan's stomach was still uncomfortable from Margaret's probing and his appetite for breakfast was gone, something that had briefly bloomed and been trampled underfoot. The humming and clicking of the central heating system could be heard over their silence, as though the machinery were whispering about them in the background.

"Hey!" Her sudden exclamation made him jump. "That chap might be there!"

He stared at her blankly. "Chap? What chap?"

"The one you said smacked you on the last day."

"Oh, him," he groaned.

"You never did tell me the details. Except his name was Ronald."

"Donald. Donald Gleeson."

"He was a bit of a bully, right?"

"Not exactly. Boorish, perhaps. Too full of himself."

"Be funny if he turned up."

"I don't see that it would be particularly funny. In any case, Gleeson was hardly the type to stay in contact with the school. He was always putting the place down. I mean, he was above me academically, but he wore this disdainful air like a medal, he'd somehow made this oikish arrogance into an art form."

"Still, you never know," Margaret persisted. "He could have mellowed, people do."

Duncan stretched behind him for a sheet of kitchen roll and blew his nose on it. "So you think we should both go? You seem interested."

"Well, it's thirty quid, but I don't see why not. It could even be fun."

He worked his lips dubiously around this possibility. School was never fun then, so why should it mysteriously have become fun fifty years on? School and fun were classic oxymorons. He had dragged himself through twelve years of school, waiting in growing desperation for the fun to begin. Finally, at Downey Hill, he realised too late that the fun package was never going to arrive.

"You seem a bit doubtful now," Margaret said. "You've gone off the idea."

"Not completely," he countered, dabbing his nose.

"That stuff's for cleaning food spills. Haven't you got a hanky?"

"Upstairs." He scrunched the paper in his fist. "I'll tell them to reserve us two places."

"Donald Gleeson," Margaret intoned. "Donald Gleeson. I rather hope he comes. I'd like to meet him. So what did he do exactly?"

"Do? He was a schoolboy."

"Don't be deliberately obtuse, Duncan. I mean, obviously, what did he do when he punched you?"

"I don't know as I really want to talk about it. It's a long time ago now, done and forgotten."

"You said he made your nose bleed. On the last day, you said."

"Well, if you know that much…"

"It wasn't anything to do with Linda Draycott, was it?"

Duncan sighed and stood up, moving away from the table as if to indicate that the conversation was aborted; but Margaret's eyes followed him round the room, underlining her determination.

"Please, can we not talk about Linda Draycott?" he growled.

"Okay. Tell me about Gleeson, then. Tell me about your last day."

He strode into the lounge and subsided into the sofa. Yesterday's paper lay folded over the arm and he picked it up and shielded his face behind it. To his great relief, Margaret didn't follow him. He heard her clattering cups and saucers in the kitchen, muttering to herself, her squashed bedroom slippers scuffing the tiled floor.

Of course, he had not forgotten Donald Gleeson, the lardy-faced boy with blond hair cropped halfway to a crew-cut, a broad, slightly flattened nose and pale grey-blue eyes oddly devoid of warmth, features which combined to give him a vaguely pugilistic appearance, an impression misleading if not entirely undeserved. For Gleeson was not a bully in the starkly physical sense; he just had difficulty in being friendly towards his peers, a symptom, no doubt, of some kind of complex. Among schoolboys, these tendencies were not commonly understood or discussed. Gleeson might demand your attention by grabbing the lapels of your blazer, breathing pungently in your face, or tugging painfully at your earlobe. He would sometimes walk off with someone else's lunch-time sandwich box and later return the empty box, speckled with residual crumbs, to the desk of its famished owner, often with a curt nod of insincere gratitude. That was Gleeson; it was how he was made.

As for Duncan Lumsden's last day of school, that he had not forgotten, either. Half a century had soothed the sore of that July day, but enough of the blemish remained for him to retrieve it from his memory like someone picking listlessly at a scab. He remembered he had a headache soon after assembly and the school nurse had given him two aspirin, to no discernible effect. Before lunch-break, in Duncan's judgment, it was game over, time to escape. What could they do to him? If they assigned him a punishment for absconding, he knew perfectly well that his meagre academic accomplishments would ensure that he could not be returning to serve the sentence. For Duncan, whose worst subject was examinations, there was no prospect of progression to the sixth form, no point in further education and no brightly beckoning career path. It was time to go home.

A morning shower had persuaded him to bring a coat, so he went to the cloakroom to fetch it. Emerging, he met Gleeson leaving the adjacent toilet. Gleeson wheeled round to face him, still fiddling with his fly. "Where d'you think you're going, Lumsden?"

"Home," came the reply.

"Can't. It's only twelve o'clock." Gleeson angled his wrist, hitching up his sleeve to show Duncan his watch.

"Get out of my way, Gleeson. I've had enough."

"Who said you can go home early?" Donald Gleeson was standing so close to his classmate, they were bumping chests.

"No-one said. And you can't stop me."

"Oh, can't I?"

"No, because you're just a kid like me, with no authority."

"Who're you calling a kid?" Gleeson snarled, and he threw one arm across to the wall to block Duncan's path.

The argument was making Duncan's head reverberate with pain. He wrenched at Gleeson's arm, but the boy lunged forward, biffing him hard in the chest.

"Look, Donald, will you please let me by?"

"Ooh, Donald now, is it? Gonna make me?"

Duncan's mistake was in trying to duck swiftly under Gleeson's arm, for in that instant the sharp buckle of the antagonist's watch strap caught his victim's ear, and in an angry reflex he kicked at Gleeson's shin, toppling him off-balance. Duncan, clutching his scratched ear, found himself bundled to the floor with Gleeson on top of him.

"Shit, Lumsden!"

"Bastard, Gleeson!"

With a hand either side of his bum, Duncan struggled to scoot backwards, away from his adversary's reach, but a couple of seconds later a very solid object, subsequently identified as Gleeson's fist, hammered into his face, spewing dark blood from his nose.

"Bastard, Gleeson!"

Both boys scrambled to their feet. Duncan scooped up his coat from the floor and ran to the door, tasting salty iron in his mouth. Donald Gleeson shouted something, but his words were lost in the manic rush of Duncan's panic. Fresh air caressed Duncan's cheeks and sweat-glazed brow, while his frenzied jogging sprayed beads of blood down his collar and on to the sleeve of his coat. He didn't stop running until he reached the bus stop.

And now the name, if not the face, was there in front of him again, incredibly or, at least, improbably, as Margaret turned to page two of the list from Downey Hill and bobbed her head, seeming to freeze, as she took in the entry halfway down the column, tapped the sheet with her fingertip and thrust the paperclipped documents under Duncan's nose, holding them there without a word.

"Eh? What's this?" Duncan, having second thoughts about the event, even though he had paid to be there, had affected disinterest in the latest mailing and left his wife to open it.

"Look, Duncan! It's him, he's on the list – Donald Gleeson!"

"What? Jeez! He can't be."

She tapped the paper again where Gleeson's name was printed. "Here, see for yourself!"

He tugged the document from her hand and read the page. "Donald Gleeson," he murmured, his voice tinged with a hollow timbre of disbelief.

"Well, well," she gloated, "just fancy. I wonder if you'll recognise each other."

"Course we will. Amazing. Donald Gleeson. The one and only."

From Margaret, a short laugh, like a hiccup. "He's probably a pacifist minister of religion now, or a solicitor or a doctor. A pillar of the community."

"Hmm. Let bygones be bygones," Duncan said, though his tone sounded mechanical, drained of conviction.

Margaret was leaning over him, reading down the list. "Oho! Look who else is coming!"

"Who? Where?"

"Here." She indicated with a tightened knuckle. "'Linda Jarvis (nee Draycott)'."

"Oh, right."

"What do you mean – 'Oh, right'?" She sat back, smirking, sucking in her cheeks. "Better make sure you've got clean pants on."

"Yes, thank you, Margaret," he said flatly.

Duncan turned back to the head of the list and studied the names in detail. Here they came, rising up to meet him like returning spirits, crystallizing out of the grey veils of almost a lifetime, people with impossibly young faces, warped by time in a sad trick of memory's light...

...Paul Arblaster. Friendly but not clever, childhood injury, limped on a wooden lower leg, excused PE. 'How come you got a wooden leg, Arblaster?' 'Cos I fancied it, dumbo. Don't ask silly questions.'

...Richard Brand. Genius with a football, mouthy, unintelligent, mud in his hair like brown dandruff.

...Penelope Bywater (nee Black). Only had to look at an exam paper to pass it, attractively severe, good legs, rose solemnly above the burden of parents who in their calamitous bankruptcy of imagination had named her after a postage stamp.

...Daniel Farthing. 'What you got for lunch, Farting? Have a good weekend, Farting?' 'Don't call me that. My name is Farthing.' 'Sorry, Farting.'

...Donald Gleeson. Face pallid and blotched like the moon, expressionless eyes, unstable, inverted ego, mad about cars.

...Linda Jarvis (nee Draycott). Dark brown hair in a ponytail, pretty, good teeth, flat chest, told off for wearing perfume to school, went out with her once to see some spaceman film, slid his hand under her skirt in the dark, cool bare thighs, then a slap on the arm just as he was sort of getting there.

...Jan Klestikoff. Polish, trousers always too short, tatty grey socks with holes at the ankle-bones. 'You sure you're not a bloody German, eh, Chestycough? Thought we'd sent your lot packing in forty-five.'

...Meryl Parsonson. Obviously not married, big nose, straggly hair, the bush-backwards style, very friendly, danced with her at the summer ball because no-one else would, held her close till his whatsit rubbed her tummy and she grinned and called him naughty.

...Liam J. Threlfall. How come he gets a middle initial when no-one else does? Stamp collector, often brought his album to class, probably quite valuable, used to exchange stamps with that goofy chap, Michael Wernett, got called Turnip. 'Bet you an't got a Mozambique Purple, Threlfall.' 'That's a butterfly, Lumsden.'

"Must be nearly two hundred names here," he told Margaret.

"I know. Wonder what you'll wear."

"Nothing too formal. Don't want to overdo it."

"Did you see that piece at the bottom, about the uniform?"

He flicked on to the last page footnote:

'You may dress as you please for this event, but preferably avoid jeans, T-shirts and trainers. You are welcome to walk the grounds at any time, but if the weather is wet, remember to bring stout walking shoes and try not to bring mud into the building. To emphasize the informality of the occasion, we would be delighted if anyone who still has one or more items of their original school uniform – hat, cap, scarf or tie – could wear it on the day, if only for a short while. We want your visit to be fun as well as nostalgic!'

He laid the sheets aside, thoughtfully rubbing his chin.

"Didn't you keep some of your old school stuff?" Margaret asked.

"I think so. In a box in the attic. Some school reports, a scarf...maybe a cap."

"Oh, bring them down!"

"Huh. Cap won't fit now, be like a yarmulke."

"That won't matter. It'll add to the fun." She prodded his shoulder, grinning. "Go on, Duncan, say you'll go and find that box."

"Okay, okay," he sighed. "Whatever you want. I'll fetch it down later."

"I'm looking forward to it now," she said, brightly. "I might even get my hair done."

"Don't let's go overboard, Margaret. Half of these buggers'll probably be bald by now."

"Well, the women won't! I want you to be proud of me."

"I am proud of you." He extended one hand. "Pass me that phone."

"Here. Who are you ringing?"

"My dad. I want to ask him a favour.

Small wonder that Duncan looked smugly content. He was driving a 1974 Signal Red Series 3 Jaguar E-Type roadster with a 5.3-litre V12 engine, red leather upholstery, special issue Nardi steering wheel with woodgrain rim and satin-finish spokes and polished wire road wheels. The airstream swooping over the Jaguar's endless bonnet lightly ruffled his hair, while across his lips played a languorous smile of self-satisfied pride.

Margaret ducked her head, tucking in her chin, to prevent the breeze from disturbing her expensive hair styling. If only

Duncan had agreed to keep the top up. Poser. Dreamer. At least there was ample room in the footwell for her long, slim legs.

"So what made you want to do this?" she asked, her words buffeted on the wind.

"Do what exactly?"

"Take your dad's car instead of our own."

"Oh, I see."

"Well?"

"It's beautiful – don't you think?"

"I suppose."

He shook his head, still smiling. Women didn't understand cars. They thought they were for running errands in, mere appliances. It was fortunate the weather was set fair. Alistair Lumsden treasured his E-Type and certainly never allowed it to be taken out in the rain. But at age 87 he had parted company with his reactions and no longer trusted himself to drive "my heavenly machine", as he called it. So he had readily entrusted the car to his son for a few hours, on pain of certain death if it should be returned with more than a speck of dust on its gleaming scarlet bodywork.

"And that was the favour you asked?" Margaret said.

"Yes. Actually, I think the favour was as much to him as to me. He knows the car just begs to be used."

"Right. You aren't going very fast."

"Do you blame me? This has to be a zero-risk expedition. Anyway, this car is part of my inheritance."

"You hope."

"What?"

"I said, you hope." She screwed up her eyes and slid lower in the seat. "This wind..."

"Nearly there," Duncan declared, and he patted the steering wheel affectionately.

Margaret was mystified. Entering the Downey Hill grounds, Duncan circled round the parked cars and took an isolated space in an area resembling an overflow car park, screened from the school building by a tall privet hedge.

"Why so secretive, all of a sudden?" she asked.

"This is fine. I have my reasons."

In the Reception lobby, two elegant ladies, immaculately coiffed, checked the Lumsdens' names against a printed list and handed them adhesive identity badges. An arrowed sign on a wooden stand directed them to the main hall, already buzzing with the muted greetings of around a hundred people. Margaret followed her husband through double doors into the hall, where he stood gazing about, not seeking out individual faces, but drawing in the sounds and smells he recalled from the past, filtering hazy remembered light from the shadows of a previous life, the way the shafts of sunlight slanting down through tall leaded windows held dust-motes in clouded suspension like searchlights penetrating mist, pooling white ovals on the polished floor.

"Amazing," he said quietly.

"Sorry, dear?"

"To be back here, in this place. Like walking into a time-warp."

Margaret nodded and touched his shoulder. Nervously, she primped her hair with her fingertips, wanting to look her best, anonymous but respectable, worthily supportive.

Standing in front of the stage, an elderly man in a striped three-piece suit rang a small handbell, calling for attention. The jumbled voices fragmented and died. People moved apart, turning to face the solitary figure, now standing with one hand balanced on the closed lid of a grand piano. The man introduced himself as David Caskill, Chairman of the Friends, and he was effusive in welcoming everyone to the seventy-fifth anniversary reunion. He alluded warmly to the school's history and fine educational record, and proceeded to acknowledge that, with the inevitable march of time, the aims and profiles of establishments such as Downey Hill must be expected to change, not always for the better, hence the imminent redefining of the school as an academy in the near future. The impression given was that Mr Caskill had reluctantly accepted the transformation without going so far as to embrace it. His words fell upon solemnly receptive ears and elicited noncommittal grunts and murmurs from a blank-faced audience. "A proud legacy of achievement in so many fields...our illustrious past spanning three-quarters of a century...noble endeavour both academic and sporting...must move with the times and eschew complacency...new horizons and a new generation..."

"He does go on," Margaret whispered.

Duncan needed a drink. There would be no beer, of course, but a glass of wine would be better than nothing. He plunged both hands into the trouser pockets of his cream linen suit, surprised to feel in the gritty depths a piece of paper which, on furtive inspection, turned out to be a long-forgotten ten-pound note. Tugging ineffectually at the creases in his jacket, he patted the bulge in his right-hand pocket, where he had hidden his battered and discoloured school cap.

"And now," Mr Caskill declared, "we shall all join together in the Downey Hill school song. Let this perhaps final rendition be a suitably rousing one. Ah, for those of you whose memories may have lapsed over the years, there are copies of the words on those sheets on the side table under the portrait of our founder, Sir Henry Margerison."

Tottering forward from an upholstered chair, one elbow supported by a minder of about Duncan's age, a little old lady crept towards the piano, whose lid a younger woman was now hoisting upright.

"We are indeed fortunate," Mr Caskill bellowed, "to be able today to call upon the musical services of Miss Cynthia Halton-Peverell, who will accompany us at the piano."

"Who's she?" Margaret hissed.

"Crikey!" Duncan blinked in disbelief. "Old Halton-Peverell. She was music teacher when I was here. She must be ninety if she's a day."

They sang the school song, all four verses. School songs, Duncan reflected, were always mad, with bizarre syntax, words you could only comprehend by reference to a dictionary and outpourings of noble purpose which no schoolboy, and very few schoolgirls, could ever be expected to honour. Duncan took a song sheet and stuffed it in his pocket as a souvenir. He croaked the words he could remember, veering wildly from one octave to another, and filled in the gaps with a series of open-mouthed gasps.

"At last," Margaret groaned, as they filed into the dining room. Duncan solicitously took her arm, her handbag bumping against his midriff. "I need to sit down," she said, anxiously.

"Best take the first seat you can find," he urged. "There'll never be enough chairs."

"What about you?"

"There's trays, look. Wait for me. I'll get food for both of us."

"You'll not get a seat."

"Well, we can't both sit down. Don't worry, I'll stand up, maybe walk about."

"Don't get me any anchovies. And no breadsticks. They're like something you might use internally."

It was as Duncan was walking slowly back with his loaded tray that he felt a hand land softly on his shoulder. Fearful of upsetting the tray, he sucked in his breath and froze, silently cursing whoever had been so thoughtless as to impede him at this moment; while in the next instant, a microsecond later, there glimmered in his brain, like a feeble light bulb, a single possibility, a suspicion converted to reality as he turned his head and met the gaze of someone who, despite the cosmetic ravages of time, could only be Donald Gleeson.

"Hello, Dunc. Good to meet." He nodded at the tray. "Won't try to shake your hand."

"Donald. Hi. Thought I might – er..."

"Course. Well I never."

Duncan shuffled ahead to where Margaret sat at the end of a table and slid the heavy tray deftly on to the plastic surface. He straightened up and reached for Gleeson's hand.

"Pleased to meet, Dunc."

"If it's all the same to you, I'd prefer Duncan."

"Course. Well I never." He widened his eyes at Margaret. "And this dear lady?"

"This dear lady is Margaret, my wife. Margaret – Donald," he added, waving a perfunctory hand.

Margaret simpered at Donald Gleeson but did not extend her hand.

"Well I never," Donald said, bending over the table. "Got a partner somewhere myself" – he glanced quickly round the room – "wherever she's hiding herself. Best go and find her, I suppose. Look, we'll have a catch-up when we've eaten – yes?"

"By all means," Duncan said, sitting down.

"Good, good." He shook his head. "Well I never, old Dunc."

Duncan pulled in his chair and watched him go, barging his way through knots of chortling, muttering people, some just holding drinks close to their chests, others struggling to balance misshapen paper plates in one hand while eating with the other. Buffets, Duncan reflected, seemed a good idea until you got there and remembered you had to be a juggler and a contortionist, or ideally one of those black women you saw in television documentaries, striding about with their worldly goods balanced on their heads.

"Eat up, old Dunc," Margaret told him, humourlessly.

The room was filling up. Gales of laughter rang out in counterpoint to the alternative music of back-slapping, *mwaa*-kissing and yelps of surprised recognition as the elderly pupils circulated, some wearing expressions of nervous bafflement, others flashing fixed grins that displayed their questionable teeth to the multitude.

"That's not her, is it?"

"What?"

Margaret was pointing her spindly plastic fork at a completely bald woman, walking past carrying a large bowl of mixed salad.

"No-one I know," Duncan said.

"Right. Not Linda Draycott, then."

"Not unless…Margaret, I doubt I'd even recognise her."

"Well, she's here somewhere. She was on the list."

"I know she was on the list. Just – don't make an issue of it."

"I'd like to meet her, that's all."

"Really? Whatever for?"

She shrugged, pulling a querulous face. "Bit of a celebrity, I reckon. First woman in history to handle your John Thomas." She licked mayonnaise off her knife. "Unless you count your mother, of course."

"Margaret, for goodness' sake!"

He drank red wine and picked selectively at his lunch, while his eyes roamed the room, bouncing from wall to wall as they sought out greying ghosts from the past. Standing on her own in the far corner, her large nose cruelly prominent, that surely was Meryl Parsonson dressed in a pink suit with matching pink-framed glasses; and the man next to her, talking to Miss Halton-Peverell in her wheelchair, looked very like Jan Klestikoff, his trousers, fifty years on, still hovering like grey flags above his shoes.

"The smoked salmon with lemon is okay," Margaret said. "Quite zingy."

"Zingy?"

"Yes, zingy. You haven't got any."

"I can go back," he said, absently. He was watching the man in the doorway, tall, slim, carrying himself well, a florid face with clear blue eyes and a white toothbrush moustache. The man was staring intently at the Lumsdens, oblivious to everyone else in the room.

Unsure though he was of the man's identity, Duncan smiled thinly and raised an acknowledging hand. There was, after all, something vaguely familiar about the lean, quite kindly face.

"Seen another mate?" Margaret asked.

"Not sure. But I think..."

His voice petered out as the tall man returned Duncan's smile and approached the table. Duncan put down his fork and gazed into the man's warm face. A pink, almost elegant hand was thrust in his direction.

"Good Lord!" Duncan exclaimed.

"Not quite," the man countered. "I think I may lay claim to some distinction here, but not quite that exalted status."

"You – you're Mr Anstruther!"

"Morton Anstruther, the same."

They shook hands, Duncan rising unsteadily to his feet.

"Class of sixty-one," Anstruther supplied. "And you are certainly Duncan Lumsden. Mind if I...?"

"No. I mean no, of course. Please."

Anstruther pulled out the chair next to Margaret, beaming down at her. "And this dear lady?"

"Oh, I'm sorry. Margaret, my wife."

Margaret turned to face Morton Anstruther and extended her hand. Anstruther took the hand and lifted it to his lips, applying a gentle kiss to Margaret's knuckles. "So pleased to meet such an attractive lady."

Duncan waited while Mr Anstruther made himself comfortable. Margaret rolled her eyes in apparent pleasure, pushing her plate away.

"Mr Anstruther taught us Biology," Duncan explained.

"Oh, really? Fancy. I thought Linda Draycott did that."

Duncan looked embarrassed. Mr Anstruther looked bemused. Margaret looked rather pleased with herself, though it was impossible for Duncan to tell whether this was because she had been complimented or because she had managed to unnerve her husband.

"You must excuse my wife," he said, darkly.

Margaret responded through gritted teeth. "Don't patronise me, dear."

Anstruther, sensing a moment of instability, placed one hand over Margaret's. "Well, it's lovely to see you both. Have you come far?"

"Far enough," said Duncan, not looking at him.

Donald Gleeson walked past, one hand on the arm of a blonde woman in an ill-fitting red dress, a tortoiseshell comb in her hair. He was as slab-faced as ever, Duncan thought, the same pugnacious schoolboy in a bigger body.

Anstruther was saying something to Margaret in a low aside, his hand still covering hers. She nodded lightly and then erupted into girlish laughter. Her eyes sparkled with tears of mirth.

"So, Mr Anstruther – " he interjected.

"Please. Call me Morton. School's out now, eh?"

"Ah, right. Morton. Yes. Not still teaching, I imagine."

"Oh no, retired twelve years ago. Man of leisure now. I'd say, leisure and pleasure." And to Duncan's startled incredulity, he folded an arm around Margaret's shoulders and hugged her briefly but warmly to his side.

Duncan cleared his throat, stalling for an appropriate response. He looked into his wife's eyes, seeing them moistly suffused with an unfocused glow of childish pleasure.

"And you?" Anstruther prompted.

"What?"

"Are you working or retired?"

"I – uh – I retired about a year ago."

"Ah. Good man. So you and I are both enjoying our freedom, the abundant fruits of our labours."

Duncan wondered about this assessment. It seemed to imply a degree of kinship which he could not otherwise acknowledge. Across the table, Morton Anstruther appeared to have claimed some fruits that did not belong to him. In another time and place, Duncan might reasonably have gone to Margaret's rescue, or at least moved to challenge the interloper; but since she plainly revelled in the attention, it was surely his own intervention that would be rebuffed as inappropriate.

"Are you all right, dear?" She had gently freed herself from Anstruther's embrace, though his hand still clasped hers. "You're looking a little flushed."

"Yes." He passed a hand across his eyes. "Wine's a bit acidic. Feel sort of muzzy-headed."

"Indeed." Anstruther nodded in genial agreement. "The red, I think, is vin very ordinaire."

"You could go outside for some air," Margaret suggested brightly.

"Right, uh...will you be okay here?"

"Perfectly. I have this rather kind man to look after me." And she squeezed Anstruther's arm with her free hand.

"So it would appear," Duncan murmured, pushing back his chair, his indignant reluctance now marginally exceeded by a sense of relief. He needed oxygen and a chance to think.

Strolling in the sunshine along the oft-remembered hydrangea walk, where they used to hang around in breaks, lolling against the brick wall to taunt the passing girls, he glimpsed the glinting red bonnet of the E-Type in the distance, a blob of raspberry jelly left melting in the sun, and he suddenly wished he could jump in and fire up that wonderful V-12, go rocketing down the road between the high hedges with only the whistling wind and the big cat's muffled roar for company. But that would have to wait, for other matters pressed in on him and there was, importantly, a hidden agenda.

Circling across the grassy border of the playing field, he rejoined the path by the gymnasium wall. In the right-angle where the windowed side wall met the older brickwork of the changing rooms, a wooden bench now stood, and Duncan sat down, tilting back his head and closing his eyes against the sunlight. Peace. A scattering of birdsong. The smell of mown grass. The lightest of breezes rustling the blue heads of the hydrangea. A waft of heat from the enfolding walls.

A cautious, perhaps inquisitive cough, from somewhere to his right. Turning, blinking into the light, he saw a silhouetted figure, a tan suede handbag dangling from one shoulder.

"Hello. Duncan? You are Duncan?"

"Oh, my!" He stood up, both arms outstretched. "You're Linda, Linda Draycott!"

There was no mistaking her. The tumbling dark brown hair was cropped short now, settling on her ears, and she had filled out comfortably; but the coffee-coloured eyes with the vivid clear whites were as arresting as ever.

They shook hands. Duncan sat down again, patting the space to his left, inviting Linda to join him.

"Thank you. Though of course it's not your seat," she said, smiling, unhitching her bag. "And you got my name wrong."

"Yes. Sorry. You're married now. Linda Jarvis."

"Jarvis, yes; married, no, not exactly."

"Oh?"

"He died this winter gone. Brain haemorrhage."

"I see. I'm sorry."

She rested her bag in her lap, both hands round it. "Don't be. Not your fault."

"I didn't mean that."

"I know. People don't know what else to say. 'Died, did he? Well I never!'"

"Right. How – how did you find me?"

"In there I recognised you across the room. I was stuck with that old bore, Halton-Peverell's minder, and I couldn't get away. Then I saw you'd gone, but I figured the lady was your – your wife?"

"Margaret."

"Okay. She seems very nice. I love the turquoise blouse. I have a hat that colour, wore it to my sister's wedding." She unclipped the handbag and peered inside. "She told me you'd gone for a walk. It's very stuffy in there."

He looked at the open bag. "Want to smoke?"

"What? No, no, I gave up months ago. Have to chomp this horrible chewing gum. Ah, here we are." She held out a stick. "Want some?"

"No thanks. I'm not keen on horrible chewing gum."

"Hmm. Not sure I am either. Save it for later, perhaps." She snapped the bag shut and put it on the ground at her feet. "So, Duncan. Fifty years, eh? Must say, you look pretty snappy."

"Thanks. I do my best. Watch my diet, walk a little every day, nothing drastic."

She sat back, tugging at her blue, knee-length pleated skirt. "It's funny, isn't it? Here we are again, after all this time, and there's really no way to catch up. I mean, if we each described our experiences since leaving school, we'd be sat here till the middle of the night."

"That would be rather nice," he said, then instantly felt foolish. He slid a hand over and squeezed her wrist. "You're still a good-looking woman."

"That's what Steven used to say. Suppose I was lucky, in a way. He fancied me till the day he died."

"Well, if you were lucky, it was cruel luck."

"Yes." She gazed thoughtfully across the field. "Yes, I suppose it was. The trouble with bereavement is, it throws up a bramble-patch of clichés. 'Life goes on.' 'Gone to a better place.' 'Out of pain now.' 'Time is a great healer.' 'You're strong, you'll cope.'" She sighed, shaking her head. "Truth is, I'm fed up to the back teeth with it all. I just want to forget. Not forget Steven, just forget about death and dying." Turning to face him, she summoned a watery smile, tight-lipped but, he felt, warily affectionate. "It's good to see you again, dear Duncan."

"Do you want to walk?" he asked her.

"Not really. Relaxing is better, I think. You know, after all this time, I still feel at ease with you."

He studied her legs. She always had good legs. Look after your legs. "I take that as a compliment," he said.

She nodded, chewing pensively at her upper lip. "We weren't exactly boyfriend and girlfriend, were we? Or were we?"

"Umm. We fooled around," he said, chuckling.

"Ah, yes. I sort of remember." She reached out and cheekily squeezed the middle of his thigh. "You were shy, but not unforthcoming. Quite gentlemanly at times, but eager when encouraged."

To his dismay, Duncan felt himself stiffening. He couldn't walk now, even if Linda wanted to. He leaned forward, hoping to disguise the distension. "Perhaps the formality earlier was a shade inappropriate," he suggested, speculatively.

"Meaning?"

"You and me. Shaking hands. After – everything."

"Oh, I don't think there was that much 'everything', Duncan. Something, but not everything."

"Even so. I'd just like to...Linda, can I kiss you?"

A quick shrug, almost imperceptible. "If you want."

98

He leaned over and kissed her softly, even primly, on the side of her mouth. She smiled, not directly at him, but with a measured awareness lightly redolent of pleasure.

"Thank you," he said.

"More formality," Linda said. "You don't have to thank me." She closed her eyes, sighing. "Funny, no-one's kissed me in a long time."

"Oh dear. Bad news. In that case..." He turned back to her and this time she moved towards him and met his approaching lips and responded with a lingering kiss that made him gulp so he had to pull away. To steady himself he had rested one hand on her shoulder, and in that fleeting moment it slipped down and cupped her left breast.

"Ah ah. Not such a good idea, I think, Duncan."

"No?"

"No. Too much water under the bridge, don't you think? Where would it lead, eh? Temptation and frustration." She grinned, shaking her head. "You never tried that when we were at school."

"You never had tits when we were at school." He sat back and stared at his hands in his lap. "I'm sorry, Linda."

She slapped him playfully. "Come on. No thanks and no apologies. Right?"

"Right."

They sat quietly for a while. Occasional ripples of laughter leaked out from the hall behind them, as though by now people had had a few drinks and become more extrovert. In the distance, out of sight beyond the trees bordering the field, a train rattled past, blowing its horn. The warm sun licked their faces, making a red mist behind their closed eyes.

Duncan glanced at his watch. "Maybe time to go back in."

"Yes, I think so."

"It's been nice."

"Yes. I don't think we can take this any further, Duncan. There'd be no point. It can't lead us anywhere."

"You're right, of course."

"Walk with me," she said, and she took his arm and held it tentatively until they reached the dining room doorway.

Margaret was still at the table. Sitting opposite her, his head close to hers, was Donald Gleeson. They drew back as Duncan and Linda approached, following the new arrivals with their eyes until the group of four were clustered at the end of the table.

"Hello, Donald," Duncan said; and to Margaret: "What happened to your friend?"

"Gone," she said. "He was no friend of mine. A man in a dog-collar appropriated him."

Duncan nodded, pursing his lips reflectively. "Well now, perhaps we could sort of swap over."

"Sorry, dear?"

"Thing is, I seem to remember, Donald, you were a bit of a car enthusiast."

"Why, that's right," Donald confirmed.

Linda pulled out a chair and sat facing Margaret.

Duncan trawled his memory. "Let's see, your father had – an Alvis, wasn't it?"

"Right again, old chap."

"I'm the same age as you," said Duncan, petulantly.

"Ah, right, of course. It was an ice-blue Alvis with grey leather upholstery. Fine motor car."

"Indeed. Today I've borrowed my father's E-Type coupe. I – uh – thought perhaps you'd like to see it – in the car park."

Donald Gleeson stood up, wiping his mouth with a napkin. "Excellent," he said. "If you ladies will excuse us."

"Then we'll let the girls get to know each other," Duncan said. He leaned over and touched Linda's shoulder. "It was good, Linda. Till the next reunion, perhaps."

"We'll have no teeth and be in wheelchairs," she said, with the merest flicker of a smile.

He winked at her. "But we'll still remember."

Duncan Lumsden and Donald Gleeson turned and sauntered through the doorway and across the hall. A curious tightness knotted Duncan's stomach. So far, so good, and there was no

100

turning back, no chemistry for a change of heart. Duncan snatched his crumpled cap from his pocket and slapped it on his head and, to his delight, Gleeson produced an identical item from inside his jacket and copycatted the symbolic gesture, the pair of them leaning backwards on the downslope to the car park, past the waste bins and the hip-high bushes, the ground levelling out after fifty yards, two big kids with daft fixed grins, their grey caps like pimples on posts, askew on the backs of their heads with the peaks stuck up sideways, pinching their scalps.

"Here we are." Duncan threw out a proudly demonstrative hand, as trembling coils of heat shimmered from the Jaguar's bonnet.

Gleeson stopped, stared, shifted hesitantly from foot to foot. "Ah, right." Somehow he sounded vacantly unconvinced.

"Handsome beast, eh?" Duncan prompted.

"Indeed, yes. It's a – it's a five point three, isn't it?"

"Correct. Magnificent vee-twelve."

"Right you are." He wandered round to the driver's door and stooped to peer inside, shading the glass with one hand to shield the reflection. "Five point three, eh?"

"Impressed?"

"Excellent condition, I'll say that."

"What do you mean, you'll say that?"

Gleeson straightened up, removed his cap and put it on again. "Thing is, old chap, well, to be honest, I always favoured the four point two. More of a classic engine, more of a classic E-Type. Know what I mean?"

"I don't know as I do, Donald. The bigger engine allowed the car to exploit its full dynamic potential, realising what was at that time a mesmerising performance. No cause to be mean-spirited about it."

"Who's being mean-spirited? I just speak as I find. The four-two's the car for me." He stroked the roof with the back of his hand. "Your dad's certainly looked after it," he added, grudgingly.

"Pride and joy," Duncan declared, puffing out his chest.

101

"Ah, but perhaps not a connoisseur's car." Gleeson's cap peak was pointing at the sky as he tipped back his head and peered critically at his fellow enthusiast through slitted eyes.

"Bollocks!" Duncan retorted, sending a mist of spittle into Gleeson's face.

Gleeson blinked against the spray. "Actually, Lumsden, I do know what I'm talking about. I'm not just your average – "

"Oh, all right, Gleeson, I can see nothing's changed here in fifty years. You always were a fucking know-it-all."

"Steady on, old chap. All I'm saying – "

"Don't keep calling me old chap!" He lunged at Donald Gleeson, prodding his chest. "I'd have taken you for a drive, but obviously you haven't a clue about Jags so I'd be wasting my time."

Gleeson rubbed his chest, blinking rapidly. Duncan's fists were curled at his sides. He could feel beads of sweat trickling down his back.

"Better go in, I reckon," Gleeson said, his voice unsteady, and he cast a quick, nervous glance at the school walls.

Duncan couldn't help himself. Boiling point had been reached. "Take your fucking hat off when you're talking to me!" he yelled.

"What? You're mad!"

With the speed of a striking viper, Duncan's arm lashed out, grabbed Gleeson's cap by the peak and in a scissoring reflex sent it skimming high over the road like a frisbee.

"What the - ?"

"Go on, Gleeson! Off you go! Run after it before a truck squashes it flat!"

Gleeson moved to run, then ducked back and dived at Duncan Lumsden, head-butting him squarely above the nose. A red weal bloomed low on Duncan's forehead, but no blood appeared. He staggered back from the blow, recovered his balance, recoiled and sprang powerfully at Donald Gleeson, aiming an inch-perfect punch at his left ear, the looping impact sending his pudgy opponent crashing to the ground beside the Jaguar's offside rear wheel.

Gleeson's groans, muffled by the asphalt as he rolled his face to and fro along the ground, were interpreted by his assailant as an unreliable barometer of pain; but this was not a time to be ungenerous, and Duncan was prepared to give him the benefit of the doubt. One arm extended, he approached the fallen figure and bent over him, relieved to see no blood on Gleeson's face, just a broad red scuff-mark peppered with black grit.

"Bastard, Lumsden!" Gleeson dragged himself upright and spat pink froth on the tarmac.

"Get up, Gleeson, you're not hurt!"

"A lot you care!"

"Here, take my hand."

"Complete bastard!"

Duncan hauled Gleeson to his feet. Together, they smacked the dirt and dust from his clothes, lunatics extinguishing a fire.

"Duncan!"

They wheeled round to find Margaret Lumsden facing them with her hands on her hips. "What on earth do you think you're doing?"

"Helping Donald," Duncan replied.

"Fighting like crazy kids! What's the matter with you?"

"Margaret, what are you doing here?"

"I was in the toilet. I heard shouting. Oh, Duncan, what a disgrace!"

Donald Gleeson was bending over, dribbling on the ground. Duncan wondered if he was about to be sick. This could be dangerous, for some of it might splash the Jaguar's wheels. *Sorry, Dad, someone puked on your car.* It didn't bear thinking about.

A groundsman in blue overalls was walking towards them. He pointed at Gleeson. "Best go to the lav," he growled. "Don't throw up out here!"

"I'm all right," Gleeson snarled.

"Go inside and clean yourself up," the groundsman told him.

With somewhat drunken strides, Gleeson complied. The three of them watched him go. Behind them, a woman towing a wheeled shopping basket came into view. Balanced on top of the basket's tartan lid was Gleeson's cap.

"This your hat?" the woman enquired, of no-one in particular.

Duncan took the cap with curt thanks and handed it to the man in overalls. He unlocked the car. "Give it back to him when he comes out. We're going."

Margaret looked aghast. "We can't just dash off. What if he's injured?"

"Trust me, he's not injured."

"Huh. I can't trust you to do anything. All this way for a punch-up!"

"It wasn't a punch-up," Duncan protested. "He insulted me. He insulted my father's car."

Margaret rolled her eyes skywards. "Out of school for half a century, and you still haven't grown up! You're pathetic!"

"Get in the car, Margaret."

"What?"

"You heard. Get in the car!"

The groundsman was shaking his head, wringing Gleeson's cap in his hands. "Fuckin' shambles!" he scowled. "Next reunion, I'm out of it."

What blissful music played in Duncan's brain as the big engine burst into life. Margaret sat stiffly solemn beside him as they swept on to the road with the hood down, the Jaguar a glinting red arrow spearing a green canyon of tall trees standing sentinel either side of the highway. For miles neither of them spoke a word. There was only the muted roar of the engine and the rush of the wind.

As Duncan slowed through a village, Margaret glanced at him, a swift double-take. "Got a big bump on your head. Soon be the size of an egg."

Gingerly, he fingered his temple. The lump was tender, sore to the touch.

"Don't know what we'll tell people," Margaret said. "'He's been back to school and I caught him fighting.'"

"I told you, I was not fighting."

"Unbelievable. One's rolling in the dirt, the other's been bashed in the head, but they weren't fighting. Geriatric schoolboys!"

Duncan waited for the derestriction sign and accelerated hard, the car squatting down on its rear wheels with a brief shriek of surprised rubber. Margaret held one hand over her nose and from the corner of his eye he could see that she was trembling, her head bobbing as if in spasm.

"Please don't cry," he said.

"I'm not."

He slowed the car and spared her a longer glance. The tears filling her eyes were surely not of despair or disappointment, but an overflowing of mirth. Margaret was laughing.

"Now what?" he asked.

"You – you've still got that ridiculous hat on!"

"Oh." He shook his head and loosened the cap with his thumb under the peak. "Good riddance!" he cried, and as the car gathered speed once more he spun the hat into the slipstream.

Margaret pulled a tissue from her bag and wiped her eyes. "Oh dear," she moaned. "Hey, this bloody car – what'll it do?"

"Not sure. Hundred and fifty at least."

"Come on then, get cracking! That food was crap and the wine was rotgut. Take me to a decent country pub. I want a steak this big" – she held out both hands a foot apart – "and a pint of John Smith's."

She started laughing again, raucously, infectiously. Duncan joined in, jolting about until he could hardly hold the wheel straight.

The Jaguar was a scarlet blaze on the grey flank of the road, powered by the sweet engines of euphoria.

Reginald Vaizey was reading the Sunday magazine supplement when he heard the commotion. At first he thought it must be the children three doors down, who habitually came out after breakfast to screech in their garden. They were aged five, six and eight, and Reginald idly supposed that, having been born in such quick succession, there must be something the matter with them, an aberration to explain their otherwise unaccountable hysteria. He was not a doctor and so could not presume to diagnose the kids' problem, nor therefore identify a clinical solution. A hefty smack occasionally suggested itself, though he was understandably reluctant to voice the proposition, even though it was a remedial treatment his own father would have administered without compunction.

It was when his ears pricked up at the yelling of his name that he realised the noise did not originate from the children. Sighing, he laid aside the fashion spread in the magazine – skeletal young women balancing precariously on legs like Twiglets – and shuffled to the back door.

"Reg! Oh, Reg!"

He pulled open the door to see his wife leaping towards him, mouth agape as if in agony. The children's kerfuffle would hardly have competed with her anguished screams. Something terrible appeared to have happened.

"What on earth's the matter, woman?" His anxiety was substantially exceeded by his annoyance.

"Snake!" Maisie almost collapsed into his arms. "Snake in the garden! Horrible stripey thing!"

Reg peered over her trembling shoulder. "What are you talking about? This is England; there's no striped snakes here."

"Y-yellow with black stripes!" Maisie quavered. She pushed past him and slammed the door, stranding him outside, cruelly exposed to the risk of fatal envenomation.

He walked down the edge of the lawn, shaking his head slowly from side to side. When he reached the ornamental pond with the fishing gnome, he bent down and picked up the length of leaky garden hose he had cut off yesterday and carried it back towards the house.

Maisie saw him and yelled soundlessly through the window, her mouth opening and closing like a demented goldfish. She opened the door an inch and shouted, "Don't bring it in here! I hope it's dead!"

Reg tossed the plastic serpent on to the patio and followed his wife into the kitchen, where she subsided into a chair and sat with her elbows on the table, hands covering her eyes. Reg pulled out the opposite chair and sat facing her. He could hear the kids up the road screeching again, as if some dreadful torture were being inflicted upon them.

"Okay, okay," he said, "I should have chucked the split hose away. I forgot."

Maisie spoke indistinctly from behind her hands. "What a fuss! I'm sorry, Reg. I had such a fright."

"Been overdoing it," he said. "All that cleaning you did last week, down on your knees from morning till night. You're done in."

She moved her hands away and stared at him. "Do I look done in? Tell me if I do. Tell me I'm just a crabby old woman who's lost the plot."

Reg nodded once. "You're a crabby old woman who's lost the plot." He wiped his nose with the back of his hand. "Get up and make me a cup of tea, woman."

Dragging the chair noisily across the tiled floor, she got up and filled the kettle at the sink. She put bread in the toaster and took something out of the fridge. Reg could hear her sniffing and wondered if she was crying, though he didn't turn to look. He never knew quite what to do when women cried. Sometimes it was best just to leave them alone. If you tried to console them with kindness, they often wept all the more. With Maisie, he found, the most successful response was to chide her for her feebleness, for surely the veiled sanctuary of tears was the refuge of the feeble-minded. Reg's army training had taught him to respect order and self-discipline, to abhor displays of emotional frailty. In Reg's world, people needed to pull themselves together.

"Thank you," he said gruffly, as Maisie handed him his tea.

"I'm making toast," she said.

"What of it?"

"Well, would you like some? There's home-made jam."

"I don't care for jam. Have we no marmalade?"

"I'll fetch some." Still sniffing, she went to the pantry. Over her shoulder, she said, "Reg, I'm sorry about the snake – about the hosepipe, I mean."

He decided to take a chance on sympathy. It was Sunday, after all. "Come and sit down. You'll wear yourself out. I'll get the toast."

Her eyes were red, he noticed, but to his relief he was able to establish that she was not crying, so in that department no further action would be required of him. Probably she was a little run-down. He made a mental note to enquire later about her medication.

They sat eating toast and English marmalade, mostly inspecting the table-top and not speaking. The neighbours' kids were screaming in ragged unison, achieving a kind of lunatic counterpoint. Reg reflected upon the physical dangers arising from madness. Grandfather Arthur Vaizey, lieutenant responsible for a unit pinned down by enemy gunfire outside Ypres in 1915, had calmly slit the throat of a young private gone berserk and liable to give away their position. He still had Lieutenant Vaizey's old tunic in the loft, the right arm dyed rust-red with the blood that had fountained from the youth's carotid artery as the knife sliced it open. It was an act as understandable as it had been unwise, motivated by monumental desperation, but almost a century later, Reg was given to ponder the appropriateness of execution in the pursuit of silence.

"I was thinking," Maisie said, and she bit off another corner of toast.

Reg waited patiently for elaboration.

"When was it we bought the caravan? Three years ago, wasn't it? Reg, we've hardly used it."

"Your point being?"

"We could both do with a holiday – don't you think? Now you're retired, we could go any time. Oh, Reg!"

"Indeed," Reg commented, evincing no obvious commitment.

"A little break would be so nice," she continued. "I've – well, I've not been feeling myself lately, if the truth be known, dear."

"Is that so?" Reg picked up the marmalade jar and studied the script on the label. "Some of us, having reached a critical age, regrettably have no recourse to any alternative gratification."

Maisie hunched her shoulders, shuffling back in her chair. "Thank you, Reg, I can quite do without your smuttiness."

Reg nodded, gazing pensively at his plate. "I stand corrected. But what about Richard and the grandchildren? I thought they were to go down there for a week."

"They were. Only it rained, then with the schools about to go back, they sort of ran out of time. They won't go now."

"Ran out of time," Reg intoned slowly. "You mean, our dear son was disorganized, as usual."

"He works, Reg. He has other things to think about."

"Oh, I see," Reg said, not seeing at all. "So what is it you think we should do exactly?"

"We could go down for a week, relax, see the sea, have some picnics in the countryside. We'll bring Norman, of course."

As if on cue, hearing his name, the Vaizeys' big black Labrador padded in from the next room, paused at the table and licked Maisie's hand, his sad, wet eyes searching her face for some vague reassurance.

"Hello, Norman," Maisie said, sympathetically.

"Actually, I'm not keen on picnics," Reg said. "Insects in your food, buzzing in your face."

"Ants in your pants," Maisie added.

"Quite," said Reg, crisply.

"Or an outdoor pub lunch would be nice, dear. With Norman under the table. We could go on Wednesday."

"Hmm. Not keen on weekdays. Have to run the gauntlet of commuters."

"Not if we wait till mid-morning."

"Not keen on late starts. Up early and away, that's me."

Maisie sighed. "Well, when would you like to go?"

"Suggest Saturday. Early morning."

"But then we'll get all the holidaymakers, Reg."

"Crack of dawn. First light. Beat them to it."

"Hmm." Maisie looked doubtful. Norman offered her his paw and she took it, moulding it thoughtfully in her palm. "Mind you, I suppose we'd be holidaymakers ourselves."

"I think not, Maisie. More specifically, we'd be recreational travellers."

"Recreational travellers?"

"Precisely. Holidaymakers: bawling kids, buckets and spades, cars festooned with bikes, tattooed blokes in England T-shirts, blinding you with their bald heads, all rushing to their concentration camps. We'll give them a wide berth, eh?"

"If you say so, dear. Saturday'll give us plenty time to get ready." She smiled brightly, nodding her head so that her perm trembled. "Time to get excited about it, something to look forward to."

Reginald grunted ambiguously. Getting excited about holidays was a condition to which he was unaccustomed. Holidays were a commitment which did not sit comfortably with Reg's concept of investment and return. People endured weeks of domestic upheaval to prepare for arduous journeys of hundreds of miles, shortly to end up back where they started, all for the speculative nugget of agreeable disorientation. It smacked of time squandered and money wasted. The best outcome the holidaymaker could reliably hope for was the prospect of eventual recovery once back at home.

"Would you like a nice holiday, Norman?" Maisie fondled the dog's paw, grinning, wide-eyed, into his rubbery face.

Norman drooled on the floor and wagged his tail. He trusted her. It was all the same to him; after all, someone else would have to do his packing.

Next day, straight after breakfast, Reg sat at his computer, pecking busily at the keyboard. Passing behind him with a duster, Maisie paused to peer over his shoulder at the screen. Reg froze, grinding his teeth, fists suddenly, unproductively clenched. He hated this kind of invasion, people standing at his back, unseen, menacingly *there*, marking his territory like sniffing dogs.

"Searching for something?" Maisie enquired.

"Don't hover behind me. You're putting me off."

"Sorry. I was only asking."

"If you must know, I'm looking for an alternative route for Saturday."

"We always go the same way – the way we know."

"And we generally get stuck in traffic. I've decided to avoid the motorway, take the A-roads."

"The motorway's faster, dear."

"Not if some idiot crashes. People are careless, they have no consideration."

"Whatever you think, dear."

"Leave this to me."

Maisie took this dismissal as her cue to move on and resume her dusting. She dusted the picture frames and the radiators and the sideboard and the top of the piano which neither of them ever played. Dusting, she felt, was quite restful, more of a pastime than a chore. From dusting, Maisie derived a calm satisfaction, a warm sense of well-being, an indefinable rightness with the world. She dusted seven times a week, sneezing contentedly behind her hand.

When her dusting was done, she crept past Reg's hunched back and noticed a different programme on the screen. He was tracing the cursor over diagrams, circling the mouse to pick up assorted shapes from the side of the display and drag them into the main frame. It didn't look at all like a route map; in fact, it didn't resemble anything Maisie had seen him working with before.

"How's the planner coming?" she asked tentatively.

"All finished. Print it off later."

She nodded at the screen. "Looks like empty boxes."

"It is empty boxes. I'm about to fill them."

"What with?"

Reg slapped his thighs and half-turned towards her. "If you must know, I've managed to adapt a neat little package young Richard sent me. To suit my own purposes, that is. Even given it a name: *MotoCube.* What d'you think of that?"

"Motorcube?"

"*MotoCube.* What it is, you see, is a one-twelfth scale representation of the interior of our car." He waved a hand dramatically across the screen. "You can drag and drop any number of different shapes into the template. So long as you know the dimensions of the luggage items you'll be loading in the car, you can easily slide them into place – a kind of virtual packing – and see if they fit the available space. If they don't, just drag them out again and slot something else in, until you get it all located. Of course, it only works if you log all your shapes and sizes beforehand. I mean, obviously they have to be to scale as well. Get the drift?"

Maisie suspected that, down this particular road, lay inestimable boredom, but just for the moment her fears were to some extent allayed by a blend of puzzlement and disbelief. "But what are all these shapes and things?"

"Our cases and bags. Our bits and pieces. The dog."

"Our – you mean, you've measured Norman?"

"Well, he has to be fitted in."

"Does the computer do a dog-shape?"

"No, obviously, it won't draw an exact replica of a dog. I've just done a Norman-sized rectangle. Then I can drag it on to the back seat."

"Oh dear," Maisie said, touching one hand to the side of her head.

"Something the matter?"

"It's just the thought of you dragging Norman on to the back seat."

"Figure of speech, woman, figure of speech." He turned back to the keyboard, clicking with renewed and merciless enthusiasm. "Not only dimensional, payload orientated as well. Super little programme."

"What does that mean, dear?"

"It means," he went on, not looking at her, "I can also adjust the load distribution within the vehicle, provided I have a record of how much the individual items weigh. In a car travelling at speed, weight distribution is a factor too often ignored."

"I see," said Maisie, peevishly. "Does that mean you've weighed the dog?"

"Not recently, no. I've used the vet's figure from the last visit."

"Should I be weighed before we depart? I wouldn't like to think that cream tea I had with Kathleen last week was upsetting your calculations, and we might all go spinning into the ditch."

Reg turned to face her again. "I do believe you're being sarcastic, Maisie. For what it's worth, no need to worry, our body weights are a constant here and I am solely concerned with the actual baggage payload. You can eat as many cream cakes as you like."

Maisie sighed unhappily. This seemed an awful lot of trouble. "It strikes me as quite complicated. Quite time-consuming."

"Preparation brings its own reward," Reg declared. "Can't just sling the bags in, slam the door and go zooming off."

"Hmm. I rather think that's what most people do all the time."

"Do they indeed? Huh. Must get themselves into a proper pickle, is all I can say."

He assaulted the keyboard in a further frenzy of clicks and mouse-strokes. A workable picture was beginning to appear. A few more minutes, and the car would be as good as loaded. Maisie's misgivings rang thinly in his ears, but they didn't disturb him. A spot of military precision, that's what was needed. Otherwise...in his mind's eye, Reg saw a crawling crocodile of overloaded cars, grinding bumper-to-bumper along the road, their front wheels pawing the air, sparks flying from grounding tailpipes, the hapless occupants leaning desperately into the wind like yachtsmen on the mad brink of shipwreck. Poor, ignorant fools. Small wonder there were accidents.

Early on Tuesday, a procedural misunderstanding – or an unsound assumption – compelled Reg to revisit his electronic diagram. Entering the kitchen, he found Maisie at the cleared table, bent over a large bag, so engrossed in her task, she failed to notice him.

"What are you doing?"

She spun round, hands poised in mid-air. "What am I doing? I'm – I'm knitting you a pair of socks. What does it look like I'm doing? Someone has to pack Norman's bag."

"But that's his big bag," Reg said, frowning. "I've only loaded *MotoCube* for the small one."

Maisie went back to her packing. "Then you'll just have to unload it. His small bag is for weekends; we're going for a week."

"Ah, right. Point taken. Negligent of me. Have to initiate a little schematic rearrangement."

"Yes, you do that," Maisie said boldly. "Hand me out those tins from the cupboard."

He brought out the dog food and went upstairs to take from the loft two suitcases, which he hoped would be capacious enough to satisfy his wife's demands. Packing for an English holiday, he reflected, was invariably a problematic exercise, for it was almost impossible to determine what kind of clothing might be needed, on account of the vagaries of the climate. Even in summer it could be hot or cold, wet or dry, calm or stormy, and sometimes a miscellany of these conditions arose in the space of a single day. This meteorological caprice was one of the more stress-inducing elements discolouring the pre-holiday anticipation, and even with an internet forecast to guide expectations, there could be no guarantee of good or reliable

114

weather. It was a most vexing situation, the more so for someone like Reg, who habitually proceeded through life according to well-defined operational guidelines. Maisie would try to convince him that escape was paramount and the availability of sunshine therefore of secondary importance; but Reg's parameters for a perfect holiday involved bracing cliff-top walks in the fresh air, followed by regenerative meals taken by open pub windows, their flavours enhanced by the brackish al fresco sauce of earth and grass.

On Wednesday he rolled the car out of the garage on to the driveway to prepare it for the journey. He connected the hose and gave the bodywork a thorough soaking, paying particular attention to the windows and mirrors. As a man who habitually cleaned his spectacles three times a day, his grim determination to see where he was going amounted to an anxiety little short of phobia. Many were the occasions Reg had catapulted Maisie's head against the side window as he swerved to avoid a dog or cyclist that had, in the next instant, revealed itself as nothing more than a smudge on the windscreen. By the time Maisie appeared outside with a mug of coffee and a melting Jaffa cake, Reg had washed the car, adjusted the tyre pressures, topped up the oil and checked the levels of coolant and hydraulic fluid. As she approached she could see his legs projecting from beneath the chassis, like a man run over.

"I'll put your drink on the wall here," she called out.

"What?" He grunted loudly and wheeled himself into the daylight, his back supported on the trolley he had built by screwing four old chair castors to a discarded breadboard.

Maisie frowned at him, licking chocolate from her fingers. "Is something falling off?"

Reg sat up and rested against the car door. "Falling off? Yes, you could say that. My enthusiasm for recreational travelling is rapidly diminishing."

His wife shrugged and held out his coffee mug. "We don't actually have to go."

"The wheels are in motion," Reg said, reaching for his drink.

"What are you looking for?"

"Looking for?"

"Under the car. What are you looking for?"

Reg sighed. "I am merely examining the exhaust system. It's a wise precaution."

"What, in case it drops off?"

"Detachment is unlikely, though not impossible. Hand me that Jaffa cake before it self-destructs."

"Here. 'Scuse fingers." She perched on the low wall and stared at him. "Something's wrong with our exhaust?"

"Not that I can see. I have been able to detect no aural distortion in the flow of gases."

"Oh. I wondered why you were running the engine."

Reg sipped his coffee, munched his cake, wiped his lips and proceeded to enlighten Maisie on the risk of asphyxiation from a leaking exhaust and the potentially fatal consequences of carbon monoxide poisoning.

"I never realised motoring was so dangerous," Maisie confessed.

"That's why I adhere to my pre-departure checklist. Safety first, Maisie, safety first. Go driving off without inspecting your exhaust, next thing you know, you're slumped boss-eyed at the wheel and careering headlong into a concrete bridge. Game over."

"Oh dear." She wiped her eyes and gazed unhappily at the weeds sprouting through the cracks in the ground. "What a performance."

"Ah, that's holidays for you," Reg said, with self-righteous satisfaction.

Thursday dawned wet and windy, but Reg was unconcerned, for he had attended to the car and planned to pack his suitcase, which was an indoor task unaffected by the weather. He opened the case on the bed and stood over it, peering thoughtfully into the empty space. A week, they would be away. Seven nights; or, more pertinently, seven mornings. The number of nights he considered an irrelevance. At night, you put your pyjamas on and went to bed. That was it; nothing happened. In the morning you got up and dressed according to the prevailing weather, your general disposition and an intuitive overview of the likely rigours of the day. The mornings were what counted, compartmentalized within a factor of seven. Reg rummaged in his wardrobe and chest of drawers, laying out on the bed a mature gentleman's recreational attire. In one combined pile, seven each of underpants, pairs of socks and neatly folded handkerchiefs. Next to these essentials he placed seven shirts and sweatshirts, before standing back to consider how many pairs of trousers and shoes he might require. It all – depended.

"It all depends," he murmured absently to himself, lost in concentration, not hearing Maisie entering the room behind him.

"What depends on what?" Maisie asked.

"Oh, hello, dear," he acknowledged, turning round, a trouser belt dangling from his hand.

"You were muttering to yourself, Reg. Something about – "

"No, I was just trying to decide what to take. You see, it's all really quite – "

"Difficult."

"Yes, I'm afraid so."

"You shouldn't get stressed. It's bad for your blood pressure."

Reg thumbed his nose and returned to his packing. "Regrettably, Maisie, stress is an ineradicable part of the procedure. In the course of our daily lives, going on holiday is one of the most stressful exercises we undertake."

Maisie stroked her temples with fingertips that trembled ever so slightly, a nervous vibration. "Yes, I suppose so. Oh dear. I hadn't thought."

"About what?"

"Well, this and that. Everything, really. Tell the truth, I'm a bit worried about that exhaust pipe."

"I have checked the exhaust system and found it to be intact and secure." He started layering pyjamas and underwear in the case. "My deliberations should allay your fears."

"Yes. Yes, of course. You're very thorough, Reg."

117

"Indeed I am. We can't just go bumbling off into oblivion."

She stepped up to peer over his shoulder. "Have you remembered your shorts? They say we could be in for a mini-heatwave."

"My shorts? I am not a man to wear shorts."

"Why not? You've got two pairs."

"I know. You bought them for me, I seem to recall, in a moment of madness."

"Buying shorts is hardly madness, dear."

"Maisie, I am not about to display a pair of spindly white legs to complete strangers."

"But your legs are only white and spindly because you don't let the sun get at them. If you were to expose them, they soon wouldn't be white and spindly any more. Don't you think?"

Reg flipped down the case lid, pushed aside a pile of shirts and sat down heavily on the bed. Frowning under beetling brows, he faced his wife with an expression which she knew from past experience could only be the prelude to one of his stern lectures on the follies of others.

"Mind you don't crumple your clothes, Reg," she said, timorously.

"Maisie, now listen to me. Listen carefully."

"Very well, dear."

"Three or four times a week I'm in the High Street."

"I know, dear."

"And do you know what I see, whenever the sun comes out? Well, I'll tell you. Teetering along in their ridiculous shorts, old buggers making grotesque exhibitions of themselves, exposing their gnarled sticks of legs like contestants in some horrible knobbly-knees competition, with their bleached walnut kneecaps and their stringy blue veins like condemned electrical wiring, some of them with legs so shrivelled it's a wonder they can walk at all, parading up and down with these ghastly white twigs protruding from their pants." He shook his head, blowing a shuddering breath from slackened lips. "And do you know what, Maisie, eh? Do you know what I want to do when I am confronted with this obscene spectacle? I want to hold up both

118

hands like a traffic cop and shout at the top of my voice: 'Go home, you crabby old fools, and put some trousers on!'"

Maisie's nodding head was tilted down at the floor, one hand shielding her eyes. A kind of moist bleating noise came from inside her palm. Reg thought she seemed unsteady on her feet.

"Have I made myself clear?" Reg persisted.

"Perfectly. No shorts then?"she quailed.

"Got it in one. Buttoned down."

Whereupon Maisie turned to leave the room, only to hear Reg call after her.

"A question, my dear."

"What is it?" she asked, over her shoulder.

"I won't talk to your back. Face me, please."

Maisie pursed her lips tightly together and, turning, leant wearily against the doorpost. "You want to ask me something?"

"I do. Will you be packing your miniskirt?"

She pulled a face upon which irritation and confusion were hopelessly entangled. "What do you mean?"

"I think my question was abundantly clear. Will you be pack-?"

"Yes, I heard you, Reg."

"Aha. And your answer is?"

"No, Reg, because I don't have a miniskirt, as you perfectly well know, and if I did, I would certainly not be wearing it at seventy years of age."

"Well, I must say I'm glad, and not a little relieved to hear it." Reg leaned forward with his hands on his thighs, smiling up at her. "That absurdity, you see, would be no less vulgar than my own, were I to go, as you apparently anticipated, tottering about in my shorts."

She clasped her hands in front of her, regarding him earnestly. "We simply don't have the legs for it – do we, Reg?"

"Yours, Maisie, are mottled and flabby, while mine, I freely admit, are thin and white like whittled sticks. They are features not suited to public exhibition. We'll be staggering about, showing our bottoms next, and then where should we be?"

"In the police station, most likely."

"Hmm, yes, quite." He rubbed his chin and gazed morosely at the floor. "Enough said, I think."

"Can I go now?" Maisie asked. "There's things to do."

"What? Oh, yes, yes, of course. Best get on."

"I shall pack my case in the morning, first thing."

He stared at her vacantly. "Cup of tea?" he enquired.

The Vaizeys always enjoyed a cooked breakfast on Fridays. That is, they habitually *ate* a cooked breakfast – a full English – prepared by Maisie and jointly consumed at the kitchen table in an atmosphere of wordless absorption too intense to be classified within the normal concept of enjoyment. They ate solemnly with their heads down, hunched over plates of fried eggs, bacon, sausages, fried bread, mushrooms, tomatoes, baked beans and black pudding, a meal which sustained them for the rest of the day after the forty-five minutes it had taken to assemble, cook and eat it.

This Friday Reg found himself at the table alone with not so much as a knife and fork in front of him. He was hungry and puzzled. For a couple of minutes he sat there, scanning an empty table, until the pointlessness of the occasion began to impress itself upon him, and he got up and moved to the foot of the stairs, where he could hear above the stairwell the scraping of wardrobe doors and the bumps and thumps of bags and boxes landing on the bedroom floor.

He stepped on to the first stair, poised with one hand on the newel post. "Maisie? I'm starving here! What's going on up there?"

Her thin voice floated down to him. "I'm making a start on packing. We're going away tomorrow."

"I'm well aware of that. Are we to have no breakfast? It's Friday."

"I know what day it is. That's why I'm packing."

"Are you cooking breakfast?"

"Not up here I'm not."

Reg closed his eyes and slowly digested this attempt at sarcasm. The holiday was taking its toll, and they had not yet left home. The pressure was on and building. The *stressometer* installed in his head displayed a flickering needle, arcing alarmingly towards the red sector.

"Reg?" Maisie's face appeared over the upstairs banister rail.

"I'm listening."

"You could at least make a start."

"What?"

"Get out the pans. Take the eggs and bacon out of the fridge. Slice some bread."

"Ah, right."

"Can you manage that?"

"And where shall I put the food?"

"Just think about it, Reg. Or perhaps you could programme the problem into your computer."

Reg returned to the kitchen and stood staring at the barren table. A low gurgling, rather like the sound of bathwater running away, resonated in his empty stomach. Crouching, he rummaged in the cupboards for a selection of pots and pans, then he rose, wincing against the protest of his thigh muscles, and searched the fridge for bacon, eggs and a pack of sausages. He laid out all the pans and food on the table, only to change his mind and sweep everything on to the nearest worktop.

"Hah. Should do the trick," he said to himself.

After a minute or two he picked up a saucepan, turned it over to inspect the base and put it down again. From the drawer he took a breadknife and carefully tested its sharpness against his thumb.

"Seems to be satisfactory," he muttered. "Wonder where she keeps the vegetables."

Further inspiration impelled him to locate plates and cutlery and set them out on the table, together with glasses for orange juice. He smiled guardedly. Things were going quite well. He pulled out a chair, sat down facing an empty plate and stood up again, checking his watch.

Maisie must have crept softly down the stairs, for he knew nothing of her arrival until she appeared beside him, carrying a large plastic box, which she placed at the end of the table.

Reg spread his hands towards the worktop. "I've made a start," he said.

"Hmm. You've started starting."

"Indeed. What's the box for?"

"To put food in. For the caravan. We don't want to go shopping the minute we get there."

"Er…no, I suppose not. Only…"

"What's the matter?"

"I'd quite overlooked the requirement. It's not entered on *Motocube*."

"Well, we need the food, and it has to go inside something."

Reg nodded with his eyes closed, pinching the bridge of his nose. It was most frustrating. Just when he thought he had the measure of Maisie, she would come up with some infuriatingly practical observation, instantly confounding all his painstakingly considered theories on female inadequacy. It was a rather bad show.

"Have to check the programme again anyway," he said. "Need to weigh your case. Have you finished with it yet?"

"No. Another ten minutes. I've interrupted my packing to do your breakfast."

"Ah, right. What can I do?"

"Not much, on past experience, aside from eating it."

She elbowed past him and lit the hob. "Go and read your paper, Reg. I'll call you when it's ready."

After they had gorged themselves on one of Maisie's elaborate fry-ups, heads bowed in silent mastication and glossy brows almost touching the plates, Reg agreed to stack the hardware in the dishwasher while his wife filled the plastic provisions box and went back to the bedroom to complete her packing. A quarter of an hour later, she reappeared, dragging a large suitcase down the stairs behind her. Reg wrested the case from her and heaved it into the hall, where he had already left the box of food. Using his digital luggage scale, he weighed the box and the case, noting the values on a slip of paper. His next task was to boot up his computer, open the *Motocube* programme and enter the remaining data for what he would now refer to as cargo. Finally, a sheet of A4 was printed, showing the plan interior of the car with the ideal location points of everything they would transport in the morning.

Reg studied the print-out with great satisfaction. "Simple, really," he puffed.

Maisie spent the afternoon in the conservatory with her feet up on the pouffe. Her eyes were closed and a cold, damp flannel was draped over her uplifted forehead. This was a time when it all began to seem uncontainable, as though even their own familiar and well-ordered house might shortly groan and crumble under the pressure of all-pervading anxiety, burying the pair of them beneath the smoking boulders of emotional chaos. By now any joyful anticipation to which the Vaizeys might conceivably have claimed access as the day of their departure drew near, had become interred beneath a veritable ordure of impending doom.

"Holidays, holidays, holidays," Reg chanted, as he opened the garage door and, consulting his documentation, began to load their cargo in the car. "Go out in a moment, get some fuel. Take the dual carriageway, test the old dynamic balance."

Maisie dozed, temporarily released from the bondage of preparation. She woke at six in the evening, wondering in a bleary daze if perhaps it had all been a bad dream. Norman slouched in and offered his head to be patted. Maisie pulled a tissue from her sleeve, wiped the strings of slobber from his jowls and told him he would have to make do with biscuits and left-over pasta for his dinner, because she had carelessly packed all the dog food in the caravan box.

Perhaps her afternoon snooze had taken the edge off Maisie's sleep span, for she woke very early on Saturday morning and peeped out to see the garden bathed in a pale wash of moonlight. How calm and peaceful it looked. For a brief moment she thought it would be the most natural thing in the world to trot down the stairs, her nightie trailing softly behind her, and step out on to the dew-soaked lawn, feeling the tingling chill of the damp grass under her bare feet.

Disturbed to sense her leaning across his face, Reg rolled over, grunting, and opened his eyes. "What are you doing?" he growled.

"Just looking at the moonlight, dear. It's beautiful, like silver on the lawn." She stroked his shoulder where his pyjama top had slipped aside. "Oh, Reg."

"What on earth are you - ? Pull yourself together, woman!"

At four o'clock they were both wide awake. Norman was snoring on the landing. They lay on their backs and tried to make out the imperfections in the ceiling. Reg extended a furtive hand under the duvet and scratched his testicles, suspecting it could be the only pleasure he would encounter that day.

"Need to make an early start," he reminded her, gruffly.

"Yes, dear."

"Let's hope we don't hit traffic."

"Did you remember Norman's water bottle, dear?"

"Filled and stowed in the pocket behind my seat to ensure it remains upright and cannot leak."

"That's good, dear."

"Merely sensible, Maisie, merely sensible."

They stared at the ceiling until half past four. Norman had a dream and shook like a black jelly, emitting a series of whoops and yelps. While the noise was at its peak, Reg seized upon the opportunity to indulge a quiet fart.

Maisie sat up, yawning. "I could make us some tea," she said.

"Excellent. Then I shall get up." He stuck one leg out of bed. "I wonder if I should have checked those hose clips. They can be loosened by engine vibration."

"I'm more worried about those holes in the exhaust," Maisie whined.

"I told you, there are no holes in the exhaust. I have examined it thoroughly."

Maisie went to make the tea. Reg sat on the edge of the bed in the dark and scratched his testicles. Everything seemed to be in order down there. Norman sneezed, firing slobber across the landing carpet. Maisie returned with a tray of tea and gingernuts. Reg dunked his biscuit and raised it to his lips. It smelled fishy. He wiped his fingers on his pyjamas.

"We could have some toast in the conservatory before we go," Maisie suggested.

With the light coming up, they sat in the conservatory, munching toast and gazing out on to the velvet lawn.

"You've made a lovely job of the garden, dear," Maisie said.

"I think maybe I should put a pack of oil in the boot, just in case," Reg said.

"Oh, I can hear the birds singing. How lovely."

"Best get weaving," Reg said, gritting his teeth. "Did you give Norman his anti-sickness pill?"

"Yes, I added it to his Cheerios."

They sat a while longer, gazing into the garden. The dew on the grass sparkled like frost.

"Hope there's no damned roadworks," Reg said.

"It's so peaceful out there." Maisie clasped her hands together as if in prayer.

"Wait till those brats come out, screaming like banshees."

"Oh, Reg. They're only children having fun. They get excited."

"They should be taught the difference between excitement and hysteria," said Reg.

A squirrel scampered across the lawn.

"Oh, look at that." Maisie leaned forward to see where the creature had gone. "Aren't we lucky to see nature at work in our own garden."

"Time we were leaving, Maisie. Fetch the dog."

Maisie didn't move. A single tear ran down her cheek. She pulled a tissue from her sleeve and blew her nose.

"Got a cold?" Reg asked.

"No, dear. Just – just thinking."

"Can't sit here thinking, woman. Roads are filling up. Bucket and spade brigade. Weekend drivers." He sighed, slapping his thighs. "Caravans skewed on the grass verges, one wheel off, leaning at a drunken angle, all the crockery inside smashed to smithereens. Welcome to recreational travelling."

Maisie nodded. "I was thinking, Reg."

"Ah, so you said. About what, exactly?"

"I don't know – such a long way."

"What?"

"Reg?"

"Articulate your thoughts, woman."

"The man says it's going to be a nice day."

"Man? What man?"

"The weather man. Lovely sunshine. Quite warm."

"Hmm. Best get moving then."

"Oh, Reg." Maisie heaved a deep sigh and shook her head. "Can't we just..."

"Just what?"

"Well, you see, I could ring Richard and suggest to him that he and Ruth go down to the caravan for the last weekend before the schools go back. The children would love that. I'd tell him I've got a cold and can't go and say can he check it out for us, make sure everything's all right."

Reg thumbed his nose, still staring into the garden.

"What do you think, dear?"

"Elimination of numerous potential stress factors," Reg pronounced.

"I mean, holidays are so nice, dear, but so inclined to put us under pressure – don't you think?"

"Got a bottle of good Rioja indoors, Maisie. Could enjoy that sitting quietly at our garden table. You could wear your new sun hat."

"Yes, dear. Oh, yes. Thing is, I..."

"You what?"

"I did promise Norman a paddle."

"Huh. Stick him in the pond."

"Poor Norman. He's beginning to look old now."

"That's because he is old," Reg said wearily. "Come to that, we're all old." He rose stiffly to his feet, steadying himself with one hand on the chair arm. "We're too bloody old, Maisie, and that's the truth of it."

Maisie looked up at him brightly, as though she had not quite interpreted his meaning. "I had an idea, Reg. If we don't go, I mean."

"Oh yes?"

"Yes. It's that box of food." She giggled girlishly, flapping a hand over her nose. "There's some nice things in it. We could bring it out on the lawn at lunch-time and have a lovely picnic. And there's your bottle of wine."

"Yes. Yes, I suppose we could," Reg conceded, and he regarded her quite tenderly.

"There'd be no-one to disturb us. No crowds, no traffic jams, no noise."

"Now you come to mention it, Maisie, it does all make a lot of sense." He reached down and squeezed her arm in a gesture not far removed from affection. "I think perhaps I shall have another cup of tea and then go and empty the luggage from the car. What do you say?"

"Surely you can do that later, dear. When you've rested."

"Ah, I think not. Unnecessary compression of the suspension, you see."

"Oh well, you know best, dear."

He unlocked the conservatory door and let in a fragrant waft of cool air.

"This afternoon, Reg, we could have a little sleep." She smiled, reaching for his hand. "We could go upstairs and lie down all cosy on the single bed."

"Steady on ,Maisie."

"Just a thought, dear."

"Best get a grip. I'll make us a fresh pot of tea."

By nine o'clock they were sitting in the garden, side by side in folding chairs. Maisie's food box was under the plastic table. Reg linked his hands behind his neck and tipped back his head so all he could see was the sky.

"Isn't this just lovely, dear?" Maisie sighed.
"First day of our holiday," Reg said.
And he closed his eyes and smiled.

Transport of Delight

She did not normally bother with the trivial banter of breakfast television, but today Marcie Willetts felt quite different. For a start, the sun was shining, after days of desultory rain. The morning's post had brought her free bus pass. On the kitchen table lay the documents which had arrived in a brown envelope last week, the final papers confirming her divorce from the tiresome Jack Willetts, an obstacle to pleasure now removed from her life for ever. For these reasons, Marcie found herself basking in a warm glow of physical and spiritual freedom, a sense of liberation, an experience that carried her on a wave of euphoria to the tantalising brink of recklessness.

On the TV screen, a smiling man in tan trousers and a checked shirt, dressed for summer leisure, promised steady improvement in the weather. "We're looking at an expansive high-pressure system moving east from the Azores," he said.

Marcie, bright-eyed, pricked up her ears.

"See how widely spaced these isobars are," the man continued. "By tomorrow this area should be virtually stationary over the British Isles."

Marcie nodded approvingly.

"Expect temperatures to be well above the seasonal average," he added, beaming in a manner redolent of the self-congratulatory, as though he were personally responsible for this happy state of affairs.

Marcie huffed and switched the man off. He was a little too full of himself. She ran her thumb over her humourless image on the bus pass. "You may be over sixty, Marcie," she told herself, "but you're still not bad looking. Hair could do with a bit of attention." She raised a hand and primped it up at the back. "Touch of pink lipstick maybe, you'd pass muster."

Upstairs, she put on a long-sleeved printed tunic in a blue butterfly design, over tailored grey trousers. Her pale blue suede shoes had a slight heel on them, but she always found them comfortable for walking. A lightweight cream jacket completed the ensemble. She admired herself in the bedroom mirror, turning artfully to left and right, lifting her arms and lowering them again. Finally, she applied a little make-up to bring her pale face alive.

"Come on, Marcie," she said, "we're going out."

From the wardrobe she took a deep canvas bag. On the side, a giraffe was drinking from a blue pool under a vivid yellow sun. The bag was a birthday present from her sister Angela. Marcie put some toiletries in the bag, together with a nightdress and a change of underwear. She carried the bag down to the kitchen, smiling broadly. Working quickly, she made some sandwiches with crumbly Cheddar, sweet baby tomatoes and a slavering of her home-made mixed fruit chutney. After she had packed the sandwiches, there was still room in the bag for a flask of hot, sweet tea. Lastly, a library book, J.D. Salinger, *The Catcher in the Rye.*

A great wave of exultation swept over her as she pulled the door shut. There was a bounce in her step as she walked to the bus stop. "I am a free woman," she said to herself, "I can go anywhere, do anything, meet anyone, say anything. My time has come."

The first bus along was a 75B double-decker. Marcie jumped aboard, waved her pass at the bored driver and climbed to the top deck. She liked the idea of travelling at some remove from the crowds and bystanders, constantly looking down upon those less fortunate than herself, their faces contorted by the grim pain of commitment. Marcie's face was suffused with a radiant flush of joyful anticipation. There was no medicine as sweetly powerful as freedom.

Damn it. She had quite forgotten to go to the toilet. Approaching the crossroads, she rang the bell, stomped down the stairs and left the bus at the public lavatories. Inside, she took her time, sitting quietly, patiently, in case there might be that last ounce of pee to come. This was not a pleasure to be hurried.

The next bus along was a single-decker, but it was heading out into the country and the driver had a cheerful face. Marcie stepped on board, brandishing her pass. "I believe you go to Henselbourne," she said to the man at the wheel.

"We do. It's about half an hour."

"Oh, I'm not in any hurry," Marcie assured him. "Tell me, is there a nice pub in Henselbourne?"

"A nice pub?" The driver thought for a moment, gazing ahead through the fly-smeared windscreen. "Ah, there's the Rose and Crown, that's a nice one."

"And where is it, exactly?"

"Find yourself a seat, dear." He jolted the bus into gear. "I'll shout out when we get there."

The bus jerked away from the kerb and Marcie lurched along the aisle to the rear, settling herself in a small seat enclosed within the curvature of the roof. She sat back, smiling, reminiscing. Back seat of the bus. Late night after the party. Squashed together with a boy. Love seat. Kissing seat. Naughty seat. How long ago would that be? Forty-five years? Longer? The recollection suited her mood. You were as young as you felt, and today she felt a young girl again, light-hearted, unencumbered, adventurous. She dipped into the bag and extracted a sandwich. It tasted delicious. At the next stop, while the bus was conveniently stationary, she poured herself some tea from the flask and drank it down. Picnic on the bus. Pulling a tissue from her pocket, she wiped her lips and brushed the crumbs from her trousers.

Opening her purse, she re-examined the photo on her bus pass. "A bit of work, Marcie, and you're still attractive," she assured herself. "Could try putting a touch of blue over your eyes, sort of bring them out. Maybe your nose could be a little smaller, but the shape's there. Nice nose, Marcie." She reached under her jacket to feel her breasts. Well, they hadn't sagged. In that respect, she was lucky. Some of her friends, hardly any older than she was, had them practically dangling out the bottom of their skirts. That Janice Walcott looked like she was carrying a couple of prize marrows about with her, ill-concealed beneath her blouse.

The bus stopped again, and a man got on carrying a fishing rod and a khaki shoulder bag. The man smiled at Marcie and sat across the aisle, a few rows ahead. Marcie stared at the back of his head. Jack had liked fishing, she recalled. In fact, he had enjoyed fishing more than being with her. He would go out all day, morning till dark, and return home triumphant, carrying nothing. Marcie decided she didn't understand the psychology of fishing.

At the next stop the driver craned his neck out of his booth and called, "Rose and Crown, my love! On the corner opposite."

Marcie waved a grateful hand, picked up her bag and walked to the door. Inhaling a gust of fresh air, sweetened by the herbal scent of recently cut grass, she realised how toxic was the air in the back seat of the bus, so close to the rear engine and its leaking fumes. It was good to be outdoors again. She strode along the pavement to the corner, swinging her bag to and fro in a swooping arc.

A few weeks ago, she might well have felt self-conscious, entering a pub alone, but today Marcie had shrugged off the shadow of her former self and stepped boldly into the wood-darkened interior of the saloon with her head held high and a determined glint in her eye. Behind the bar, a young man with a ponytail was pouring a beer for a well-dressed, grey-haired gentleman in a checked jacket and green cords. Marcie waited, smiled and ordered a large glass of white wine and a menu, while the smart man moved round behind her and sat at a table by the open window.

"I'll have a prawn salad baguette," Marcie declared.

The barman pushed her wine glass towards her. "I'll bring the food over."

She sat at a table in an alcove, put down her bag and sipped her wine. It was cool in the pub and agreeably quiet. Reaching for her book, she found the bookmarked page and began reading, with her glass in her spare hand. After a couple of pages, she became aware of some attention from the man in the window seat, who seemed to be staring at her over his raised pint glass. Marcie flicked her eyes in his direction for the briefest of moments, then continued reading as if she had not noticed his interest.

"Such a beautiful day!" the man called out.

"Absolutely." She offered him a tight-lipped smile above the rim of her glass.

"Nobody much about."

"I like it that way," she said.

"Ah. Does that mean you're one for solitude? Only I uh..."

"What?"

"I was going to ask if I might join you."

Marcie lowered the book and studied the man's face. He had grown his grey sideburns down to his earlobes and his hair curled in a loose quiff over his forehead. His skin was surprisingly unlined, softly suntanned, lending his open face an expression kindly yet prosperous.

"Be my guest," she said.

He came over, set down his beer and almost bowed as he extended his hand. "Rupert," he said. "Rupert Branston."

Marcie grinned mischievously. "Really? I bet you're a bit of a pickle."

The man rocked slowly back and forth on his heels, allowing her a weary smile which suggested that he had endured this joke many times before. "I decline to comment," he said, sitting down.

"I'm sorry. Forget I said that. Pleased to meet you, Rupert."

"My pleasure also. Now, are you to leave me guessing?"

"Pardon. Oh, no, of course. I'm Marcie Willetts."

"Marcie. A rather attractive name – for a rather attractive lady."

Marcie dropped her book in the bag, keeping her eyes on Rupert Branston's face. He was quite good-looking, she thought. The breeze from the open window brought her the lemony tang of his after-shave.

"Thank you. Just passing through?"

"No, actually this is my local. I'm on my way to meet an old friend. Thought I'd pop in for a quick drink." He smiled and raised his glass. "I'm glad I did."

"Old school friend, perhaps?"

The barman appeared with Marcie's baguette, and Rupert waited until he had gone. "Something like that. Trouble is, I'm not sure it was such a good idea now."

She cut her baguette neatly in half and rearranged it on the plate. "Why's that?"

"Chap can be a bit eccentric. Lovely day like this, I'd bet you he'll be sitting indoors with the curtains pulled and we'll be peering at each other in semi-darkness. That's why I need the drink."

Marcie chuckled politely and offered Rupert a piece of baguette.

"No thanks. I had a big breakfast."

They sat in silence for a while. Rupert drained his pint and Marcie drank most of her wine. The baguette was larger than she had anticipated.

Rupert stood up. "Another drink?"

She picked up the glass and tilted it thoughtfully to and fro. I wonder if he's trying to get me drunk, she thought, hopefully. "Oh, go on then."

He returned with another pint, another large glass of white wine and a local magazine from the end of the bar. The last of the lunch lay abandoned on Marcie's plate. She fingered the corners of her mouth in case any crumbs adhered there.

"So. Haven't seen you in here before," Rupert said breezily, rubbing his hands together. "Going somewhere in particular?"

"I just fancied a day out. My new bus pass came today. I love the sunshine. And" – she tipped her glass at him – "I'm celebrating the completion of my divorce proceedings. The papers came through last week."

"Well, well." He chinked her glass with a conspiratorial wink. "That's two things we have in common."

"Meaning?"

"Drink up. Sold the car when I retired, go everywhere using my bus pass now. Wonderful piece of plastic. Plus, I divorced Irene in 2010. Oh, we're still casual friends, but – well, you know. Water under the bridge."

"I see. Does that make us kindred spirits?" she asked daringly.

Rupert stared at her, his mouth slightly open. "Not sure, dear lady, not sure. Can't discount the possibility. Anyway, where are you off to?"

"I thought I'd get the 441 from here. It goes to Hampton-on-Sea. I might even stay there the night."

Rupert rubbed his chin speculatively. This woman seemed like fun, yet she had to be taken seriously. He had only come in for a swift drink, but now the momentum of the day had changed, and there were certain measurements to be taken, priorities to be reassessed. He started the process by offering her another glass of wine.

"I don't know. Well, maybe just one more. Then I really must go." She reached out and touched his hand. "You're very kind."

"And you're very appealing," he said.

Marcie smiled appreciatively but tried not to simper. She watched the way Rupert Branston moved as he went to the bar, approving of his upright, almost elegant stance and the manner in which his ash-coloured hair, left long at the back, flicked up in a duck's tail above his collar. Whatever his age, she thought, he was not an old man.

He placed their two glasses carefully on the table and sat down, stuffing notes into his wallet. Clasping one more generous measure of chilled wine in both hands, Marcie considered her position. If Rupert had not specified his intentions, his inclinations were beginning to become apparent, slowly taking form out of a mist of respectable amiability.

"I was thinking," he said. "I was standing at the bar and it came to me."

"What did?"

"That perhaps I should – er – go along with your plan."

135

"What plan?"

He sighed, absently stroking a wet mark on the table-top. "About going to the sea. I thought – what I'm saying is, if it's all the same to you, dear lady, I should very much like to come along with you."

Closing her eyes as an aid to concentration, Marcie pinched the bridge of her nose, head lowered as if in prayer. Though her mind was clouded with alcohol, she could see that the time for a decision had arrived. Here, surely, was an end to idle banter. Rupert Branston appeared before her in a different guise, a bull to be taken by the horns.

"Are you looking for an assignation, Mr Branston?"

"Oh, I think we're already having that. I'm just looking towards the next phase – if you get my meaning."

Marcie felt rather pleased with herself, and quite pleased with Mr Branston, though she was reluctant to show it. There was still room for subtlety.

Rupert tugged his ear-lobe, as if this were some kind of signal. "What I'm saying is, I'd like to come to Hampton with you. On the bus. We could stroll on the beach. I'd buy you an ice-cream. Or a silly hat."

"Do I look like I need a silly hat?"

"On the contrary, Marcie dear, you look, if I may say, self-assured and sophisticated. I was merely offering you a little harmless entertainment."

"I see. What sort of entertainment had you in mind?"

He coughed discreetly and his eyebrows rose nearly an inch, which seemed to Marcie the most eloquent reply she could expect or require. She threw back the last of her wine and reached for her bag. "Come on then, Mr Pickle," she said. Then, at the door, she hesitated, holding up one hand.

"Something the matter?" Rupert enquired.

"Your friend."

"What friend?"

"The man with no name in a darkened room."

"Oh, you mean Osbert."

"Osbert? Do I?"

"Fancy calling a child Osbert." Rupert shook his head in mock despair. "Some parents have no consideration."

"That's as may be. You were supposed to be visiting him, not chatting up strange women."

"You're right, of course." He scratched his head and quickly checked his watch. "Wait here a minute. Sit on the seat outside. I shall return with the problem solved."

She settled herself on a weather-scarred bench beneath a hanging basket and watched as Rupert hovered in the doorway, clasping his phone to his cheek. His free hand danced in the air as he spoke, and he alternately nodded and shook his head, sending ripples of light through the silvery waves of his hair. Marcie admired the taut straightness of his back and the way the cuffs of his well-cut cords broke fashionably over the sides of his leather loafers. This was not a man to whom the term 'pensioner' could be applied with any sensitivity.

She stood up as he returned. "Well?"

"All done, dear lady."

"What did you say?"

"Nasty old tummy bug. Something doing the rounds, you know. Poor old Osbert, he wouldn't want to catch that."

He took her arm and she did not resist. Bumping softly against her, he guided her to the bus stop, thoughtfully carrying her bag in his suntanned hand.

It was mid-afternoon when they reached the beach. Hampton sands were alive with sunbathers, swimmers, scampering dogs and couples strolling hand-in-hand with their heads down in a sun-gilded world of their own. Rupert took her hand and held it lightly as they strolled along the beach.

"Are you enjoying your freedom?" he asked her.

"Very much, thank you."

"I see. And may I enquire, is that 'thank you' for asking or 'thank you' for being your escort?"

"So you're in the escort business now?"

"Hardly. I was trying to determine, if you like, a level of intimacy."

Marcie stopped and peered at him, speculatively. "Mr Branston, I've only known you a couple of hours. Intimacy is something I've not had time to consider."

"Of course. Am I rushing things, perhaps?"

"It rather depends what things you mean," Marcie said, and she poked her tongue in her cheek to show him that, given their circumstances, she could be prevailed upon so long as the issue were not forced. She would be amenable but in control.

At the pier kiosk he bought two ice-cream cornets. Perched on a rigid metal seat twenty feet above the waves, they gazed down through the planking at the clouded green jade of the incoming tide surging round the pilings, hissing and gasping as it sucked at the shingle. Suddenly aware of his unabashed laughter, she looked up to face her companion, seeing his eyes bright with merriment.

"What's so funny, Rupert?"

"You. Your face."

"What?"

"You've got a blob of ice-cream on your nose."

"Oh."

She felt in her pocket for a tissue, but he stopped her, producing a crisp white, folded handkerchief, which he shook loose and gently applied to the end of Marcie's nose.

"There! All better."

She appreciated his calm, old-fashioned tenderness. This, she thought, was not only a gentleman, but a gentle man. His blue eyes radiated the warmth of kindly amusement, but his sense of humour betokened a desire to share fun, never to poke fun or make a joke at another's expense. This assessment led her to wonder about the circumstances of his divorce, the inevitable apportionment of blame. Straying into this area would risk exposing her to the disappointment of a harsher perspective on a friendship which, however fleeting it might be, she was beginning to enjoy; she would not venture along that pathway, for fear of disillusionment.

"I know," she exclaimed, biting off the last inch of her cornet, "we could look for shells! Souvenirs!"

"Souvenirs?"

"Of our day on the beach. Don't you think?"

"You mean seashells or explosives?"

She slapped him playfully on the thigh. "I mean shells. Pretty shells to take home."

"Come on then." He helped her up, taking her bag again. "Let's fill our pockets."

They walked on along the shingled beach, heads down, stooping occasionally to pick up a pink or grey or mottled seashell, pale colours delicately reminiscent of birds' eggs. Rupert hid his shells in his jacket pocket; Marcie dropped hers in the bag swinging from his hand.

"You know, this puts me in mind of my father," he said, "a story he once told me."

"Go on. I like a story."

"Oh, it's a true story."

"Even better."

They drew apart for a moment, each taking a different route to skirt round a couple sunbathing face-down on two towels, the man with a sun-bronzed, muscular back, his wife or girl-friend lying with her face sideways on her outstretched arms, her slender white back protectively oiled and the top of her bikini draped on the towel beside her.

"We meet again," Rupert said, as they stepped together, and he took her hand.

"A lovely day. You were saying..."

"Ah yes. My father."

"What was his name?"

"Is it important?"

"Yes. I like to know these things."

"Okay. His name was Charles. Charles Royston Branston."

"Good names. Solid, reliable names."

"Shall I go on?"

"Please. Is it a funny story?"

"Depends how you look at it. Anyway, it was a couple of years after the war. Dad was shambling along the beach, much as we are now, at Prestwick in Scotland, and there was no-one much about. Then he spied a figure coming slowly towards him – grey, stubbly face, baggy old clothes, didn't look English. When they got close, the man hailed my father in what sounded at first like a German accent, only it turned out he was a Polish airman. So they stood and chatted for a while, pausing now and then to look around them, and suddenly the Pole's attention focused on something dark, sticking half out of the wet sand at the water's edge. Well, Dad wasn't too sure, it looked to him a bit suspicious, the kind of thing you'd leave alone, but this airman chap, he strolls over, nonchalant as you like, and pulls it out with both hands. Just stands there, brushing sand off it."

"Don't tell me!" Marcie looked scared and delighted.

"Quite. Explosive device, either unearthed or washed up. 'Is that what I think it is?' my father says, nervously. 'Okay, is a mine,' replies the Pole. 'Is anti-tank mine, not dangerous.' And he carries right on, slapping the sand off it. By now, Dad's beginning to back away, wondering about legging it. So the airman fellow, he points to these probes on the flat surface. 'Can only explode by impact on these points,' he says, 'not just by holding. You just not touch points.' Dad sort of swallows, feels his hands sweating. 'That's all very well,' he says, as calmly as he can, 'now you know that and I know that. But does the mine know that?'"

Marcie laughed, resting one cheek in her hand. "Extraordinary!"

"Yes, it was, rather. Anyhow, the Polish chap somehow tucks the mine under his arm and starts walking with it. Dad looks incredulous. 'Where do you think you're going?' The chap shrugs. 'Is okay. Anti-tank mine. I take to police station.'"

Marcie shrieked. "No!"

"And that's what he did, apparently. Can you imagine the wonderful scene at the police station when this bloke wanders in with his find and plonks it down on the counter? Bet they all went scuttling for cover. Love it!"

Marcie loved it, too, loved the story, loved the expression she could imagine on Charles Royston's face, loved Rupert Branston's serene grin as he recalled the incident and the way her new friend's perfect teeth flashed white in the sunlight as his animated face moved in time to the music of his memory.

"Perhaps we've got enough shells," she said.

He laughed.

Sometimes holding hands, sometimes just rubbing shoulders, they walked on for half a mile, until they came to a flight of steps opposite a small parade of shops across the road. Under a red awning, the bright lights of a fish and chip shop glimmered invitingly. Rupert looked at the shop window, then at Marcie. She smiled and nodded.

In the mellow early evening light, they sat side by side on a barnacled breakwater, munching haddock and chips from sheets of paper. They ate slowly, without talking, wanting the supper to last as long as possible, the intense pleasure of this moment to be as a time suspended, something with no meaning outside itself.

"You know, Marcie." He wiped his lips with his fingers and screwed the chip paper into a greasy ball. "I doubt I'd have enjoyed that meal more if I'd taken you to a posh restaurant."

"Perfect," she agreed.

They gazed quietly at the sea, the lowering light dancing on the wave crests. Rupert sneaked a glance at his watch. He didn't want this to end, not yet. He took her hand and squeezed it tightly.

"What happens now?" Marcie asked cautiously.

"Up to you, I think. This was your outing, originally. Is this your overnight bag?"

"Sort of. I can do one night, if I want."

"And do you – want?"

She sighed, feeling the warm grip of his hand again. "I'm not sure what I want. It's a bit late to be catching buses back."

"Some of them stop by evening. You could get stranded."

"I know."

"I saw – there was a little place we passed about ten minutes back. Lobelia Cottage, I think it was. A B and B place with hanging baskets outside. It looked welcoming."

She stood up, brushing her clothes. "Will you walk back with me?"

"No, I shall just saunter off and leave you to go stumbling back in the dark on your own." He picked up her bag and swung it back and forth. "Of course I'll come with you."

It took them barely five minutes to reach Lobelia Cottage. They stood staring at it over the road. There were yellow lights on in the downstairs windows, reflecting from copper-coloured ornaments hanging on the walls. You have to make a decision, Marcie, she thought. Or maybe more than one decision.

She turned to Rupert Branston, reaching for her bag. "Rupert, what are you going to do?"

"What?"

"Right now. What are you going to do?"

"Can't say I'm in a hurry," he said flatly. He narrowed his eyes. "Sign in the garden says 'Vacancies'."

Marcie wondered about the import of the plural. The sign in her head said 'Caution'. Signs could be tactfully ignored, of course. You could treat them with disdain or throw mental stones at them. Marcie was looking for relaxation and fulfilment, not for warnings.

"Let's go and ask," Rupert said.

"What are we asking?"

"How many vacant rooms they've got."

"You mean – ?"

"Like I said, I'm in no hurry. That's if you don't mind me hanging around."

"What if they've only the one free room?"

"Well, let's enquire first. No harm in that."

He led her across the road and up the narrow path to the front door, where he rang the bell.

A small, plain woman in jeans and a long floral-print blouse opened the door. Rupert directed his thumb at the sign outside. "Good evening. I was – that is, my sister and I were wondering if you might have two vacant rooms for tonight."

The woman smiled thinly, shaking her blonde head. "Afraid not. Only the one left. We only have four in all, you see."

Rupert looked at Marcie. Marcie looked at Rupert. The woman looked blankly at the pair of them. Marcie blinked rapidly. "Go on," she murmured.

"I think we'll take the last room, then," Rupert said.

The woman peered at Marcie's bag. "Is that all your luggage?"

"Travelling light," said Rupert. "What's the room like?"

"Take it or leave it. It's a single really – well, a large single, but there's a put-you-up as well. If it's just the one night, I mean."

"That's fine," Marcie said, edging into the doorway.

"I'm Margaret Thompson." She stood aside, then closed the door behind them. "And you are?"

Rupert took Marcie's bag again. "I'm John Royston and this is my sister, Claire. We'll have the room, thank you. What time do you serve breakfast?"

"Eight o'clock until nine. Full English available. Details in the room. You're in room three, top of the stairs and turn right. I'll bring up towels shortly."

Marcie followed him up the stairs and waited on the landing while he found the light switch and beckoned her into the room. She looked around quickly and sat on the bed. It felt rather squashy, but it would do for one night. Along one wall, at right-angles to the main bed, stood a primitive-looking Z-bed with a single pillow and a spartan duvet. Rupert sat down carefully on the odd bed, with Marcie's bag between his ankles.

"What do you think?" he asked her, apprehensively.

"Well, brother," she replied, "I think it'll be good when morning comes. But" – she broke into a smile – "we're here and I'm happy and I'm certainly not about to let a rather dismal room spoil my day."

"I'm much relieved – Claire."

"Don't mention it, John."

"Do you think she suspected anything?" he asked.

"All she wants is the room paying for," Marcie said boldly. "Anyway, what's to suspect?"

"I don't know. Am I – uh – leading you into bad ways?"

"I really can't say. Are you? Define bad ways."

Rupert stood up and fiddled with the fragile bed. Some possible bad ways jumped out at him, but he fought them off, at least for the time being. There was no sense in rushing things. When he had adjusted the bed to achieve the most comfort he could reasonably expect, he heard a knock at the door, and Margaret Thompson handed him a pile of white towels for the tiny bathroom in the corner.

"I hope you'll manage," she said, angling her head into the room.

Next to the aged, bulky television there was a meagre hospitality tray, from whose components Marcie made them coffee and biscuits. While Rupert watched TV, she lay back on the bed, her shoulders supported by pillows, and tried to read her book, though her concentration wavered and drifted, requiring her to read the same page several times to absorb its meaning. Her eyes kept floating away from the page to swim around the room, while a small, coy smile creased her lips. What was she doing here? Who was this man? How could this have happened? Should she be admonishing herself for her waywardness, or indulging in self-congratulation for embracing the concept of a free spirit?

The sky darkened at the window, throwing their dim reflections into the room. Marcie was tired. She took her bag to the bathroom and emerged in her nightdress, toying with her hair. Rupert looked at her and smiled. "Time for bed, sister," he said.

Having left home with no intention to be out overnight, he could only undress down to his boxer shorts and slip unobtrusively under the duvet. "Goodnight," he called softly into the darkness.

A church clock struck ten.

"Wake me by seven," Marcie told him.

A breeze sprang up and an errant tree branch thrashed the window.

Marcie started. "What was that?"

"Ghosts," he intoned.

She sat up and threw a cushion at him, making him laugh. As her eyes grew accustomed to the gloom, she looked over and saw him folded awkwardly into the flimsy bed. He was a foot too long for it, adopting a foetal position to gain the necessary support. For the first time that day, she felt sorry for him. He had made her day for her. He deserved better. She rolled over, sighing, realising where this would lead her.

"What's the matter, dear lady? Can't you sleep?"

"Oh, brother of mine."

"We're alone in the dark. I think we can dispense with the subterfuge for now."

"I suppose. Poor Rupert." She clicked on the bedside lamp. "That bed looks so uncomfortable."

He stared at her, absently scratching his head. "It's fine, really."

"Rupert, how can it be fine? It's only fit for a child."

For several seconds, neither spoke. Laughter sounded downstairs. Someone shouted in the street.

"So what do you suggest?" he ventured, optimistically.

She sighed once more, a gesture of mute submission, a concession not to the man in the other bed but to her own scarcely sublimated wishes.

"Marcie?"

"There's not a lot of space, but it's got to be more comfortable than that – that ridiculous apology for a bed."

"Marcie, you don't have to be - "

"Oh, for goodness' sake, Rupert! Will you for once stop being a gentleman? Come over here and get into a proper bed."

He pulled a face in the shadows as he swung towards her, but his eyes were alight with a lustre of anticipation. A vision flashed in his mind: Osbert stolidly installed in his sagging armchair in the half-dark, ready to pour tea for two. Then this. *Thank you, Osbert, for the invitation, for bringing me out. I owe you one.*

There wasn't a lot of room, of course. Of this drawback, might be made a virtue. Pulling himself quite close to her, he lay on his side to maximise the available space. The bed was warm. He was warm. Marcie Willetts was warm.

"Shall I put the light out?" she asked.

"In a minute."

"You've no pyjamas, then."

"Why would I have pyjamas? I was only going to lunch with a friend."

"I remember."

"I should say, my boxer shorts are quite new, they have no extraneous holes and are securely all-enveloping."

Marcie snuggled into the pillows. "A surfeit of information," she mumbled.

For what seemed to Rupert like a long time, they lay breathing softly together with their eyes closed. Marcie fed herself faint threads of his after-shave. Rupert nuzzled closer to her cheek, inhaling the lightest hint of ylang-ylang. She reached for the light switch.

A single *bong* from the church clock told them redundantly that it was half past ten.

"Does that thing go bonging away all night?" Rupert asked wearily.

"How should I know?"

"I know you don't know. I was merely articulating a thought, dear lady."

"Well, you shouldn't articulate in bed," she chided him, and they giggled like infants and surreptitiously adjusted their positions.

The next *bong* might almost have been a starting pistol. His travels for the day may have been over, but Rupert's hand chose this moment to embark hopefully on a journey of its own, caressing the side of Marcie's cheek, the smooth planes of her neck and, with slow inevitability, the conveniently gaping vee of her nightie.

"Rupert, what are you doing?"

"Just keeping you warm, dear lady."

He sighed, folding himself against her. The journey continued uninterrupted.

Her sharp intake of breath concerned, but did not alarm, him. Now his hand had come to rest, laden with a cool orb, a velvety pudding, pliant and cherry-topped.

"Are you all right, Marcie? Am I hurting you?"

"What? No, no, of course not. It's just – no man has touched me there in a long time."

"Indeed? The land of lost opportunity."

"Hmm. You don't seem to have allowed the opportunity to escape you." She flinched, drawing up one leg. "And certainly not down there!"

"Oh, Marcie!"

"Oh, Rupert!"

His manhood crept stealthily from its hiding place. Her trembling fingers encircled him.

"That your prize marrow, Mr Branston?"

"That your honeypot, Mrs Willetts?"

They gave each other gentle pleasure until the next *bong.* Rupert wondered where to go from here. The odd hour of sleep suggested itself. It was amazing. He never knew he could feel excited and relaxed at the same time. Reaching up, he touched her cheek and felt her eyelids fluttering.

"Are you asleep, Marcie?"

"Of course I'm not asleep. My heart's banging away worse than that clock."

"Marcie?"

"What is it?"

"Perhaps we should – you know."

"Well, we've done everything else. And the last thing I had from you was a bag of chips."

"Oh, Marcie, sweet lady!"

"Come on then, Mr Branston. Let's do some gentle *bonging* of our own. Then we can sleep the sleep of the just."

At the kaleidoscopic, whirlwind end of fractured dreams, seven *bongs*, vibrating the window-pane, drew them up from the fragrant morass of slumber.

"What time is it, Rupert?" she burbled into the pillow.

"Eh? Can't you count?"

"Don't be cheeky."

"Seven o'clock. Soon be time for a nice greasy sausage."

"Mm. Had one of those last night."

"Now who's being cheeky?"

Marcie chuckled without opening her eyes. Rupert turned the TV on with the sound low. "I'll let you doze a while," he said. He opened the curtains a few inches, hardly enough to brighten the room. In the bathroom, he showered, dabbed himself quickly with Marcie's deodorant and put on yesterday's clothes. When he came out, a girl on the screen with big glasses – in her thirties, he would guess – was reading the news. He studied the girl's face. When she got to Marcie's age, he wondered, would she look anything like as attractive as the woman now lying on her back in the bed. A flicker of sadness touched something inside him then, as he looked at Marcie's face, the confident, trusting set of her mouth, the uncomplicated stillness of her. For he realised that he had not treated her fairly or honestly. He had not abused her, but he had used her, had misled her by avoiding a lie and calling that the truth. The white lie he had told Osbert had been a small, innocent device; but his deception of this delightful woman seemed, in the stark light of a new day, an act of shameful meanness.

"What are you staring at?"

"Sorry. I thought you were asleep."

"Hmm? I was asleep. I was sort of asleep."

He made her coffee with a stale biscuit in the saucer.

"Do you want to use the bathroom, Marcie?"

"Soon."

They watched the national news. They watched the local news. He drew back the curtains and flooded the room with sunlight. Taking the accommodation card from the bedside table, he sat on the edge of the bed with his back to her.

"Would you want a full English?" he asked.

"Had a full English last night, Mr Branston."

"Very funny, Mrs Willetts."

He let her doze a little longer. It hardly mattered. She was tired. Her eyes were closed and the corners of her lips quivered with the moist undercurrent of an incipient snore. He leaned over and kissed her cheek.

In the end he had to wake her, even though she resisted, groaning, and simply lay gazing up at him, slack-eyed, as if trying to remember who he was. Clasping her upper arms, he drew her upright, encouraging her with kindly words, until she fell loosely against him like a life-sized doll.

"Time for brekkas, dear lady."

"Oh. What time is it?"

"Quarter to nine."

"Quarter to nine? Quarter to nine? Why didn't you wake me?"

"I did. Then you fell asleep again."

Pulling her rumpled nightdress straight, she stumbled to the floor. "I'm in the bathroom. Ten minutes. Shower and change of underwear."

In the breakfast room they found a table by the window and sat tugging awkwardly at their unclean clothes. Two other tables were littered with napkins and dirty plates from departed guests, but one last couple still sat in the corner, idly munching triangular toast.

"You're late," Margaret Thompson said brusquely, as she fussed with their cutlery.

"You're ugly," retorted Rupert, under his breath, and winced as Marcie kicked him under the table.

Marcie ordered a boiled egg, Rupert a poached egg on toast. They helped themselves to orange juice and cornflakes. The sun came streaming in, daubing the fresh tablecloth with dazzling panels of white light.

Rupert sipped his juice, regarding her sombrely over the glass. "Any plans for today?"

"Actually, yes. I saw a notice on the pier about a doll's house exhibition in Lestwick. It's only ten minutes on the bus."

"Hmm. Good idea." He fiddled with his knife and fork, appearing preoccupied.

"Tag along if you want."

149

"What? Oh, I see." He fumbled for a small nugget of salvation, a tiny plaster on the gaping wound in his conscience. "Fact is, dear lady, I really ought to be getting back."

"Up to you," she said brightly.

"Yes."

"Things to do, eh?"

" Well, you see... Jean will be wondering where I am. I turned my phone off."

She frowned, holding a spoonful of cereal in mid-air. "Who's Jean?"

"Jean. She – she's my wife."

"What?" She sounded the 't' with indignant emphasis.

He sighed, gazing unhappily at his empty plate. "Jean'll be waiting for me."

"Jean – you told me you were divorced!"

"Sshh. Keep it down." He glanced at the couple in the corner, morosely masticating their toast. "I'm sorry, I should have said."

They sat back while Margaret Thompson, grunting, delivered their eggs.

Marcie stared blankly at her food. "You told me," she said quietly, "you were divorced from someone called Irene."

"So I was, in October 2010. Then I met Jean at a family party. We were married last Christmas."

"You didn't tell me!"

"You didn't ask me," he said feebly.

"Oh, come on, Rupert! That's no excuse, and well you know it."

"But we've had such a wonderful time, Marcie. We've had a day by the sea, we've had supper on the beach, we've had – "

"We've had sexual intercourse!" she hissed.

"I'll grant you that," he allowed, loftily.

The woman at the far table peered at him solemnly, chewing with her mouth open.

"Rupert Branston, I can't believe this." She shook salt on her egg, grinding her teeth. "That is, I can believe it, because I have to. You couldn't make it up. I don't know," she added wearily, "I feel as if I've stepped off the set of a Channel Four play."

He slid a hand cautiously across the table and stroked her fingers. "You're right, of course. I should have explained. But – well, look at it as a victimless crime."

"A victimless - ? Rupert, don't you think perhaps your wife is the victim?"

"Oh, not really. I mean, she won't know anything about it." He speared his egg and watched the yolk run. "Life goes on."

She ate her breakfast, eyes downcast. She could accommodate his logic but had a problem with the morality. "Do you love her?"

"Certainly. She's my wife."

"In your case, I'm not sure one is a natural consequence of the other."

"What?"

"It doesn't matter. So you're going home?"

"I must. We've got a nice little bungalow on a new estate by the park."

"Sounds very cosy."

"As I said, Marcie, I am really very sorry if I took advantage of you – of your trusting nature, your innocence."

"Hmm. Married man or not, I wasn't so innocent last night."

"Ah. You were – shall we say? – not in full possession of the facts. I surmise that would have made a difference."

"Too damned right it would!"

"And I could have expected no less of you."

"That sounds dangerously to me like someone struggling for a moral high tone," Marcie told him. "I rather suspect that opportunity elapsed some time ago."

The corner couple scraped back their chairs and left. Rupert and Marcie sat facing each other but not looking into each other's eyes. Rupert traced invisible shapes on the tablecloth with a stuttering finger. Marcie slowly, listlessly transferred her gaze to the street outside, where the sun was already gathering heat, bringing out the holidaymakers, clutching the idiotic comforters of their bottles of water.

151

Freeing her hand from his tentative grasp, she mopped a paper napkin over her brow and wiped some crumbs from the corners of her lips. She looked at him and smiled. Her smile broadened into an impish grin; and then, to Rupert Branston's utter amazement, Marcie Willetts began to rock with uncontrollable laughter, shaking the table as she lurched helplessly back and forth in her creaking chair. Her gaiety filled the room.

He insisted on carrying her bag as far as the bus stop. "I shan't see you again," he said. "May I kiss you?"

"After last night, it's a modest request," she said.

He kissed her on the side of the mouth. She could still smell his after-shave, or perhaps she only imagined it. "Goodbye, dear lady."

"Goodbye, Mr Pickle."

She waited until his bus came, and waved at him as he sped away, growing smaller, smaller, disappearing out of her life. Then she crossed the road and sat on a plastic bench in the bus shelter, laughing silently into her hand. The bus to Lestwick would be another fifteen minutes. She opened the neck of her bag and peered thoughtfully at her dirty underwear, decorated with scattered seashells. The number 115B was right on time. She hopped aboard, holding out her pass to the driver.

"Going far?" he enquired, pleasantly.

"I don't think so," Marcie replied. "In fact, I've gone quite far enough already."

To Feed the Ducks

"Come on, come on, let's get you all sorted, shall we? I've got your warm coat, your scarf and your woolly hat – will you want your gloves? – and if you can just help me get them on you, we can have a nice little outing, only it's cold out there and we don't want you catching any nasty surprises." Annie Mulligan bent over the old man, prodding and fussing like a small bird pecking for crumbs. "Now what about your blanket, you'll need it today. Would you like the red one or the blue? They're both clean, so it's your choice, see."

George Hobbs sighed, shifting awkwardly on his wooden chair, managing to be grateful to Annie whilst wishing she would leave him alone. "Not the red blanket," he growled, "it makes me look like I'm going in an ambulance."

"Well, we're not putting you in no ambulance, so the blue one it is. Here, get your sleeves in for starters and I'll do up your buttons, then the scarf and – "

"I can manage, I can manage. I'll do me bits. Just fetch the blanket."

George's wife Elsie, watching these preparations with her back to the kitchen sink, unfolded her arms and side-stepped to the cupboard above the washing machine, where towels, teacloths and wheelchair blankets were stored on a shelf over the boiler. She took out a neatly folded blue blanket and handed it to Annie Mulligan, then she leaned back on the sink again, crossing her ankles, content for the moment to watch this small twice-weekly spectacle played out before her. Elsie, if truth be known, did not particularly like Annie, considering her a fusspot and not the sharpest tool in the box, but the girl was kind and trustworthy and touchingly fond of the old man in her occasional charge. She came early on Tuesdays and Fridays to give George his bath, help him dress and, if the weather was fair, take him to the park in his wheelchair, where he liked to watch the people coming and going and feed bread to the ducks on the big pond. When it was wet, Annie would sit indoors with him and play Scrabble – which George easily won – or listen to music hall songs on the elderly record player. On winter days like today, when it was cold outside, Annie always took the thoughtful precaution of allowing a restorative interval between the hot bath and the chill outdoors, by reading out extracts from the *Daily Mail* while George's fragile metabolism slowly rebalanced itself. Annie was nothing if not careful.

George had found little of interest in today's paper and was keen to get out. The sky had a steely sheen to it and the leafless trees looked darkly brittle, but he knew that Annie would wrap him up warmly with the blanket bound tightly around his thighs and chest, almost like a straitjacket.

Elsie Hobbs nodded her head slowly, nearly imperceptibly, as she studied Annie at work. Annie wasn't bright, but she wasn't expensive either, and for sure she was what you might call 'a good sort'. She was reliable, punctual and invariably pleasant. She generally ignored Mrs Hobbs and got on with the job she was paid for. In return, Elsie spoke sparingly to the carer and was quietly confident that the old man was safe in the girl's hands. She could leave them alone, hovering aimlessly on the periphery of their vision.

"I've put a brown bag of bread on the table," she told Annie.

"Sure, I see it, thanks," Annie said, not looking up. She placed one hand on George's back and the other on his shoulder and, with a little gentle coaxing, managed to manoeuvre him into the wheelchair, where she secured him in his blue blanket, tucking the loose folds under his legs. "Snug as a bug in a rug," she declared.

"This chair's wobbling about," George grumbled.

"Ah, it's only me making it wobble. Reckon these brakes could do with a bit of tightening."

"I'll get my son to see to it," Elsie said.

"Right you are, Mrs Hobbs."

Elsie moved to the table and handed Annie the bag of bread. As usual, the girl had made a neat job of packaging George for the journey; she had to give her that much. Maybe

Annie wasn't what you'd call clever, but she was good at what she did. Elsie thought it wasn't ideal work for a young girl, but they paid her and she got on with it and that was all there was to it. She didn't seem to mind George's bubbly farting in the bath or the way his withered grey-haired balls and penis flopped against her wrist as she dried between his legs, cheerfully ignoring his grunts and idle complaints as she eased him into his frequently threadbare clothes. Frankly, the world could do with a few more of Annie Mulligan.

"Well, I think that's you fixed," Annie said, and she tugged George's red wool hat down firmly over his ears. "Let's be going then. Oh, your arms. D'you want them outside or under the blanket?"

"Outside for now. I've got me gloves."

"So you have."

She reached down to release the brakes and deftly rotated the old man towards the door. Elsie, watching them go, came close to managing a smile, the merest breath of approval.

A brave white sun had left its thinly quivering disc hanging in the muslin clouds, its meagre warmth already streaking the frosted grass with vivid deltas of renewal, islands of green amid a carpet of spiked silver. On the surface of the pond, dark pools the colour of old oil had spread between the melting skeins of ice, affording the darting, quarrelsome ducks a brief prospect of adventure.

"Here, stop, right here, this'll do! D'you hear me?"

"I hear you, George. Don't shout. Don't fidget."

She parked the wheelchair on the flagstones a few feet from the water's edge and applied the brakes. From her coat pocket she took the brown bag and dropped it in George's lap. His eyes fixed on the water, the old man rummaged in the bag, tore off some rags of crust and tossed them clumsily on to the thinning ice. Out of nowhere, spontaneous as rabbits from a magician's hat, a squawking flurry of ducks pelted into view, pecking wildly at the bread and at one another, beating their wings on the treacly water. George shook his head, dredging up a guttural laugh.

"Will you just look at them!" Annie bent to his ear, cocooned in the wool hat. "You'd think they was starving!"

George smiled, open-mouthed. He loved to see the ducks. Paddling in frantic formation behind their mother, a phalanx of tiny ducklings, soft down striped like tigers, arrowed into view, homing in on the floating bread. Father was not far behind, his crackling quacks urging order and caution. Sunlight speared the mallard's glossy head and drenched his chestnut breast in a glowing inflorescence of burnished gold. Where else in nature, George wondered, could you see such rich blue-green iridescence as gleamed upon the male duck's velvet head? Perhaps it was only the cold, perhaps not, but tears collected in the old man's eyes, and he ripped at the last of the bread and, drawing back his thick-padded arm, aimed his throw at the mallard's dusky bill as it shovelled the murky water.

Annie, standing behind him, reached down for the paper bag. "Is that your bread all gone?"

"What? Yes. All finished."

She took the bag and screwed it into a ball. "George, your hands'll be freezing. You've no gloves on."

"Took them off. Couldn't get at the bread."

"Well, they're going blue." She grabbed the gloves, stuffed down the side of the chair, and began tugging them over George's icy fingers.

"All right, all right, I can do it meself."

"Have it your own way."

She waited patiently while he struggled with the gloves, then she grappled with the blanket, managing to bind it down smoothly with his hands underneath to keep warm. The clear blue sky was so pale it was almost silver, the low sun drained of warmth. Annie pulled him back a couple of feet from the edge, bending to jiggle the brake levers.

George half turned, scowling. "Don't fiddle with the brakes!"

"Who's fiddling? I'm just making sure they're on. Sure, they need seeing to."

Some days they could watch the kids playing with their toy boats. When there were no ducks about, George liked to see the boats bobbing on the water, the quietly tolerant smiles of the mothers and fathers, the innocent excitement on the children's faces. Sometimes there were sail boats, sometimes a few motor boats powered by batteries. Today he saw only a single child, snugly bundled in a red anorak, crouching at the pond's edge with his mother, shapeless in an oversized sheepskin coat, bending anxiously at his back, while he prodded a yellow yacht across the splintered ice to the darkly dimpling water just beyond his reach.

Annie drew back her sleeve to check her watch. In her raincoat and no hat, she was feeling the cold now that a breeze had sprung up, ruffling the surface of the pond and twisting the skeletal limbs of the trees. George, warmly wrapped, would sit here for as long as she let him, but it was time to move on, and she leaned into the wheelchair, stamping her feet, flexing her arms on the handlebars.

"Getting chilly, George. Shall we get us a hot drink?"

Her words hardly penetrated the lumpish folds of the wool hat. "Do what?"

"Should we get a hot drink?" Annie shouted.

"Don't yell at me, I'm not deaf!"

"It's okay. I'm sorry."

"What?"

"Would you like a tea or a coffee? There's the hut open."

George cranked back his head to peer up at the opposite grass bank, where the corrugated iron roof of the workmen's shed was visible over the blue box of the refreshment hut with its open hatch and silver-gleaming tea urn.

"Do they do soup?" he asked. "I think they do soup."

"I believe so, George. We can ask."

Annie released the brakes and pushed him round the end of the pond and up the slope to the hut. A small boy, his mother *tutting* in frustration, reached up to the hatch for an ice-cream cornet he insisted on having, despite the cold.

"Don't expect you'll be selling many of them today," Annie said to the girl serving, as she moved up to place her order.

"Kids!" The girl shook her head. "What'll it be for you, dear?"

"Coffee, two sugars. And is there soup today?"

"Tomato or mushroom," came the reply.

Annie called out the options to George beside her.

"Tomato!" he barked.

While the girl disappeared into the gloom to make the drinks, Annie bent her head and fumbled in her purse for some change. The boy and his mother had wandered away, the girl stood with her back to the hatch and Annie was concentrating on her purse. George was unattended, gazing downhill at the deserted pond. He squirmed awkwardly in the chair, trying unsuccessfully to free his blanketed hands, ready to hold his soup when it arrived.

The girl turned and placed the coffee cup on the counter. She gasped. "Look out for your man!"

But her cry had come too late. Strained by the tilted weight against worn blocks, the wheelchair brakes had freed themselves, sending the chair and its helpless passenger bumping over the rutted grass, across the flagstones and into the pond with a duck-scattering explosion of brown froth. George's strangled cry, as he plunged into the freezing water, rang out above the frantic quacking of flapping ducks and the horrified shrieks from the kiosk.

"Oh my God, no!" Annie clapped a hand to her mouth, her falling purse raining coins on the ground.

Marooned in the pond with his back to her, George kicked his legs uselessly underwater, stirring up brown sludge. The water was up to his waist. His cries carried on the breeze, savage, uncomprehending, like the mad bleating of a tortured sheep.

Annie was at the pond's edge, tearing her hair. "My God! Will someone help me?"

The tea girl was out of her hut, running behind her. "I'll get somebody. They'll get him out!"

158

Annie waded into the water, instantly feeling an icy surge filling her shoes. "Hold on, George! We're getting help. Don't you worry now."

The old man shouted something, but his words were unintelligible, grotesquely distorted by fear and panic. He rocked back and forth in the wheelchair, his arms still trapped beneath the waterlogged blanket. Underfoot, the bottom of the pond was slippery with mud and duck mess, and Annie dared not advance any further for fear of skidding into the deeper water. Slowly, trembling with shock and cold, she stepped backwards, one footstep at a time, until she could lift herself on to the paving stones again, flapping her arms in anguished frustration. Already her feet, squelching in her shoes, felt like two blocks of granular ice. Tears brimmed in her eyes, but she forced them back, knowing that she must be strong and focused; she could not break down or cry, for George was in her charge and needed her now as never before.

Over her shoulder, a man shouted. Rapid footsteps thumped the ground. She turned to see two men in yellow tabards over donkey jackets rushing down the grass slope towards her. She cried out, gesticulating wildly at the chair and its half-submerged occupant. The men wore tattered jeans and work boots and stumbled into the water with massive strides, their arms held wide for balance.

George threw back his head and wailed madly at the sky. The wheelchair rocked under him, threatening to overturn. Reaching him, the first man slid on the dark filth beneath the water and grabbed the back of the chair to keep himself upright. His mate approached more cautiously and went to George's side to reassure him. The other man stood with one hand on George's shoulder. By now the chair had crept forward and water was lapping at the old man's chest.

"Oh, please!" Annie screamed at them, balled fists thrashing the air.

The men waved at her to be quiet. "Have to get him turned," one of them yelled. "Can't pull him out backwards."

They conferred, heads close together, nodding, flexing their arms. Annie stamped her sodden feet, feeling nothing there, just a viscous numbness. Grunting and gasping from exertion, the men managed to drag the wheelchair round in a circle, until at last George could see Annie and Annie could gaze in desperation at George.

"Can you move him?" she cried. "Can you push him to me?"

But the chair had embedded itself in the mud and slime, its wheels sunk to the axles in a toxic slurry of mashed leaves, duck droppings and organic mulch. No matter how hard the men fought to move it, their efforts were useless against the dead weight of the obstacle and the obstinate suck of the polluted water. Across the pond, their snarls of breathless anger rang out in unison with George's terrified screeching.

"Stay here! Stay with him!" One man left the chair and came stomping out of the pond, breaking into a lumbering run as he scaled the bank.

"In God's name, what's happening?" Annie squealed, as the man brushed past her.

"Park warden! Rope!" the man shouted, and he vanished behind the tea hut.

In the pond, the remaining man had freed George's arms and was yanking the saturated blanket aside to prevent it from becoming entangled in the wheels. A moment later the blanket was spreading out like a blue oilslick on the heaving water.

"Get me out!" George screamed. "Get me, get – I'm – I'm – "

"Keep still! You hear me?" He squeezed George's shoulder hard. "We can't carry you. There's no safe footing. We'd only drop you."

George cried out, beating the water to a scummy foam with flailing fists. "For God's sake get me out of here!"

Annie was back in the water, almost up to her knees. Her arms hung limply at her sides. Tears blurred her vision. She felt sick, as if she might vomit in the ice-flecked brown tide. The girl from the hut reappeared beside her, clad in green wellingtons, clutching at her arm. "What on earth's happening?"

"What? I don't know." Annie was staring into the pond. "Something about a rope."

Ahead of them, where George had fed the ducks, the commotion had brought a knot of onlookers to the water's edge. Small children stood gazing in puzzlement at the man sitting in the water. Their parents waited behind them, anxiously clutching the little ones' shoulders, lest they too should topple forward and become part of the spectacle. A boy sucked absently at the yellow nozzle of a plastic water pistol. His father raised a pair of binoculars surreptitiously to his eyes, the better to view the old man's plight. No-one was feeding the ducks now; here was superior entertainment, something ludicrously terrible enacted before their eyes, free of charge or commitment.

A harsh diesel rattle vibrated from beyond the iron roof of the long shed. Swerving down the grass slope, a grey Land Rover pickup roared into view, belching smoke, the park insignia on the driver's door. Annie, chewing her knuckles, watched the driver wrestle the wheel as he hauled the vehicle round to face the shed and then, revving furiously, reversed it to within a few feet of the pond. Doors slammed as the driver, a short man with a stubbled face and a bitter black moustache, dressed in green overalls, jumped to the ground, accompanied by the workman in the yellow tabard.

Annie shrieked, pointing at the accident. "Over there! You gotta get him out!"

"All right, all right, I see him." The driver reached into the tailgate and pulled out a coil of thin green rope. "Stand back, please."

"Are you the park keeper?"

"I'm the warden. You keep right back. Okay?"

Annie walked back and sat down on the concrete step in front of the kiosk, moulding her hands in her lap. The crowd opposite had grown to about thirty people, jostling one another for the best vantage point. Some of them had brought sandwiches, which they clutched in raw hands and crammed into their mouths in the bitter cold.

161

The warden stooped to tie the rope to a hitch at the back of the pickup. The rest of the coil he passed to the other man. "Tie it to the front of the chair, both sides so it's balanced. The two of you stand by to steady him when I pull."

The man nodded and went loping back into the water, kicking up spray. Out in the pond, his mate stood with both hands on George's shoulders, as if to reassure him. The old man's face was ashen, pitted like the moon with the searing pain of the freezing water engulfing him. Annie watched the men work, looping the rope around the uprights below the armrests, dragging it tight. Rather than risk knotting the rope and having it come loose, destabilising the wheelchair, one man gripped the end in his hands, while the other shouted to the warden on the bank.

Quickly, the driver was back in the cab, applying power, slipping back, inching forward again, grinding the clutch as the rope sprang taut. At last it was happening. The Land Rover gained momentum. In the pond the old man's body jerked violently as the wheelchair bucked under him, each workman seizing an armrest to steady its motion as the wheels squirmed in the mud and were suddenly freed, and inch by inch the chair and its pathetic cargo began to plough through the roiling water, scattering sticks and leaves from the blackened spokes. Annie shuddered and wept. George was on his way.

A thin cheer rose up from the crowd as Annie moved down to the water. George heard the people's desultory acclaim and managed to lift one hand in brave acknowledgement as his chair bumped on to the paving, showering detritus. The warden leapt from his seat and soon there were four of them there – the two workmen, the warden and Annie Mulligan – fussing with the half-drowned man, rubbing his grey face, pummelling his lifeless legs.

"Oh, thank you, thank you." Annie flapped her hands over George's waterlogged body, not knowing what she was doing. "Can you undo the rope and I'll get him home."

The warden frowned, shaking his head. "Not so fast, young lady."

"I have to get him back to his wife."

"Not in this state, you don't. You can't wheel him through the streets like this. He'll catch his death." He lowered his voice. "If he hasn't already."

"Then what'll you have me do?"

"Come on. We'll take him to the workshop, get him some dry clothes. Poor guy's freezing."

They all took a hand, pushing the wheelchair. A man from the dispersing crowd ran up to help. George seemed to float across the grass like a man in a sedan chair, dirty water spewing in his wake. He made no sound.

The warden kicked shut the workshop door and slapped his hands together. "Right, I'm Arthur. What's your name, my friend?"

"His name's George," Annie told him. "I'm looking after him."

"Are you now? That why he fell in the pond?"

"It was an accident," Annie said, her voice on the point of breaking.

"I see. We gotta get him out of those wet clothes." He moved up beside George and spoke gruffly in the old man's ear. "Can you walk, George?"

"If we help him up," Annie said, "he can walk a little."

"Can you hear me, George?" Arthur asked.

"He's not deaf," said Annie.

"Can he talk?" asked Arthur impatiently.

"Of course he can talk. He's not stupid. He's just scared, that's all."

"Okay. Electric fire in the office there." He pointed to a half-open door in the corner. "Let's get him in there. Then you can take over. Undress him rub him down with this." He handed Annie a grubby towel. "Spare overalls on the back of the door. Put 'em on him. Understood?"

Annie nodded.

"While you're doing that, I'll be making him a hot drink. Then we'll see about getting you home, George."

Annie gazed miserably at the wheelchair. "His chair's a terrible mess."

"Don't worry about that. I'll put both of you and the chair in the back of the Land Rover and run you home. He needs to get to bed quick as possible."

"You're a kind man."

"Yes, well. I've got work to do, so let's press on with it." He stretched down his top lip and rubbed his moustache. The little black stub made him look severe, Annie thought, but when she looked at his brown eyes, the warden appeared calm and reasonable, almost compassionate.

The yellow-jacketed workmen were hovering uncertainly in the doorway, faces clouded with doubt as to whether their responsibilities in this matter had now been discharged. Arthur flapped a dismissive hand in their general direction. "Get back to work!"

Over her shoulder, Annie acknowledged them with a fleeting, brittle smile. "Thank you both. George won't forget you."

The taller man, who had waited with George in the pond, waved a perfunctory farewell. "Hope the old guy's all right. Good luck, my friend."

There was a swivelling chair in the office, and Annie managed to sit George on it with his back to the cobwebbed window. Piece by piece, she pulled off his sodden clothing, while a dark pool spread over the wood floor. By the time she had reduced the old man to total nakedness, Arthur had thrust a hand round the door to pass in a steaming mug and a black sack. Annie took the mug and placed it on the paper-strewn desk, before bending to stuff the wet clothes into the bag. A halogen fire burned orange at her back as she worked. From a peg on the door she took down a set of green overalls, shook them vigorously and held them in front of George, shivering violently in his naked helplessness.

"Now you've to stand up, George," she said quietly. "You have to help me, see."

"I don't know. Don't know as I can," he whispered.

"Course you can. Just lean into me so's you don't fall."

"What do I do? What do I do, Annie?"

She pulled him, heaving with both arms behind his biceps, and slowly, gradually, he found the faltering strength to move towards her, until his grizzled face was level with hers and his white-haired chest nestled in her coat.

"Lean on me and lift your leg. Come on, George. Nice warm overalls."

"Oh no! Oh no!"

"What is it? What's the matter, George?"

George's thin white legs were flapping from side to side, like sails in a rising wind, slowly at first, then more rapidly, as if driven by some uncontrollable electrical force snapping through his lower body. He stood pinioned against Annie's chest, teetering on the awful brink of subsiding to the floor.

"Oh no! I can't stop it!"

And Annie instinctively held his quaking body away from her at arm's length, balancing his shoulders on her fingertips, as a tawny cataract streamed down the old man's legs, splashing from his ankles on to the already-puddled floor.

She drew in an anguished breath. "Oh, George!"

"Couldn't help it," he moaned.

"All right, all right, never mind." She grabbed the dirty towel. "Hold on to me, I'll wipe you."

George clutched fiercely at her shoulder, whimpering like a child, while Annie mopped his legs with the bunched towel. A movement at the window caught her eye, and she blinked in angry dismay as a small boy peered into the room, his nose flattened obscenely against the glass. She mouthed "Go away!" at the child, furiously shaking her head.

The boy's cry squeaked into the room. "That old chap! I seen his bot, all shrivelled!"

Annie pushed George on to the chair and dashed to bang on the window. George cried out in confusion, grabbing her arm, pumping the flesh.

The door opened and the warden peered in. "Got a problem? D'you want – oh!"

Annie turned to face him. "I'm sorry about the mess. I'll clear it up."

"It's okay. Worse things have happened. Just see to him, give him his drink."

"I'm really sorry."

"I'll sort it, don't worry."

"You're a good man, Arthur."

"Five minutes. I'll make space in the Land Rover."

"His wheelchair..."

"It's in already."

"Bless you."

He closed the door on them. Despite the cold, Annie worked up a sweat as she struggled to dress George in the overalls. She left him barefoot, tossing his shoes and socks in the plastic bag. The filthy towel, dropped in the stinking puddle, would absorb some of the water. She forced him to drink some of the warm tea the warden had made, holding the mug to his quivering lips.

"Come on, George. Let's get you home."

They sat him next to the window in case he was unwell on the short journey and had to be got out in a hurry. He sat quietly, panting, with his head rolling against the glass. Annie travelled squinting at him nervously from the corner of her eye.

"God almighty, I wondered where on earth you'd got to!" Elsie Hobbs met them at the gate, drying her hands on her apron.

"The park, of course," Annie said, stiffly.

Arthur carried the wheelchair up the path and leant it against the fence. He went back for the bag of clothes and handed it solemnly to George's wife. "That's it," he said. "I'm going. Best give him a hot bath."

Annie touched his arm. "I'm – we're grateful," she said. "Really."

Together, the women ushered George into the house, hesitating as he stumbled on the step. Annie closed her eyes in relief as the warmth of the living room enveloped her. The radio was on, a man's stern voice warning of snow on the way.

George capsized on to the sofa and lay there in a bundle, grey-faced. Saliva shone on his chin.

"You could have phoned me," Elsie said.

"What would have been the point?" Annie retorted, splaying out her hands. "You couldn't have got to us. You could have done nothing."

"What happened exactly?"

"Not now, please."

"Why's he in those overalls?"

"Fell in the duckpond," George murmured.

"For Christ's sake!" Elsie blinked ferociously, grinding her teeth. "I thought he was going to feed the bloody ducks, not jump in with them."

"It was an accident – okay? I told you about those useless brakes."

"The chair went in?"

"I turned my back for a second, that's all. It happened in a flash."

"You were supposed to be looking after him!"

"So I was. I was just paying for a mug of soup for him. I was talking to the girl."

Elsie lowered her head and gazed forlornly at the carpet. "I thought you were looking after him. I pay you to look after him."

"And so I was, Mrs Hobbs. After it happened, I got help, I got it sorted. I did my job."

George squirmed awkwardly on the sofa, whinnying like a distressed horse.

"Did your job, did you?" Elsie smacked her thighs defiantly. "Tipped him in the pond, ruined his wheelchair."

"All right, all right, so I was distracted, only for a moment. It happens. Look, shouldn't we be attending to George now, not arguing about what's over and done?"

Elsie worked her thin lips in a petulant circle, staring at the dishevelled figure on the sofa. She sighed, shaking her head. The man on the radio promised gale-force winds and a wind-chill factor of minus ten. He managed to sound rather pleased at this development. Annie imagined him sitting smugly in a warm studio, snug in a cable-knit sweater, with a cup of coffee and a chocolate biscuit in front of him, his wife cooking a tasty casserole for him at home. Some people had all the luck.

"You could run him a bath," Elsie said, testily. "Then come down and help me get him upstairs."

After his bath, George was put to bed with two hot water bottles. He slept until six the next morning, when Elsie heard him coughing. An hour later he was able to get himself up and come downstairs in his pyjamas and dressing gown. He looked pale and complained of chest pains, though he managed to eat some porridge sprinkled with brown sugar. Sitting in his armchair, he read the paper, wheezing as he turned the pages.

Elsie stared at him accusingly. "Could you manage a shave, do you think?"

"Why? I'm not going anywhere."

"Maybe. You make the place look scruffy, sat there with half a beard."

"I'm not well. My insides is all mixed up."

"I could ask Annie to come over and give you a nice shave. Freshen you up, sort of."

"I can do it myself."

With mottled cheeks and the lamplight sparking in the bristles on his jaw, George retired to bed again at seven that evening. He had refused any food after the breakfast porridge. Elsie helped him up the stairs, one hand resting ineffectually in the small of his back. She brought him up two more hot water bottles and touched his forehead as she eased them under the duvet.

"You're all sticky," she said.

"Chest feels like someone's sitting on it," he grumbled.

She sat up, reading. Before midnight she heard a thumping on the floor above her head and went up to see what was wrong. George was lying half out of bed, his chest heaving, dragging in great draughts of raucous breath. Perspiration gleamed on his brow and cheeks. His walking stick hung limply in his dangling hand.

"Is it your chest?" Elsie asked.

"Course it's my chest."

She stood in the doorway, staring at him. Annie might know better what to do, but she didn't want to ring the girl at this late hour.

"Should I get you a hot drink?"

"Don't want a bloody drink."

She heaved him back into bed and covered him up warmly. The sweat was coming through his pyjama jacket like thin grease. "I'll leave the light on," she said.

She went downstairs and thought about her predicament. What should she do? When ought she to do it? If only Annie Mulligan were here, she would know what to do for the best. She didn't particularly like Annie, but she respected her. She hoped Annie hadn't felt her rude when she brought George home from the park. That hadn't been her intention. The accident – for that, surely, was what it was – had really not been Annie's fault, not after the girl had already warned her about the brakes. You had to be fair with people.

At one o'clock she checked upstairs again. George's head had lolled sideways on the pillow and his face was bluish-grey. There was a patch of vomit on his chin and on the bedclothes. She nudged him but he didn't wake. That's when she called the ambulance.

George lay flat and motionless in Intensive Care, apparently comatose, his waxen face distorted by a plastic oxygen mask. From the quiet corridor, Elsie watched through the window as a nurse adjusted the fluid lines attached to his arms and peered at the red and green traces flickering on the screens behind the bed. Less than human now, George seemed to hover in white space, reduced to a buzzing, bleeping robot, helplessly marooned in suspended time.

The nurse came out, closing the door carefully behind her. Elsie turned her back to the window. "It doesn't look good, does it?" she said softly.

"He's warm and he's resting," the nurse said, touching Elsie's arm. She indicated the wooden bench against the wall. "Why don't you sit down a minute."

"I suppose." She sat down slowly, folding her coat under her. "Is it pneumonia, d'you think?"

"Probably. How long was he in the water?" She didn't wait for an answer. "Dirty water, full of bacteria. He may have ingested some."

Elsie gazed hopelessly at the floor. She felt she should be asking medical questions, evincing an intelligent concern, but somehow there seemed little point. They would do the best they could, and that was the end of it. George was her husband, one half of her, her closest friend, and she had abandoned him to strangers in case perhaps they could help him, when she herself had nothing more to offer him. No abdication of responsibility could have cut her more deeply.

The nurse beckoned to a pink-uniformed orderly and asked her to bring Mrs Hobbs a cup of tea. Elsie carried on staring at the floor, until the patterns in the vinyl seemed to swim up to engulf her. Accepting her tea, she lifted the cup in a trembling hand, rattling it in the saucer. Parched with shock and apprehension, she drank down to the last dregs and rested the cup and saucer on the seat beside her.

"Mrs Hobbs, I think you should go home. You're tired out. There's nothing for you to do here. George is resting and you need to do the same."

Elsie looked up and read the nurse's name badge. Janet McAllister. She had the faintest dark moustache, Janet McAllister, but her brown eyes were warm and kind. They encouraged Elsie to be brave in spite of her fears.

Nurse McAllister fiddled with the buttons on her uniform. "Try and get some sleep. It'll be hard, I know. We'll ring you at once if there's any change."

"Please, I'd like to talk to the doctor."

"Of course. Tomorrow. Come back after nine o'clock."

She stood up. "You'll ring me then."

"Certainly. How will you get home?"

"What time is it?"

The nurse glanced at her watch. "It's nearly two-thirty. Shall I get you some transport?"

"If you could. I can't afford a taxi at this hour."

She sat down again and waited. She resisted the temptation to turn and look at George; it hurt too much. She thought, am I being selfish? Is my pain smaller or greater than his? Could I have prevented this? Could anyone have prevented it? The world turns, spinning us off into the void.

A man in brown cords and an anorak was bending over her. "Come on, I'll run you home," he said.

A pool of yellow lamplight mitigated the darkness of her strangely cold bed as she lay tethered to a tenuous sleep by the frailest thread of mindless fatigue. Without him next to her, she woke more than once and wondered where she was, burying her face in the pillow as the recollection swarmed over her. With no little gratitude, whatever might be its import, she sprang into wakefulness soon after seven at the sound of the telephone.

"Hello. This is Mrs Hobbs."

"Ah, Mrs Hobbs. I'm sorry to call so early. It's Sister Maynard at Saint Giles."

"It's about George?"

"Yes. I think perhaps you should come in, if that's possible. George is causing us some concern."

"I will come," Elsie said, already swinging her legs out of bed. She went to the bathroom and splashed cold water on her face, then pulled on her clothes from the night before.

Annie Mulligan answered the phone with surprising alacrity.

"Annie, it's Elsie Hobbs. I'm sorry to ring you like this. It's about George."

"Oh my God! What's happened now?"

"He's in Saint Giles. They've just phoned. It's not good, Annie."

"Elsie?"

"I was wondering. Could you run me back there? I need to see him, in case –"

"Surely, Elsie. We'll go together. We'll be together. We'll do this together."

Respectfully restored to a modicum of privacy, George now lay in a quiet corner of the geriatric ward, his bed shielded by a green-curtained screen. With sombre intuition, Elsie reasoned that he had been moved because, as a clinical exhibit, he could no longer be expected to benefit from the sophisticated paraphernalia surrounding him. The transfer, though humane, was an admission of something darkly inevitable.

Elsie and Annie sat side by side on upright chairs, watching the rise and fall of the old man's blanketed chest. Once he shuddered and coughed into the oxygen mask, but his eyes remained closed.

"Will you look at him?" Annie said, her voice hardly more than a whisper. "I don't know what to say."

"There are no words," Elsie assured her.

"Do you think he can hear us, Elsie?"

"Doubt it. He's dead to the world," she said, prophetically.

Annie rummaged in her coat pocket. "I brought us a muffin each. It's not much, but..."

They sat eating muffins and dropping crumbs on the floor. A nurse parted the screens and took George's pulse and temperature.

"Has he woken up, do you know?" Annie asked her.

The nurse shook her head, not looking at them.

"I could find a machine, get us a hot drink," Annie suggested.

"Up to you," said Elsie.

Annie found a KitKat in the depths of her pocket and broke off a finger for each of them. "Breakfast," she pronounced. The drink was forgotten. Anyway, she didn't want to leave Elsie on her own, not yet.

"Do you know, there was − " Annie checked herself and clutched her throat.

"Know what?"

"I don't remember. It doesn't matter."

"Let's just sit quietly," Elsie proposed.

172

They didn't speak for several minutes. Occasionally Annie glanced at Elsie from the corner of her eye, but she didn't want to be the one to break the silence. Small talk just seemed to make the situation more uncomfortable.

George opened his mouth and moaned, and his head rolled to one side. The women sat forward, each meeting the other's gaze. Annie twisted her hands in her lap.

"Think I'll get the nurse," Elsie said, standing up.

A different nurse came in. She removed George's mask, prised open his eyelids and took his pulse from his wrist and his neck. She stared at him solemnly.

"He's gone, hasn't he?" Elsie regarded her sternly.

"I'm afraid he has, Mrs Hobbs. I'm very sorry."

Annie chewed her knuckles and a tiny whimper escaped from her lips.

Elsie patted the girl's thigh, but it was almost a slap. "Don't, please."

They stared at George, defying him to move and confound them.

The nurse pulled the blanket up under George's chin, as if that would make him more comfortable. "I'll leave you for a moment," she said. "Sister will come in shortly."

Sister Maynard appeared five minutes later and peered at George as though seeing him for the first time. "Dear me," she said, picking up the discarded oxygen mask. "Well, we did what we could, Mrs Hobbs. Unfortunately we were always fighting a losing battle."

The three of them stared at the old man in silence. Elsie, unblinking, chewed her bottom lip, breathing deeply. Annie sat with her face clasped in her hands, grinding her teeth to stem the tears. A thin whistling noise issued from George's colourless mouth, like a final parting breath.

"What happened to him, exactly?" the sister asked, her eyes still on George's face.

Elsie shook her head. "Don't let's talk about it," she said, "not now."

Sister Maynard nodded and lowered her eyes in sympathetic acquiescence. "Of course. Well now. Someone will come to take George in about half an hour. You're very welcome to stay until then." She smiled sadly at each of the women in turn. "I'll leave you in peace in the meantime."

Annie murmured "Thank you" to the sister's retreating back. "Did he have a watch?" she asked Elsie.

"A watch?"

"A watch. A wedding ring. You should have any jewellery."

"He didn't usually wear a watch. There's a ring. Don't worry about it. I'm sure they'll see to that."

They sat quietly, gazing at George, idly studying the red marks the plastic mask had imprinted on his sallow face.

"It seems all wrong," Annie said. "All he wanted was to feed the ducks. Then he asked for some tomato soup. Just some soup. Is that too much to ask?"

Elsie thought about this but didn't reply.

"How will you manage?" Annie asked her.

Elsie frowned, beetling her brows. "What d'you mean, manage?"

"Without him, I mean."

"How will I manage?" Elsie repeated the words with laboured slowness, as though she didn't understand them or couldn't believe them. "I've been managing him for five years, since he had his stroke. That's it now. There's nothing left to manage."

"I see," Annie said, emptily. She decided not to press the point.

Elsie sighed softly and shook her head.

"I forget how old he was," said Annie.

"Eighty-five." She tossed her head in a short, snorting laugh. "'I'm eighty-five, you know – eighty-five!' he used to say, as though that was how fast he was going. Quite proud of it, he was."

Annie smiled warmly and looked at her watch and shuffled her chair back to the wall. "Look, Mrs Hobbs, I really ought to be

174

going. You deserve some time alone now." She stood up and buttoned her coat.

"I won't be long myself," Elsie said. "I don't fancy watching strangers taking him away."

Annie stepped forward, bent over and kissed George lightly on the forehead. Tears welled in her eyes. "Will you get home all right?"

"Ah yes. There'll be a bus soon. Come and see me some time," Elsie told her. "We'll have tea. I'll bake a nice cake."

But Annie couldn't respond. Rubbing her eyes with her sleeve, she hurried out, walking quickly with her head down.

Elsie pulled her chair closer to the bed and held out her hand, pressing the backs of her curled fingers gently against George's cheek. It felt cool but not cold. She ran two fingers through his tousled white hair, lifting it away from his brow.

"Now you listen to me, George, you listen good. It'll be my turn before long and I don't want to be wandering about on my own. Understand? So you be sure and wait for me at the big gates. That's where I'll meet you. 'Till death us do part', they say. Well, I'm not so sure about that. 'Till death us do reunite', I reckon. Fifty years we've been together, and that's a long, long time. I think we're in it for keeps – don't you? Know what I'm going to do? I'm going to leave the light on in your room. We're not shutting each other out, see. This is not the end of anything, just like a turn in the road. We're moving to a different place. You go first, me next; it's as simple as that. Okay, enough, enough."

Elsie stood up slowly and patted George's shoulder. "Oh, my dear love," she whispered.

Along the deserted corridor, her rubber heels squeaked on the polished floor. A single tear rolled down her cheek, and she brushed it away with a knuckle. She pushed open the heavy doors and stepped out into the cold half-light. Under the orange beam of a car park lamp, bright sparks of sleet slanted sideways before vanishing into the gloom.

She hunched down into her coat, tugging at the collar. "Lovely weather for ducks," she said.

The Confessions of Miss Antonelli

Today I received a letter from my brother Antonio in Italy. It is not a very interesting letter, but as my brother is not a very interesting person, that is only what I would have expected. It is quite a long letter, but Antonio, predictably, has not recently been anywhere special or done anything unusual, which means, unfortunately, that his four closely-typed pages are a rather dull monologue of routine family behaviour and unchanging local events. Antonio is two years younger than me – he is 25 – and still lives at home with my mother and father in their small house near Livorno. He is a good-looking boy but, for some reason, he has never had a serious girl-friend and remains single and, I suspect, quite innocent and unworldly. This naivete I find strange, although it hardly matters to me as we are living separate lives now, in different countries.

I suppose my brother's letter is timely, in that it prompts me to write to him and to my parents and it also comes a few days after a most – shall I say, improbable? – incident here, which I fully intend to relate to my family, as I am now doing to you. I flinch a little when I recall the event, but I admit also to finding it rather amusing. I suppose, in a way, it is an eloquent comment on my true character.

To begin at the beginning: my name is Antonia Antonelli and I am 27 years of age. Straight away you might be forgiven for deducing that my parents have little imagination in the matter of naming their children, but I can only say that they are educated and intelligent people and our names are simply the ones they jointly favoured. My father made his money in the dairy industry – I think cheese, particularly – soon after the war, and he has always been a kind and generous man, with appreciative friends in many European countries. He speaks several languages, including French, English, German and, I believe, a little Spanish, as well, obviously, as his native Italian, and both my brother and I were brought up to be fluent in

English and French. I would not say we were spoiled children, but we were well cared for.

I came to England in 2005 and, with some funds from my well-wishing father, set up home in a rented apartment in south London. Later that year I secured a post at Shelbeck College, teaching Italian to English students. I work there still and love what I do, for Italian is a beautiful language and it brings me great pleasure to introduce other young people to something that is both useful and lyrical. Sometimes, at the end of a class, I can see the elegant euphony of my language reflected in my students' faces, and that is worth almost as much to me as the modest salary I receive.

After five years, I began to find the flat quite confining, and I recently moved into a small terraced house a few miles away, still conveniently situated for the college. This was about three weeks ago. Dear Papa, he has sent me some more money, to offset the higher rent I now have to pay and to buy some new domestic items, mainly for the kitchen. I tell him I am well regarded at work and my salary has increased, but he ignores this information and insists upon remitting money from Italy. Believe me, I realise how fortunate I am.

I am very happy in my new home. I have a larger kitchen than before and generally more space to move around, with an upstairs and a downstairs. That feels quite a novelty. There is only one bedroom, but that does not worry me. My most recent acquisition is a double bed, not because I am planning to sleep with anyone – I have no boyfriend at present – but so that I can enjoy the luxury of stretching myself out at night and sleeping in a starfish shape, which seems to enhance my total relaxation. How I love my big bed! Oh, and also I now have a small garden, I would say about twelve metres by ten, with a paved patio and a rectangle of lawn. At the bottom of the garden is an old shed and inside, when I forced open the broken door, I found two deckchairs and a slightly rusty lawnmower. If the mower does not work, when I get around to trying it, there is plenty left from Papa's last gift for me to buy another one. I am not what you would call a gardener, but at least now I can sit outside when it is fine, for being Italian I am something of a sun-worshipper and enjoy the warm weather.

The weekend I moved in here was the start of a week's holiday for me. I wanted to get used to my new surroundings and sort out my possessions, empty my packed boxes, all that kind of thing, and to do so without hurry. A senior colleague at work, Mark Travis, has a van, and he kindly offered to transport my belongings for me. I promised I would prepare for him a nice Italian meal by way of thanks.

As Mark and I were carrying boxes up the front path – we must have made ten journeys each – I became aware of an elderly couple next door hovering by their doorstep. After perhaps ten minutes, the lady introduced herself pleasantly. "My name is Norma," she said, "and I am your neighbour." She was smartly dressed but with a pinafore over her clothes, and a vaguely blue colour in her hair. "And this," she added, putting a hand on the shoulder of the gentleman next to her, "is my husband, Harold." Whereupon Harold turned and gave me a most lovely smile, showing perfect teeth – though I accept that they may not be his own – and sparkling blue eyes, below a thatch of snowy-white hair.

I could not shake hands as I might have liked, as I was holding a heavy box of crockery; but I returned their generous smiles. "Norma and Harold. So pleased to meet you!" I told them. "My name is Antonia."

The lady nodded enthusiastically. "Norma and Harold Brownlow," she said.

We carried on unloading the van. When the job was done, I made Mark a cup of tea with my brand-new kettle, and he left, wishing me good luck. I was quite touched when, half an hour later, the doorbell rang, and there stood Norma Brownlow holding out a plate of home-baked apricot jam tarts as a small welcome gift. English people, I have invariably found, are at heart very kind and considerate of others, and not insular in the way they are often unfairly and inaccurately portrayed. So I found an empty tin in a kitchen cupboard and stored the jam tarts in it to keep them fresh, for there were too many to eat all at once. I must not forget to give Norma back her plate.

Now we come to last week, and the curious incident I was going to describe to you. It was mid-morning and the sun was coming out after early rain. I was well ahead in my unpacking and housework, and I thought I deserved a short break from my deliberations. Naturally, I decided to take my library book and sit for a while in my little garden. First, I went to the shed and dragged out a deckchair, brushing off the accumulated dust and cobwebs and setting it up on the patio, facing the fence at the end of the garden. I had taken off my old, all-enveloping clothes and put on a cropped T-shirt and a pair of pink denim shorts – for, as I mentioned before, I like to take advantage of the sunshine. No sooner had I settled down than I realised I was facing the wrong way, for the sun was behind me and I was in shadow; and so I turned the chair round and sat facing the houses, even though I would really have preferred to keep the windows at my back.

The garden smelled vibrant and earthy after the rain and I soon became immersed in its scents and engrossed in my book. I was reading 'The Sea' by John Banville, a quite beautiful novelist. I wonder why the Irish make such wonderful writers. Anyway, I read about fifteen pages and then suddenly became aware of a movement at the upstairs window where the Brownlows lived, the flickering of a curtain and a glint of light catching my eye. Distracted from my book, I peered up at the window and saw what appeared to be a lens, a reflective spark in the glass, and for a moment I thought I was looking at a camera; but then, in the next instant, I noted the outline of a second lens, convincing me that this was, indeed, a pair of binoculars. All this took no longer than three seconds, but I was quite sure I had not been mistaken; somebody was spying on me through binoculars.

You may find my reaction quite interesting. Had I believed I was being photographed, I would have been indignant, feeling that a part of me was being abducted without my permission, presumably for some unsavoury purpose. Yet once I had

179

determined beyond reasonable doubt that I was, in fact, being studied through binoculars, I could not prevent a slow, knowing smile from playing across my lips, and I did no more than raise my book again and continue reading as if nothing untoward had happened. In the space of a few seconds, I had decided that one of the Brownlows — and I strongly suspected that it must be Harold rather than his wife — was covertly examining me while I lay in the sun, deriving some small pleasure from this furtive act. Voyeurism, in my view, is at worst mildly distasteful, but it also presents its comical side, and I have never been accused of lacking a sense of humour. I carried on reading and shortly forgot what I had seen.

The weather next day was overcast and cool. This gave me an ideal opportunity to continue with my work indoors, cleaning floors, hanging curtains, re-arranging bookshelves and setting up my music system. It was a day well spent. In the evening Mark telephoned to ask if I was all right and comfortable in my new home, which was thoughtful of him. I decided not to tell him about the invisible spy next door, for he would be bound to worry. English people are quite caring, I think, even when they do not know you well.

By mid-week the sun had returned and it was very warm. I was loving my book, and of course fond of my garden, so I did a little work in the morning and then changed my clothes, ready to go outside. The dirt on the deckchair had left a black mark on my pink shorts, so I tossed them aside and, instead, undressed completely and slipped happily into my dark blue silky bikini, keen to add to my tan. I drew my dark hair back tightly from my face, clipping it in a bun behind my head, and picked up my book, a pair of sunglasses and a towel, which I intended to drape over my upper thighs and belly, mindful that my bikini pants are cut rather high and occasionally, when I unthinkingly part my legs, a few stray dark hairs peep out at the sides. When I have time, I will arrange a waxing session and ensure that this tiny problem is attended to.

The garden was bright and fragrant and I could hear birds singing nearby. A burst of radio music sounded briefly from an adjacent open window, but after a minute or two it was switched off and the attractive birdsong was once again my only accompaniment. I need hardly say that I felt relaxed and content there in the garden, just me and John Banville. Again the sun was at an angle over the rooftops, and I lay facing the houses as before, except that this time I had moved my chair back a few feet, so that I could feel the cool grass under my bare toes. Adjusting the chair so that I was reclining at a shallow angle, I revelled in the liquid warmth, settling the towel across my midriff, my sunglasses perched atop my head. How peaceful it was. I felt rested and happy. I thought of my parents in Livorno and wondered if they might be sitting in the sun like me. I reflected upon my good fortune in having found a rewarding job close to home, with friendly associates and eager, responsive pupils. I knew well that I had much to be thankful for. Mark Travis, too, I rather liked, and appreciated his helpful attentiveness. I must gather ingredients, I thought, and check my recipes for the supper I owed him, before he might suppose that I had negligently forgotten my offer. Mark was quite good-looking, about thirty, I would say, very quiet and perhaps a little shy. Somehow I felt that he was, in some indefinable way, not my type, although he spoke nicely and, as far as I could see, had a good, slightly muscular body. Perhaps he went to a gym, or just adhered to a sensible diet. Yes, I could almost admire his body, although of course much was necessarily left to my imagination, as I had not seen him naked and would surely not expect ever to do so. Still, there in the sweet air, sinking slowly into my easy reverie, I was gently possessed of a moist tingling between my legs as I pictured this gentle man, and I confess that I sought momentarily to relieve that not unpleasant, but perhaps unwanted, sensation by sliding my hand under the towel to loosen the elastic of my bikini bottom and touch the pad of my middle finger against my ripening bud. *Hello, Mark.*

Breaking into my idle daydream, there came again that wink of light from the Brownlows' window. No, I did not imagine it. I saw the net curtain swish aside and the brief stab of that dull lens. This time I fancied I also saw behind the glass circle, or circles, a faint white cloud, which could only be Harold Brownlow's hair. I pulled down my sunglasses and looked through them, disguising the exact direction of my gaze. Oddly, the pair of binoculars – for that is what I certainly saw – seemed quite high above the window frame, bearing in mind that, as I recalled, Mr Brownlow was not a tall man. Well, well, I thought to myself, here surely is a man come back for more of distant happiness, a further instalment of uncommitted pleasure. Here, no less, is a man to bring out the demonic tease in me. He knows himself, his wants and weaknesses, but – alas! – he does not know Antonia Antonelli.

Very well, I realise now that it was not a good or wise thing to do. It was unnecessary, childish and irresponsible. But I assert that I had no reasonable means of knowing what the consequences might be, so I do not entirely blame myself. It was silly, but not malicious. Perhaps, in a way, I felt sorry for Mr Brownlow, sorry that he needed this small, unsatisfactory pleasure to ease him through the day. Most assuredly, I did not feel anything of anger or insult. So I decided to play along with him and his little game, because that is how I am made. I am simply Antonia Antonelli. Laying down my book on the grass, I threw the towel aside and drew up my knees so that the soles of my feet rested wide apart on the front bar of the deckchair. Through my darkened lenses, I saw the curtain twitch again. With the merest flicker of an inward smile, I pretended to scratch an itch beneath my left breast, then tugged lightly at my bikini top to release that golden orb into the sunlight, bronzed hillock, cherry-pink nipple, suddenly, briefly warming in the sun, only to be as swiftly recaptured and concealed from view.

Within a microsecond of that playful exposure's cruel cessation, the silence was shattered by a loud crash. Looking up, I saw the net curtain swing down like billowing smoke and half of a black hole appear at the window. It is fair to say that for a moment I did not know what to think. Removing my sunglasses, I stared at the empty space, screwing up my eyes, but I could not make out anything or anyone, only a ragged patch of darkness. A little later, just as I was about to abandon my vigil, I thought I dimly discerned a moving shape behind the glass, though it was but a fleeting apparition, something I might almost have imagined, and I went back to my book and tried to ignore the incident. Then, as I reached the end of a chapter, I heard the wail of an emergency siren in the distance. In this area such disturbances are not uncommon, and this one hardly impressed itself upon me; until, that is, I saw through a gap in the fence the reflection of a flashing blue light in the Brownlows' downstairs window, a beacon shining inwards from the street, and I was set to thinking all over again.

The sky had clouded over and it was no longer so warm. A thin breeze ruffled my hair and pricked tiny goosepimples on my arms. I left the deckchair where it was and went indoors. Still wearing my bikini, I made myself some tea and sat at the kitchen table with a steaming mug and a plate of Mrs Brownlow's jam tarts. I tried not to dwell on what might have happened next door. I turned on the radio, but I found it difficult to concentrate on the programme and quite soon switched it off again. By the time I thought to go into the front room and look out of the window, the road was almost empty and there was no sign of the vehicle with the blue light.

It is only a few minutes' walk from here to the corner shop, and next morning I went up to the corner to buy some milk. As I came back to my gate, I saw Norma Brownlow sweeping her doorstep. I said "Good morning" and offered her a friendly smile.

Mrs Brownlow stopped sweeping and stood with her broom-handle clutched in both hands. "Hello, Antonia," she said. "Are you settled in yet?"

"Very nearly," I replied, fumbling for my key. "Are you well?"

"Yes, thank you."

"And Mr Brownlow?"

Whereupon Mrs Brownlow's smile withered on her face and she took to rocking to and fro, balancing on her broom. "Not so good, I'm afraid, dear. He's met with a bit of an accident."

"Oh dear. What's happened?"

"A fall, dear, he's had a nasty fall."

"Oh no! Is he all right?"

This, I immediately realised, was an inappropriate question, for I had already been told that Mr Brownlow was not well. My mind was suddenly spinning with jumbled reflections, and I even felt the onset of a kind of panic.

"He's in the hospital," Mrs Brownlow said. "He's broke his arm and banged his head. He's in Saint David's."

"Oh, Mrs Brownlow!"

"Yes. They'll keep him in for a day or two longer, in case of his head, see."

"Of course."

"Says he fell off a chair."

I remembered how tall the short Harold Brownlow had appeared in the window. He must have been perching on a chair to gain a better elevation into the garden. I briefly held the cold milk against my forehead to cool me down, for this was the worst possible news.

"Him and his brother," Mrs Brownlow continued, "they was going to the horse racing. Lingfield Park. That's what he said. Harold, he likes a bit of horse racing."

I nodded unhappily.

"Wanted his old binoculars. They was on top of the wardrobe, in the alcove next to the window. So he stands up on the wonky chair, grabs his binoculars, overbalances – pow! – busted arm and broken binoculars, lens smashed."

"Oh, Norma, I am so sorry."

"Not your fault, dear. Did you like them jam tarts?"

"Pardon? Oh yes. I – I must return your plate."

"Only a plate, dear, don't you worry about it."

"He's in Saint David's, you say?"

"Right. Tumbrell Ward." She waggled the broom about, shaking her head. "Tell you, I laughed. Tumbrell Ward. Very suitable, seein' as he's taken a – a *tumbrell*. If you get my meaning. Sorry, dear – know you're Italian."

"Norma, will you please give him my very best wishes. And may he have a speedy recovery."

"And not go balancing like a circus act on no more chairs," Mrs Brownlow added, pumping her broom on the ground as if to indicate that enough had been said on the matter.

Although I do not know Mr Brownlow and had met him only once, it will probably not surprise you to learn that I felt concerned for the old man's welfare and constrained to visit him in hospital, to see for myself the extent of his injuries. I am not a selfish person, and my conscience told me that I could not comfortably absolve myself from a degree of responsibility for the situation in which my neighbour now found himself, for I had knowingly taunted him and manipulated his weakness, with no other objective than my own idle amusement. The following evening I went to the hospital carrying a shopping bag, containing a pack of mixed fruit, a local interest magazine and a small gift wrapped in brown paper.

They had put Mr Brownlow in a side room with a large window next to his bed and his own television fixed to the wall. I tapped my knuckles nervously on the open door and waited. The patient was spooning yoghurt into his mouth whilst peering at a newspaper folded against his blanketed, upraised knees. In case he had not heard me, I knocked again, a little louder, and he looked up, blinked several times and sat upright with the spoon poised in mid-air. His face was a picture of bafflement, a frozen landscape across which a slow dawning light began to spread as I moved into the room.

"Good Lord!" Mr Brownlow gasped, letting the sticky spoon drop into his lap.

"It's me, Mr Brownlow – Antonia from next door."

"Well I never. Miss Antonelli! What on earth - ?"

I stood beside the bed, lowering my bag to the floor. "I saw your wife. She told me of your accident."

He pointed vaguely to a plastic chair under the window. "Please. Don't stand."

I pulled the chair towards him and sat down. As far as I could make out, he had quite easily used the spoon with his right hand, and he was resting a plastered left arm on the bedclothes, so I felt somewhat relieved in assuming that he was right-handed and would therefore be only moderately inconvenienced by his fracture. I needed some reassurance, some justification for convincing myself that I had not unwittingly landed the man in a desperate position.

"I can't stay long," I said, "I have a friend coming later this evening."

This was untrue, but it would allow me to make a prompt exit if the situation should become embarrassing for either of us.

"It's very kind of you to come at all," Mr Brownlow assured me. "I have seen little of you, Miss Antonelli, but clearly you wish us to be good neighbours. Most encouraging."

Inwardly, I smiled, reflecting that, indeed, far from seeing little of me, Mr Brownlow had recently enjoyed a more comprehensive view of me than most people I knew. In that respect, he had placed himself in a privileged position, but now he was paying for the experience in the currency of pain and discomfort. Inclining my head, I saw that the right side of his face was blotched with dark red and blue swellings from the edge of his eye to his jaw-line. It looked very painful.

I reached into my bag. "I've brought some things for you, Mr Brownlow." I laid the fruit and the magazine on the bed but left the wrapped parcel concealed for the moment.

"Please, call me Harold."

I patted the hand on his broken arm. "If you will call me Antonia."

He nodded, extending his other hand to turn over the fruit pack and the magazine with a tight-lipped, dazed smile. "Well, thank you for these – Antonia." He glanced up at me. "There was really no need."

"Is your face very sore?"

"What? Oh, my face." He touched his right cheek delicately with his fingertips. "Nothing broken, they say. Tender, yes. If you must know, it's not so much that it hurts, it's more that I feel quite stupid – a silly old man."

"Harold, you are not stupid. You mustn't say that."

"Causing all these people all this trouble."

"You had a fall, Harold. It happens all the time."

"Not to me, it doesn't." He shook his snowy head and I saw the glitter of tears in his eyes. "Daft old man," he muttered. "Lucky I didn't break my neck."

In silence, I gazed into his eyes and saw him watching me, almost studiously, perhaps recalling that brief moment before the fall. It felt quite strange, my being there with him, face to face, closely exposed to each other in such surreal circumstances. I knew what Harold Brownlow had been doing that afternoon, despite his contrived explanation to his wife, and he also knew the awkward truth of the matter. I knew that he knew the real story, but of course he did not know, could not know, that I shared that intimate knowledge. In a sense, that gave me a hold over him, an upper hand, if you like; yet this advantage, if such it was, did not afford me any satisfaction. I simply felt sorry for him, and not in a deprecating or disrespectful way; there was no need for that.

We discussed for a while the usual trivial subjects that are part of the minutiae of hospital visiting: the noises that interrupt sleep; the inadequacy of the food; the brusqueness of some nurses and the kindness of others; the endless round of pills and probing; how much of the changing weather he could see from his window; the mind-numbing tedium of daytime television. After half an hour or so, the old man's face took on a greyish appearance, and I checked my watch as a prelude to leaving him in peace.

"Now you must take care," I told him, picking up my bag from the floor. "I have to go. Ah, here, I nearly forgot." I took out the brown paper parcel and placed it next to his broken arm. "Please don't open it till I've gone."

"Another present? But – what is it?"

"Just something you may find useful."

Again, tears welled up in his eyes. He made no attempt to wipe them. I think he wanted to thank me once more, but he couldn't find the words, just lay there, propped against a bank of pillows, gazing at me, thinking, wondering.

I went to the door, turned, smiled, waggled my fingers at him and stepped into the corridor. My job was done. I was glad I had made the effort. The point was, it had meant something to each of us.

What was in the package? Think carefully. What could it possibly have been? Yes, of course, I had bought Mr Brownlow a new pair of binoculars. After all, it was in some small measure down to me that the first pair had been broken. I was partly responsible. Nothing and no-one will convince me otherwise. I may be mischievous, but I am not immoral.

Having told Mr Brownlow a white lie about someone visiting me put an idea in my head. When I got home I picked up the phone, stared at it for a moment, as if in disbelief at what I was about to do, and rang Mark Travis. I reminded him of the authentic Italian supper I owed him and invited him to come for the evening, next day. Mark sounded genuinely pleased and said he would be delighted to come. I promised myself I would be the perfect warm and welcoming hostess, no holding back, no aimless small talk, just a readiness to tell him about myself and to listen when, as I sincerely hoped, he would tell me all that I wanted to know about him. However, I somehow doubted that I would say anything about Harold Brownlow.

You see, Harold is an old man. Very well, I know little about him, but I truly believe that he is not stupid or cunning or even particularly lascivious. He is simply an old man who likes to look at a pretty girl. That is natural and harmless. To be honest, I am sorry that I teased him and, however indirectly, despatched him to hospital. I suppose, really, it is me who is the stupid one, leaving him nothing more than a victim.

I think that, as we grow older, we are travelling inexorably through the scenery, leaving behind all the familiar places and faces, all the long-loved buildings and happy heartlands, and moving out into a different region, where life exists in a more arid, less friendly environment, the experiences we knew and cherished now fewer and farther between, like a scattering of isolated houses and unrecognised people standing by them. Until? Until we come rushing into a cold place where there is almost nothing to love any more. So, dear Mr Harold Brownlow, perhaps I can stand firm and try to be the last house on your long journey, the place where you had the quickest, lightest touch of pleasure before the day's end. Perhaps.

You will want to know about Mark. He stayed with me till midnight, and we had a wonderful meal with red wine and white wine and much easy laughter. Long before he left, we were both quite inebriated, so I insisted on calling him a taxi to get home. I had taken the precaution, earlier, of changing the bed sheets and putting on my most exotic red and black underwear. I was, to be truthful, acting right out of myself, but I had decided most emphatically not to do anything he might construe as seduction. We had no music and I deliberately avoided turning the lights down low. I was interested, for sure, but I wanted Mark to, as it were, make the running. I kissed him as he left and he complimented me on my perfume.

The trouble is, inevitably, when you allow a man to make the running, sometimes he runs. That is the way of the world. But we have time on our side, and I will wait and see what happens. A bit like with Mr Brownlow, you might say.

Yes, we will see what happens.

M alcolm J Tompkins, aged twelve, in the station, on platform four, with a threepenny platform ticket and a bar of Fry's *Five Boys* chocolate in his blazer pocket and, clutched in his left hand, a well-thumbed Ian Allan booklet of locomotive numbers, ready to be blue-lined with the ballpoint pen lodged behind his ear in the manner of a junior grocer.

He had been there an hour this summer afternoon, straight from school, his face a mask of serene concentration as he patrolled the concourse, weaving among the waiting travellers, his time perfectly, comfortably his own. A few trains had passed through, some stopping, others hustling past at self-important speed, shaking the platform with their brutish noise. A slow goods train trundled by at half past four, trucks trembling and clanking, pulled slowly enough for Malcolm to count the smut-smeared hulks in the long crocodile: thirty-five of them, including the empty brake van at the tail.

It depended on his mood. Some days he liked to be on the station, mingling inconspicuously with the embarking or alighting passengers, vicariously allowing himself a small share of their bustling importance as he peered into soot-streaked windows or open doors; while sometimes, preferring a wistful solitude, he would climb the steps to the iron bridge over the broad valley of tracks a mile away and stand there, leaning on the metal parapet, watching for the upward swing of a semaphore signal beside the cleared line. Last week, from the open bridge where the thundering behemoths roaring beneath him flung smoke and grit in his face, he saw the *Duchess of Atholl* and *The Kings Royal Rifle Corps* and later on *Oliver Cromwell* with smoke deflectors quivering. That was the day the leather-capped driver of *Duchess of Hamilton* waved a gloved hand at him, the briefest communion amid so much speed and splendour. He went home happy with a blackened face, his hair matted and tousled by too many warm winds.

Malcolm J Tompkins, aged sixty-seven, in seat 14, coach C on the 12.15 from Leeds, with a greetings card in his coat pocket and one of his mother's home-made egg sandwiches on the flimsy table in front of him. Every few miles he would reach in his pocket and finger the sealed envelope, wondering why the elderly Mrs Tompkins had instructed him not to open it but to hand it immediately to his wife on his arrival home. Very well, Malcolm's birthday was not until the day after tomorrow, but the fact remained that it was his birthday card, inexplicably vouchsafed to someone else.

The rattle of the refreshment trolley drew his attention, and as the girl propelling it appeared at his shoulder, he ordered a coffee to go with his sandwich. Dear Mother, she had insisted on making him a snack, even though he would have happily relied upon the trolley service. The day before she had taken an early morning taxi to the butcher's to buy best-quality beef for a casserole, its humid fragrance filling the house when he arrived. Her ninetieth birthday, a few days before Malcolm's, had been the occasion for his journey. A large bunch of flowers from the florist next to the station had brought a youthful radiance to her furrowed face. There were quick, dry kisses and a brief blinking of tears.

"Honestly, you didn't have to go to all this trouble, Mum."

"Trouble? Is it trouble to look after my own son? Especially when he's come all this way."

"I could have gone for fish and chips."

"You could. And I could have sat here feeling guilty because I hadn't made an effort. Responsibility doesn't vanish with age, Malcolm."

That was one of the treasured pearls of his mother's wisdom. She held fast to a duty of care, a lifelong commitment. A strata of maternal affection was richly overlaid with a deep bedrock of practical devotion to her only child, a bond which daily reminded her that her parental obligations to this man

191

could finally be discharged only when one of them died. April Tompkins took life seriously, at ninety still working at motherhood.

His eyes moistened again as he thought of her, alone in the big house full of memories and cold rooms. He shook himself, chomping hard on his sandwich, feeling the thick slap of pulped egg as it coated his tongue. Come on, Malcolm, he told himself, get yourself together, you're going home, hold your head up, clear your brain, no wallowing in regrets, no old man crying on a train, dropping egg down his front. We'll have none of that.

Although the train had slowed, approaching the end of its journey, his weary eyes, tired from a night of shallow sleep in his mother's chilly, fusty-smelling spare room, were not up to the task of reading the fleeting name boards at the next station, but he could see the dishevelled knots of train-spotters clustered at the downslope of the opposite platform, some with rucksacks, one brandishing a camcorder. It surprised him how old they were. When he had solemnly entertained himself with this most pointless of activities, more than half a century ago, it was a youthful pursuit, something he did because – his passion for trains aside – he did not know enough of the ways of the world to embrace anything else. But now? Now here were grown men in shapeless jackets, men with grey faces and thinning hair, loitering with the grim intent of paedophiles, gazing at the identical bulks of passing power plants, generators towing metal centipedes, because there were no fire-breathing locomotives any more, no hollering monsters wreathed in smoke. He closed his eyes and smiled, knowing he had had the best of it.

An empty bus was waiting, engine throbbing, outside the station. He collapsed into the nearest seat, running one hand over the outline of the birthday card warmly buckled in his pocket.

"Give it straight to Dinah. Don't interfere with it."

"But it's for me – yes?"

"It's for her first. You understand me?"

Dear Mum. Of course he understood her. Ninety and sharp as a razor. Her self-awareness and cognizance of the world around her were so powerful as to be intimidating. How he loved and envied her for that unfailing strength.

So he handed the envelope to his wife and watched her take it into the next room. Dinah Tompkins carefully picked it open, slid her fingers into the card and removed the contents.

"Ah, she's put cash," she said to herself. "That's good. Thoughtful."

She licked the flap again, hoping to repair the damage, and resealed the envelope, placing it behind the mantelpiece clock. Then she took the money upstairs to her bedroom.

Malcolm selected a disk from his DVD collection and slid it into the player. *Mallard* rumbled across the screen, belching grey smoke, huge connecting rods thrashing in winter sunlight. This was a limited edition film; few people had one. He kicked off his shoes and rested his feet on the coffee table. He was home. Life was good. He smiled.

Malcolm J Tompkins, aged sixty-eight, sitting in the kitchen, with a buttered crumpet in one hand and a birthday card from Dinah in the other. Still in her dressing gown, Dinah stood at his shoulder, idly studying the sparse hair on her husband's head.

"Oh, I almost forgot," she said, and she went through to the lounge, picked up the envelope from behind the clock and brought it to the kitchen table.

"You've opened it," Malcolm said, fingering the flap.

"I know. There's a reason."

He read what his mother had written in the card. "Says I have to ask you about a present."

"That's right. That's why I kept the card."

"Why? It's my card."

"There was money in it, money for me."

"She's giving you money on my birthday? Will I get money on your birthday?"

"Poor love." She touched his shoulder.

"That's not an answer."

193

"The answer is in my pocket," she said.

Malcolm grimaced, shaking his head. "This is a strange birthday."

"Feel in my pocket," she told him, urging her hip towards him.

"What's in there?"

"Feel in my pocket."

"What's in there?"

"Feel in my pocket."

Malcolm wiped his buttery lips with his fingers. "This is a strange birthday," he said.

Dinah jiggled her hip. "Just fancy. Sixty-eight. Your dad died at sixty-eight. It makes you think."

"Don't remind me."

"I'm just saying."

"It was an accident," he reminded her.

"Even so."

"It doesn't count. He didn't die; he was killed."

"I know. Malcolm."

"What?"

"Feel in my pocket."

"What's in there?"

"Just feel in my pocket."

He swung round in the chair and looked up at her. "She should have got more, you know, my mum. The compensation, I mean."

"She got nine thousand, Malcolm. Nineteen years ago. A lot of money then."

"But not much for a man's life."

"Well, it's done now. I don't hear her complaining."

"It's not Mum's way to complain," he said sullenly. "So what's happened to the money?"

"Oh, I don't know, Malcolm. But knowing your mum, I'm sure she used it wisely. Maybe she invested it. It could be for your future."

"What? No, not that money. I mean the money you took from the card."

"Ah. I'm keeping the money. It's spent already."

"You've spent my birthday money?"

"So I have, Malcolm, every penny of it."

"How much did she send?"

"Sixty pounds, if you must know."

"Six-? What did you spend it on?"

"Not what. Whom. I spent it on you."

Malcolm rested his head in his hands. "I can't get to grips with this birthday."

She moved closer and hugged him. "Here." She pulled a piece of paper from her pocket and laid it on his sticky plate.

Malcolm picked up the square of paper and read what was printed on it. Dinah stood with one hand gently squeezing his shoulder. "Your mum and me, we've gone halves," she said.

He leaned back and held the paper up to the light as if he could look through it. His mouth fell open and his eyes grew wide. "This is – is this for me? Are you giving me this?"

--- *The Glory of Steam –*

Join Blue Vista Travel and a select group of rail enthusiasts for an unforgettable 100-mile journey through the English countryside aboard our specially chartered train, steam-hauled to Bridgweston and back by one of two classic locomotives – either **Sir Nigel Gresley** *or* **Red Prince.** *We will arrange for your train to be powered by whichever of these great engines is available on the date you select. Book now for our first memorable excursion departing July 24th at 10.30 am. N.B. Light refreshments are served at the halfway station while the locomotive is watered and turned. Do come and experience this wonderful opportunity! Details of prices and dates are given below.*

**

Dinah gave him a hug, bending to nestle her cheek against his. "Two tickets in my top drawer upstairs," she said. "From Mum and me. I'll come with you, of course."

"But this is marvellous. I can smell that smoke already." He shook his head in blissful disbelief. "It's the day after tomorrow, look."

She tugged the downy lobe of his ear. "We'll take a picnic. A packed lunch."

"I'll bring my camera."

Malcolm was still shaking his head. His hands were trembling. This was the best present ever. He would take his little dictaphone to make notes and then transcribe them into his diary. These excursions were few and far between; it might never happen again. Tonight he must remember to recharge the camera battery. On the radio they were forecasting summer storms. He hoped nothing beyond his control would happen to spoil the day.

His excitement was tainted with anxiety that night. At two in the morning he awoke to hear the wind booming in the chimney and the bedroom windows rattling. Something rasped and clattered overhead, surely a roof tile sliding loose. That was the nervous, irritable end of sleep. For a while he lay on his back, listening to the gale, imagining a desolate landscape of felled trees.

Dinah touched his arm. "Can't you sleep?"

"No. Windy nights always wake me." He sat up, swinging his legs out of bed.

"Where are you going?"

"To the toilet."

"You went at eleven. Your prostrate?"

"What are you talking about? I was on my back."

"I mean, your prostrate gland. You should see the doctor."

Malcolm fumbled for the bedside light switch. "I think you mean *prostate*."

"Do I? I get those confused."

"Yes, we're old and confused," he said testily, reaching under the bed for his slippers. On his way to the bathroom, he hummed tunelessly so he couldn't hear the wind. As he stood at the lavatory, he heard rain peppering the window like buckshot. In the morning he would ring the travel company, just to make sure the railway lines were clear.

Soon after breakfast, subdued by apprehension, he telephoned the tour company. The high winds had abated, but the radio news reports told of transport delays and some structural damage. A bus had been blown over and a top-deck passenger killed, lacerated by broken glass.

A pleasant-sounding girl did her best to reassure him. "I don't think you should worry, Mr Tompkins," she told him. "We've had some early reports of minor trackside damage, but nothing serious. I believe – wait a minute – yes, in the wooded areas the line passes through there are apparently some trees down, but I'm not aware of anything interfering with the railway. So really, I don't see any need for concern."

"So the trip will go ahead as planned?"

"Don't you worry, Mr Tompkins. Just enjoy your day out."

Replacing the receiver, Malcolm walked slowly back to the kitchen, rubbing his hands together. Dinah, washing dishes at the sink, turned and touched his face with wet hands. "You all right?" she asked him.

"I'm fine, thank you."

He shook his head. Through the window, he could see the sun coming out. He could almost inhale the smoke, feel the drumming of the wheels on the rails, hear the gasp of escaping steam. It was good to be sixty-eight, after all.

Malcolm J Tompkins, aged sixty-eight and two days, in the waiting room at Bridgweston station, with a warm sausage roll from the kiosk and a Styrofoam cup of coffee, a camera strung round his neck. The Tompkinses had thoughtfully shared their boxed lunch with a small boy and his mother on the outward run. While the railmen joined forces to rotate the locomotive laboriously on the turntable – Malcolm was pleased that *Red Prince* had been chosen as the motive power rather than *Sir Nigel Gresley*; he preferred the aspect of the 2-10-0 engine with its imposing smoke deflectors and sculpted boiler to the expressionless slab front of the A4 – an animated group of enthusiasts gathered in the dingy room, eight *aficionados* of the era of steam, all except Dinah Tompkins somewhat shabby in appearance, if button-bright in both recollection and anticipation.

Tom and Barry Maynard, identical twins from Shrewsbury, perched like bookends, one at either end of a ripped leatherette bench, three other travellers between them. Next to Barry was Bella Monk, the only woman anyone had seen on the train apart from Dinah, Bella with pitted grey skin on her greasy face and a shapeless red cardigan scarcely containing her melon-sized breasts. To her left sat James and Jules, holding hands, thighs chafing together, sweet boys of indeterminate age, plainly in love with each other as well as with the railway. On chairs in the corner, Malcolm and Dinah sat leaning forward with a tall, thin man, Owen Partridge, darkly bearded, standing behind them, his brown eyes searching the row of faces opposite.

The separated twins craned their necks to fix each other with earnest stares. "What about that acceleration before the one-in-four!" Tom exclaimed.

"I know." Barry's head was bouncing with delight. "Hey, did you get any smoke?"

"Not so far. On the way back I'm standing on the seat."

Tall Owen, scratching his beard, addressed no-one in particular. "Quite a few trees down in that copse we passed."

Bella nodded. "I saw that. Upsetting. It's like nature arguing with itself."

The gay boys smiled up at Owen, showing their teeth. James' hand rested lightly in Jules' lap.

A whistle sounded, shrill and close by, as the reversed engine chugged past on its way to pick up the tail carriage.

The lofty man was watching the happy boys. James was more affectionate now, caressing Jules through his trousers. "You two known each other long?" Owen enquired darkly.

"Long enough, by the looks of it," Bella said. She turned to Dinah. "So are you a steamie too?"

Dinah pursed her lips, rolling her eyes. She wasn't sure she liked Bella, but courtesy cost nothing. "I'm supporting my husband." She clasped his hand. "I bought him this trip for his birthday."

James grinned and gave her a thumbs-up with his free hand.

The door opened and a young station official with a ponytail dangling from his railway cap looked in. "Need to be moving," he said. "Heading back in five minutes. Just coupling up."

Bella, peering at his receding back, tugged thoughtfully at her ear. "I wouldn't mind coupling up with him."

Malcolm's coffee had gone cold and he swigged it down and tossed the cup into a bin. "Think I'll grab some of that smoke myself," he told Dinah. "She'll be powered up approaching that incline in the cutting; that'll be the place."

Bella kept close to them as they traipsed along the platform. "Mind if I share your compartment? I came down with the icky-sticky boys. Don't fancy it going back."

"Suit yourself," Dinah said.

Facing the chipped, clouded mirror on the compartment wall, Dinah worked her mouth, touching up her pink lipstick, idly noting Bella's distorted reflection hovering behind her. Both women teetered, almost overbalancing, as *Red Prince* snorted a fierce jet of steam and took up the load with a graunch of protesting couplings. Outside, daredevil lads with camcorders, yelled at by platform staff, crouched filming the huge driving wheels as they spun under power on the wet, leaf-slicked rails, then with seconds to spare ran back along the departing train to be yanked aboard by waving, outstretched hands before the gathering speed could defeat them.

"Foolishness," Dinah grumbled, watching the commotion beyond the window.

"Five sets of driving wheels," Bella pointed out. "Only chance they'll get, most probably."

"Huh." Dinah scowled. "Wheels going round. I ask you."

Malcolm had dragged down the door window, admitting mingled scents of smoke and grass. Running slightly downhill, they picked up speed, the driver sending two warning blasts of his whistle as the train approached a level crossing. Dinah sat close to where her husband stood, envying the rapt expression on his face as he gazed across the green and gold blur of rushing fields, white tendrils of steam coiling past the window in moistly spiralling clouds, balletic wraiths quickly to be atomised by breeze and sunshine.

"Don't put your head too far out," Dinah told him, sternly.

"I want some of that gorgeous, nutty smoke."

"Hmm. Reckon *nutty*'s the right word," she observed. "Mind you don't get grit in your eye."

Malcolm shut his eyes for a moment. "Lovely sweet smoke," he murmured.

A few minutes later, with a brief shudder of brakes, the train began to slow. Bella, standing in the corridor with her back to Mr and Mrs Tompkins, turned and swung into the compartment, clutching at the luggage rack for stability. "Signal against us?"

"Don't know," Malcolm called over his shoulder. "Not as I can see."

Bella wiped her nose with a knuckle, sniffing aggressively. "Poofter on the line," she snarled.

Dinah, reading a timetable, looked up reproachfully. "Hardly necessary," she said.

"Oh. Sorry. Trouble is, I hate poofters." She slumped into the seat next to Dinah. "Know what I'd do if I had a son and he turned out to be a queer?"

"Well, I'm sure you're about to tell me," Dinah allowed, wearily.

"If he was home with me, I'd wait till he was asleep, then I'd creep into his room and I'd throttle him with my bare hands. I'd call that doing the world a favour."

"Would you now? I'd call it murder."

"Hmm." She shook her head slowly from side to side, studying the grubby floor. "Bring back the old standards, I say. Bring back the steam trains, bring back the blokes with barrows that clean the streets, the milkman with a horse, the concept of punishment, a respect for morality. That's how I was brought up."

"Surely that depends on your definition of morality," Dinah said. "Morality's an abstract commodity, my dear. One man's meat, and all that."

"Cop-out," Bella grunted. She leaned back, yawning. "So what's up with this train?"

The train had slowed to walking pace. Leaning forward, Malcolm saw them approaching from the middle distance, three yellow-jacketed track workers, plodding along the row of coaches. One man carried a spade, hoisted over his shoulder in military fashion, the handle in the palm of his hand, the blade pointing at the sky. As the group drew near, the train jerked to a halt. There was the hiss of wasted steam and the burbling of a small brook under the trees.

Malcolm thumped the window down as far as it would go and called to the spade-carrier. "Problem?"

The man stepped up to the door. "Nah." He glanced to left and right, as if measuring the train. "That gale the other day – some trackside signs came down, we had to clear them away."

"No debris on the line," Malcolm said. "We came through fine this morning."

"Right you are. Got to mind these signal stands, though." He pointed behind with his thumb. "They've mostly got flat steel plates carrying the lamps. They catch the wind like sails. Some's been blown sideways."

"Towards the track?"

"Right. Think we got them all."

Malcolm nodded.

The man lowered his spade and leaned on it. "Anyway, don't worry, mate. There's a few lads crossing the line up ahead. We'll just wait for them to get clear and then we'll get you on your way. Shouldn't take long."

Malcolm thanked him and withdrew, sitting down opposite Dinah. The three workers moved on, pausing briefly to talk to passengers in the next carriage. Dinah looked at her watch and shuffled her feet. Malcolm pulled his dictaphone from his pocket and clicked the switch on and off.

"Made any notes?" Dinah asked.

"A few. And I think I've captured some engine music."

Bella was on her feet, peering in the mirror. "Christ, look at me! I look about sixty." She looked at Dinah. "Could I borrow your lippy?"

Dinah fumbled in her bag. "Here. How old are you, then?"

"Not sixty."

"I see."

"If you must know, I'm forty-one."

"Perhaps you've had a hard life, eh?" Dinah said, not looking at her.

"Something like that." She stroked pink crescents on her lips, pouting like a fish.

"You got a date?" Malcolm ventured.

"Don't rightly know. Thanks." She gave Dinah the tube back. "My old history teacher. I'm seeing him tonight at this wine bar. Whether it'll lead to anything..."

Dinah popped the lipstick in her bag and gave Bella five seconds' critical appraisal. The application of a pink smear, she reasoned, could be but a marginal improvement. Next there was the putty complexion, the matted hair and sagging breasts. Without further remedial work, perhaps a programme of sympathetic structural repair, no discerning man would look twice at Bella Monk.

The train jolted, inching forward. Malcolm, grinning, clenched his fist and raised it to his cheek in boyish pleasure. A playful toot of the steam whistle contrasted absurdly with the monstrous panting of the locomotive under power, rhythmically percussive as it strained against the weight of its stock, a bellowing beast at last unleashed. Track workers' jackets flashed yellow against the windows as the speed built, some of the men gazing morosely at the fleeting faces, others offering a languid, perfunctory wave.

Malcolm was back at the open window, craning his neck to see ahead. The rising wind fanned his face, filling his eyes with tears. He saw a grey-painted signal stand lying on its side in a gully, chalk marks scrawled on the muddied post. A black and white gradient sign lay on its back in a bush, where the wind had tossed it.

"Malcolm!"

He ducked his head inside at Dinah's call.

"What is it?"

"I told you, don't hang so far out. Look at your face!"

"How can I look at my own face?"

"There's black on your forehead."

He hunched close to the window again. "There's worse than a black forehead," he muttered.

Dinah rolled her eyes at Bella. "Suppose he won't be washing his face for a week."

They had the momentum now. Malcolm reckoned they were doing forty, and he knew that would have to increase within the next couple of miles, because then the train would be entering the cutting at Skeffington Bank, an uphill stretch requiring maximum effort. That would be a good time to catch some smoke, when the engine was being urged to deliver ultimate power in readiness for the steep climb ahead.

Dinah was tugging crossly at the back of his jacket, and he reached round to slap her hand away. If only she would understand.

"Malcolm, please!"

In the distance he could just make out the dark line of trees enclosing the cutting. Before that streak of green, he saw that the train would have to follow a long left curve atop a raised promontory, the coaches looping back on themselves through the radius of the bend. This, he realised, would be the perfect opportunity for a photograph of the dark red engine as it angled into full view. It could even be the day's most inspiring picture. A fresh thrill of anticipation pulsed through him.

"Dinah! Camera, quickly!" He turned, pointing up at the luggage rack over her head.

Sighing, she took down the camera and handed it to him.

He hung the strap round his neck and thrust his head and shoulders out into the slipstream. *Red Prince* was charging now, up around seventy, the gigantic muscles of his connecting rods flashing in the sunlight, towering eruptions of leaden smoke mushrooming magnificently into the sky. Malcolm waited, hands trembling, for a moment in history, lifting the viewfinder to his eye, hunting for the best light, bringing *Red Prince* into focus against the horizon. Just a little longer.

A workman in a red tabard, legs astride on the grass bank, shouted at this man suspended in space at fearsome speed, but Malcolm's ears were full of the wind and he didn't hear the warning cry. The workman's arms threshed the air, palms towards the train, but Malcolm eyes were locked on *Red Prince* and he didn't see the waving man. Here, now, surely was the shot he craved, sun-bronzed bank, cerulean sky, great red engine roaring at the hills. He leaned a final inch and fingered the shutter.

The half-capsized signal post, beaten inwards, presented its steel plate to the rush of the carriages, no room to spare. In that microsecond of terminal velocity, Malcolm must have felt the hideous blow, but in an instant, as the world whirled, the pain was gone, and there was nothing but nothingness and the scream of silence.

"Come on, Malcolm! How long does it take for a photo?" Dinah yanked his jacket, on the verge of anger.

"What's that?" Bella gaped at the red swatch on the window.

"Malcolm, it's not safe!"

"He's hooked up on the frame," Bella told her. "Pull him in!"

Between them, they dragged Malcolm back through the window. He thudded on to the floor, spewing blood down the door. Bella screamed, deep, guttural howls, in and out, in and out, like a bellows. Dinah, staring, icily paralysed, scrambled back from the broken heap as a torrent of blood pumped from the livid core of the axed neck.

Bella held up both hands, scarlet fingers shaking. "Oh, Jesus! Sweet Jesus!" She lunged for the communication cord.

204

Dinah tasted the iron of his blood as it welled against her cheek, but there was no way she would let him go now, her arms enfolding his pulsating chest, squeezing hard, blinded by tears as a red storm engulfed her.

Malcolm J Tompkins, aged sixty-eight and two and a half days, in the peaceful fields of light, with a sky-blue butterfly perched on his scalp, slowly opening and closing its wings. His lips were creased in the merest of thin smiles, a feather-flicker of memory. His eyes were open, reflecting the clouds. Over his nose, a red gash from the shattered camera. The butterfly danced away, carefree, unknowing, searching the woods for the rest of its short life. Under the jagged stump of Malcolm's chin, the grass shone crimson, the stubbled earth rejuvenated by the richness of his departing blood.

Above him, the train stood with doors flapping open. Birds still sang in the copse below the field, but their small voices were drowned by the shrieks from the open doorways and the faltering breath of the stalled engine.

Already there were volunteers. Two men were combing the long grass, heads down, stumbling. One of the men carried a black bag. By the track, someone shouted, pointing, shaking his head, turning away. The first man, not the one with the bag, slithered down into the field, walking slowly, hardly daring to walk at all. When the man holding the bag arrived, the other man had fallen to his knees, covering his eyes, as he vomited into the rough grass.

Dinah Tompkins sat on the step of the carriage with her feet on a wooden sleeper and a blanket draped about her, held in place by the encircling arm of a man whose pale face was tracked with tears.

A grey patch of roadway showed through the trees below, and somewhere down there, not so far away now, the wail of a siren rose on the air.

Red Prince shuddered like a frightened animal against the sky. Soon, men in green suits were seen walking out of the

205

trees, uselessly carrying bags. They talked to the men who had come from the train. Then there was no talking any more.

A Touch of Gold

March 5th, 1960, that was when it happened: Doris Marlene West entered into holy matrimony with Morris Arthur Clough at All Saint's Church, Pendlebury-in-the-Marsh, at 2 o'clock in the afternoon, those present proceeding afterwards to the Reception in the back room of the *Fighting Temeraire* opposite the village green. By a munificent gesture of her father, the bride arrived at the church in a snow-white carriage drawn by a pair of white horses, with two brocaded footmen perched precariously behind the rear wheels.

Roy Sparkes, the Best Man, sheltering from a stiff breeze in the huge stone doorway, watched Doris and her father arrive in theatrical splendour. Roy thumbed his nose, scarcely concealing a contemptuous scowl. "Huh. Come in a 'orse an' cart."

That was fifty years ago to the day. Now Morris, descending the stairs, tugging his tartan dressing gown tightly about him, reflected ruefully upon the achievements of half a century. Two children, Raymond and Josie, both educated to a modest standard and now moved down south; a pleasant semi-detached on the outskirts of Lancaster, mortgage discharged; an elderly Ford Focus in the driveway, seldom cleaned now the boy scouts didn't come round; a temperamental cat called Loony with one ear unaccountably bitten off; a placid history of dutiful loyalty, as prescribed by the Reverend Stanley Hurbiston, now certainly dead. Given the circumstances he was about to expose, Morris wondered whether the vicar's departure might possibly go some way to conveniently invalidating the requirement for fidelity.

Already up and dressed, Doris greeted him with a curt Good Morning nod from her seat in the upright armchair beside the simmering gas fire. Her orange crimplene suit perfectly matched the glow from the artificial coals, and her blue-slippered feet lay crossed at the ankles. Doris was relaxed, blissfully unaware of the torment about to be visited upon her.

"Ah, happy days." Morris slid, puffing, into his facing chair and offered his wife a weary smile.

"Well, some of 'em were," Doris allowed. "Not sure about the golden bit."

"Ah well," Morris said.

"I didn't get you anything."

"I got you a card," he said, brightly.

"Did you now? Where is it?"

"Don't rightly know. I got it last week and put it away. Tried to find it last night."

Doris lowered her gaze and nodded reflectively, as though this lapse were only to be expected.

Morris looked at Doris. Doris looked at Morris. A soft puttering seeped from the gas fire. Doris uncrossed her ankles and crossed them again the other way.

"Fifty years," said Morris, more to himself than to Doris.

Gazing at him, Doris narrowed her eyes, bringing her eyebrows close together. "You've got that look," she said, accusingly.

"What look?"

"Sort of – edgy."

"Edgy?"

"It's the sort of look you get when you've done somethin' you shouldn't have, or you haven't done somethin' you should."

Morris sighed, shifting awkwardly in his chair. "Ah, right," he said.

The letterbox rattled and a series of soft thumps sounded on the mat.

"P'raps the kids have sent us a card," said Morris, but he didn't get up to look.

Doris was staring at him intently, gripping the arms of the chair. "I know that look," she said. "I've lived with it fifty years."

Morris swallowed, and Doris saw his Adam's apple bob in his scrawny neck.

"I'd say there was somethin' you 'ad to tell me, Morris. Somethin' as is buggin' you."

Morris pulled a well-used handkerchief from his pyjama pocket and blew his nose. He warmed his hands briefly in front of the fire.

"In case you 'adn't noticed, I'm waitin'."

Morris tugged the furry lobe of one ear, averting his gaze. "Warm in 'ere," he said.

"Never mind that. If you've somethin' to tell me, you'd best – "

"All right, all right." He cleared his throat and ran a liverish tongue over his lips. "Fact is, I've – uh – got some news."

"What sort of news?"

"Well, you see...the thing is, I've been 'avin an affair."

"You what?"

"I said, I've been – "

"I heard what you said, I'm not deaf. I'm just incredulous!"

"Ah, right," Morris said.

Doris stared at Morris. Morris stared at the carpet, both hands dangling in front of him.

Doris worked her thin lips round and round in a ragged circle. "Go on then."

"What?"

"Who is she?"

"You – you really wanna know?"

"Of course I do. That's the first thing any woman'd want to know."

Morris swallowed again and waited for his throat to unlock. "I think maybe you'll be surprised," he said.

"Surprised? I'm kind o' surprised already." She shook her head. "Jeepers, it's not Kylie Minogue, is it?"

"No."

"And am I to be supplied with a name?"

"Well, if you must know...it's Alice Farrington."

Doris' face was contorted as if in pain. "Alice Fa-"

"We bin seein' each other."

"Yes, well I 'ad gathered that much." She held a hand listlessly in the air. "Blimey! Alice Farrington!"

"You know who I mean?"

"Oh, I know who you mean all right. Her with the orange face and the bottle-blonde hair and all them gold bangles and earrings big as bicycle wheels. Well, they say men like a bit o' rough."

Morris momentarily considered offering a defence by proxy, but relented. It would only inflame the situation. He chewed nervously at a thumbnail.

"Alice Farrington," Doris murmured. "Funny, I saw her in Sainsbury's the other day. I thought she give me a shifty look."

"Ah, right," said Morris.

"So 'ow long 'as this bin goin' on exactly?"

"About two weeks."

"Two weeks? Two weeks? Sounds like 'Brief Encounter' wi' no trains."

"You see, we agreed to end it. It wasn't right."

"Most perceptive of you."

"It was by mutual agreement."

"What, doin' it or stoppin' it?"

"Both, I suppose," said Morris, miserably.

"I can't believe it. After all this time." She pinched the bridge of her nose between her thumb and forefinger. "Why today of all days, eh? Answer me that."

"How d'you mean?"

"What I mean is, why did you wait till our anniversary – our Golden Anniversary, mind – to let me in on your grubby little secret?"

"I suppose that's the point. It's our anniversary, our special day. It's not a day for lies and deceit."

"Well, couldn't you 'ave told me before?"

"I tried to. That is, I was sort of workin' up to it slowly. Next thing I knew, well, March 5th were tomorrow, and I still 'adn't done it." At last tears brimmed in his eyes. "Truly, Doris, I am just so sorry."

She sat with one hand covering her mouth, gazing into the fire. "Well, 'ere's a right old fandango, an' no mistake."

"Shall I fetch the post?"

"Leave it. I don't want to read people's cheery congratulations."

"Ah, right," Morris said.

"You've turned a celebration into a disaster," Doris informed him. "I 'ope you're satisfied."

Morris scratched the back of his neck, not looking at her. There were no suitable words. A single tear trickled down his cheek, resting saltily on his lower lip.

"So what is it you get up to? Do you, you know, go all the way?"

"Yes. Round to 'er 'ouse."

"No, no, no. I mean, is it the full act?"

He sighed, hunching his shoulders. "Pretty well. Mostly."

"What happens on the 'pretty well' days? Do your teeth drop out or you forget who you are or you get your palpitations?"

"Don't," Morris said quietly.

"You're a bloody marvel, you are." She sat back, glaring, as if to bring him into a different focus. "Is she married?"

"No. He died. She's got a son, visits sometimes. I think he's a paramedic."

"Huh. S'pose she has him standing by, in case of spontaneous traumatic calamity."

"Well, I've told you, anyway," he said, lamely.

"Thereby ruining one o' the most important days in our lives."

"I can't – what do you want me to say, Doris? What do you want me to do?"

"I want nothing from you. Nothing."

"I can't turn the clock back."

"Wouldn't make no difference. You'd be at it again, just the same. You men, you're weak as water. Useless as puppets."

Morris nodded, resting one trembling hand on the top of the fire. There was a strange taste in his mouth, sour and acidic.

211

"You gonna get dressed?" she snarled.

"What? Yeah." He rubbed the bristles on his jaw. "Could go up and have a shave."

"Right. Before you go, 'and me that phone book."

He reached into the glass-fronted bookcase behind the chair and gave Doris the directory. "Who're you ringing?"

"Hairdresser's for a colour an' cut. I deserve it."

Morris slouched to the door, head bowed. He turned, holding on to the door-frame, and looked back at her. There was a spreading grey patch in the middle of her auburn hair, but she was still a good-looking woman. The tears stung his eyes again. She deserved better than this, today, any day. After fifty years, all he had left them with was damage.

"Do I disgust you?" he asked her, in a faltering voice.

She peered at him speculatively. "No. Because disgust is like when you lift the dustbin lid off and there's mess inside, all crawlin' around. You bang the lid back on and forget it. This is different, Morris. This is disappointment. Disappointment has a 'abit of lingerin'. It'll still be there tomorrow an' the next day an'… Well, anyway, there y'are. I can't put a lid on this."

She turned aside and listened to the slow tread of his footsteps on the stairs. She heard the bathroom door click shut. On a small trolley next to her chair was a pile of magazines, the telephone and a pen and notepad. Riffling through the phone book, she found the number of Romoldi's salon and noted it down on a piece of paper. Then she flicked to the back of the book and searched the residential numbers.

She moved her lips as she turned the pages. "Farrington, Farrington…" The first Farrington said 'Window Cleaner', so she moved on, tracing a finger with its chipped pink nail slowly down the small print. Here, surely, was the name she wanted: 'A.L. Farrington'. The only other Farrington was a T.J. Doris dialled the likely number and waited. Only three rings, and the phone was picked up. She hugged the phone close to her face.

A somewhat gravelly voice, though clearly a woman's, announced the number.

"Good morning. Is this Mrs Farrington?"

"Speaking."

"That's good, because I believe we 'ave a mutual friend — Alice. You don't mind if I call you Alice?"

"A friend? What friend?"

"Mr Morris Clough."

There was a hesitation at the other end of the line. "I do know him a bit, yes."

"Hmm. It's what bit you know as most concerns me," Doris said.

"Meaning what exactly? Who is this?"

"This is Mrs Morris Clough."

The line went dead.

Without delay, Doris re-dialled. Alice Farrington answered. "Hullo."

"Yes, it's me again, Alice. Now don't you put the phone down, or I shall make rather a lot o' trouble, an' that's a promise."

"What- what is it you want?"

"What do I want? Well, I think perhaps it's time you an' me 'ad a little chat."

"I'm not seeing him any longer," Alice Farrington said quickly.

"So he tells me."

"I see. He's admitted it to you, then."

"That's the bare bones of it, yes."

She could hear Alice Farrington's anxious breathing, dramatically amplified by the receiver. A radio was playing in the background, a banal pop song supplying a ludicrous counterpoint to this toxic exchange.

"It just happened," Mrs Farrington said, at length. "It's — well, it's history now."

"You'll be 'istory, my dear, if you don't listen very carefully."

"I'm listening," Alice said.

"Good. Now about that little chat I mentioned. What I – "

"Mrs Clough, I can only say –"

"Don't interrupt me, please. Just listen. I want you to come round and see me so's we can all know where we stand. Come 'ere at eleven-thirty. No need to get dolled up, just come as you are, which in my personal estimation is mutton dressed as lamb, no offence, of course. Do we 'ave a deal?"

There ensued a brief silence while Mrs Farrington digested the insult. For perhaps ten seconds, Doris, imperious in her occupation of the moral high ground, was content to wait for capitulation.

"Do you mean today?" Mrs Farrington asked, wheezing.

"I do."

"Only you see…Friday is my coffee morning."

"We got coffee 'ere," Doris told her.

"I do rather like to meet up with my friends, you see. Sort of therapy."

"Therapy?"

"Yes. Helps me – regenerate. You know how it is, things getting on top of you."

Doris sniffed. "Yes, well, accordin' to latest reports, the thing as bin gettin' on top of you is my 'usband."

"Oh dear." For the first time, Alice Farrington sounded tearful. Sniffing and a little moist panting filtered down the wires. "Oh dear," she said again.

"So that's agreed, then?"

"Will Morris be there?"

"He will."

"Oh dear."

"We shall 'ave a cosy little get-together. I'm quite lookin' forward to it."

"I'll come," said Mrs Farrington, in a voice scarcely removed from a whimper.

"I thought you would. Do you know our address?"

"Yes."

"Splendid. I'll 'ave the coffee pot simmerin'."

Re-appearing, clean-shaven, Morris faced a wife apparently much mollified, becalmed by events beyond his knowledge, though his relief was tempered with suspicion. What, he wondered, had transpired in the past twenty minutes?

"Glad to see you've made an effort," Doris said, looking him up and down.

He had put on a crisp white shirt and grey flannels. Doris lifted her head, testing the air. Yes, he had even applied some after-shave.

"That the stuff I gave you?" she enquired.

"What stuff?"

"After-shave. Hints of cinnamon and aloe vera, as I remember. Bet she was all over you, wi' that on."

He sat down, stroking his face, checking for residual stubble. For a man of his age, he had a good complexion, unpitted, just a few wiry lines under the eyes. He always used a good-quality shaving cream, none of your aerosol gunk, mixed with natural oils. Sitting facing Doris, he dared to think of Alice when they were in bed, the way she reached up and took his head in both hands, moulding his cheeks in her warm palms. Passion fruit.

"Did you get a hair appointment?" he asked her.

"Not yet."

"Oh. Thought I heard you talking on the phone."

"You did."

"Ah, right. One o' the kids?"

"No. A friend. We got a visitor."

"Who? Where?"

"Half-eleven. Nice you got yerself spruced up. She'll be impressed."

"She?"

"Thought we'd all 'ave coffee an' biscuits."

"Who're you talking about?"

"Use your imagination, Morris."

Morris sat back, looking worried, using his imagination. It didn't bode well. He didn't care for the stoical resolve on Doris' face. Now what was she up to? She didn't even seem to be that angry. So who was this unspecified guest? "Use your imagination", she had told him. On the face of it, that could only imply one thing. But surely not. She couldn't have. She wouldn't. Or would she? She might. She would. Was this the

215

calm before the storm? Was Doris about to make him a helpless pawn in some awful game?

He propelled himself rapidly from the chair and ran upstairs to the bedroom. Perched on the window sill, he slid aside the net curtain and peered down into the street. People were passing by, on foot or in cars, going about their daily business quite normally, which made him feel resentful. How had he allowed this to happen? Could it ever have been worth it? Might he even have simply kept his mouth shut? After all, everyone had secrets. You never knew another person, no matter who they were, deeply and completely. It was like trying to squeeze the last few millimetres of toothpaste out of the tube; in the end, you gave up, because what was hidden in there was inaccessible. It would never see the light of day.

Of course, he reflected, he didn't love Alice Farrington, didn't even feel that much affection for her. It had nothing to do with his feelings towards Doris; they remained completely unimpaired. His brief dalliance with Alice had been a matter of curiosity, enhanced by a patina of adrenalin. He recalled the February evening when it had all started; that is, not the affair itself, but the first casual sowing of the seeds of attraction. Doris had gone to the pictures with her sister – he couldn't remember the film – and he decided to go out for fish and chips. Mrs Farrington was in the queue ahead of him, wearing a rather smart tan Antartex coat with the collar up. When they had lived round the corner in Cromwell Crescent, the Farrington woman, as Doris was somewhat contemptuously inclined to call her, was a near neighbour, occasionally acknowledged in the paper shop, where she parked her silver Volvo with two wheels on the kerb and the engine running. That was before the Cloughs moved to a larger house in Barley Street. So Morris waited for the queue to move up, drawn to a commotion at the front as Mrs Farrington, panting in dismay,   rummaged in all her pockets for the purse she had obviously left at home. Partly out of chivalry, and also to see the obstacle removed, Morris stepped forward to pay for the woman's parcel. It was a small gesture, invisibly loaded with burdensome consequences.

216

She had waited for him outside. "So very kind of you. It's Mr Clough, isn't it?"

"That's right, Morris Clough. We used to live opposite you in Cromwell Crescent."

"I remember. You had yellow curtains and a lantern over the porch." She thrust out her free hand. "Alice Farrington."

Morris shook her warm gloved hand.

"So, so silly of me. I must have left my purse in my other coat. You're my saviour."

"Ah well. It's only a few chips, eh?"

She looked critically at both their moist bundles. "Both got singles, by the looks of it."

"Wife's gone out. How about you?"

"Husband's gone out."

"Oh. Somewhere nice?"

"The cemetery. He died four years ago."

"I see. I'm sorry to hear that."

"Don't be. I'm over it." She turned and tugged at her collar. "Let's walk, our suppers are getting cold."

Somehow it had seemed only natural for Morris Clough and Alice Farrington to keep each other company on a winter's evening by eating their haddock and chips at Mrs Farrington's kitchen table. They didn't bother with plates, just ate straight off the greasy paper, breaking up the hot fish with sticky, flickering fingers. When the food was nearly gone, Mrs Farrington, as though feeding a child, popped a chip in Mr Clough's mouth, and Mr Clough did the same for Mrs Farrington, watching the chip slowly disappear in a thin haze of pink lipstick.

"By 'eck!" Morris declared. "I enjoyed that."

"Enjoyed what exactly?" Mrs Farrington enquired, fixing him with a cunning smile.

"Poppin' it in yer mouth. Sort of – I dunno."

She fed him her last chip, pursing her chubby lips as it slid on to his tongue. "There now!"

For Morris, who had never before considered fish and chips an erotic experience, there was soon a price to be paid beyond the fish fryer's tariff, and one which he was more than happy to meet, for an understanding had been fashioned across the kitchen table, and their next meal together was a bottle of wine upstairs, two glasses next to the pinkly glowing bedside lamp, while they touched each other's bare shoulders and mutually admired their underwear.

Jolted from his reverie, Morris saw the familiar long tan coat, set off with a rolled Burberry umbrella, advancing up the front path. Alice Farrington was precisely on time. He headed for the stairs, hearing the doorbell ring as he swung round the top newel post.

Doris called from the kitchen. "Let her in and bring her through. And no whisperin' in the hall."

Their visitor looked flustered. She stepped inside, glancing briefly, nervously, at Morris Clough, unbuttoning her coat. "I've been summoned."

From the far end of the hallway, Doris appeared, wiping her hands on her pinafore. "Mrs Farrington, how good of you to come." Her grim smile somehow left her eyes unaffected. "Morris, take the lady in and find 'er a seat. I shan't be a moment."

Morris took Alice Farrington's coat and told her to sit in the green wing chair. He sat in his usual chair and examined the pattern in the carpet as if he had never seen it before. Mrs Farrington's face was clouded with the palpable discomfort of someone unused to being told what to do, but too compromised by opprobrium to retrieve her habitual assertiveness.

"Don't worry," Morris whispered.

"I can't believe it's come to this, Morris. Why ever did you tell her?"

"I just – I don't know, Alice."

"You've gone and got us both into shit. How could you?"

Morris shook his head, vaguely attempting to determine which was worse, the revelation or the act itself. He peered anxiously at Alice Farrington out of the corner of his eye.

Doris flounced into the room, carrying a loaded tray, which she placed on the glass top of the coffee table. "Coffee, biscuits an' apricot jam tarts," she announced.

Morris and Alice stared dismally at the tray without moving.

"I shall leave you to 'elp yourselves. Morris, pour the coffee, please."

Morris did as instructed, handing Alice a cup of coffee with a gingernut in the saucer.

"The tarts are 'ome-made," Doris said. "Come on, Morris, they're your favourite. 'E likes a tart, does Morris," she added caustically, casting a reproachful eye over Alice Farrington's swollen bosom.

They munched in silence for a while. Morris covered his mouth to stifle a burp.

Alice leaned forward, replacing her cup and saucer on the table. "Mrs Clough, I feel I should speak up for both of us by – "

"No, no, dear, I 'aven't asked you 'ere to apologise. It's more in the nature of an enquiry, see."

"An enquiry?"

"Yes. For instance...I was interested to know, from what you might call a technical point of view, whether you prefer 'im to be on top o' you or underneath."

Morris choked violently, spraying coffee over his trousers.

Alice wrung her hands, averting her eyes.

"Oh dear," Doris said flatly. "Shall I fetch you a cloth, Morris?"

He slumped back, shielding his eyes with a limp hand. "I don't want a cloth. I just – Doris, what is it? Why are you doing this?"

Doris curled her lip, her gaze roaming coldly from her husband to Alice and back again. "Why am I doin' this? Why am I doin' this? It's what you're doin' I'm concerned with!"

"We aren't doing it any more," Alice said brightly.

"Thank you, Mrs Farrington, I think the damage is done." She stared fixedly at Morris again. "And if I'm embarrassin' you, Morris my dear, I assure you it's small beer compared with the humiliation you have 'eaped on me. Have you any idea how I feel, knowin' you've betrayed me, turned our marriage into some kind o' music hall joke? Well, do you?"

Alice Farrington spread her hands before her, as in hopeful supplication. "We were just friends, Mrs Clough. It just happened – we strayed, and we're truly sorry. We weren't thinking."

"Friends, is it? Oh, I don't mind 'im 'avin' friends. I don't mind 'im 'avin' a gun so long as 'e don't go about shootin' people. I let 'im 'ave a friend, an' 'e abuses my trust. It's taken me fifty years to find out 'e can't be trusted."

Morris dabbed ineffectually at his trouser-legs with a paper napkin.

"A further line of enquiry," Doris said.

Alice screwed up her eyes as if in pain.

"Why? That's my question. Why?" She picked up a jam tart and sat back. "Take your time."

Morris tilted back his head and studied the ceiling for inspiration.

Alice glared at him. "Morris!"

"What?"

"Say something, for God's sake! This is your house!"

"What's that got to do with it?"

Doris chomped mechanically, dropping crumbs down her front.

"It was something different," Morris said. "I just wondered what it would be like. Sort of like seeing something in a window you don't really want, but you fancy giving it a try."

Alice bristled visibly. "Thank you, Morris – for giving me a try. I shall remember to be grateful."

Doris, sucking her teeth, glanced randomly from one offender to the other. They seemed to have arrived at a defining moment. In her perception, if Morris had humiliated her, he had also insulted Alice Farrington, and it was possible to view these misdemeanours as equally distasteful, if only she could persuade herself to stand outside the situation for long enough to fabricate an impartial judgment. The trouble with men, she realised, was not women, but other parts of the men themselves.

"I think he's talking about variety," Alice said.

"Variety?" Doris repeated it very slowly, pronouncing each syllable as though she had never heard the word before. "Va-ri-e-ty."

"You know what I mean," said Alice.

"I know what variety means. Before you do it, you sing a song, wear a funny 'at."

"That's not what she means," Morris said.

"I'm still not clear what the attraction was." Doris steeled herself to imagine Morris in bed with Alice Farrington, and shuddered at the vision. She wondered if that orange stuff came off on the sheets. Or on Morris. "I am still waitin' hopefully for enlightenment."

"I'm not in love with him," said Alice, shaking her head. "I'm not wanting to steal him from you."

"Hmm. That must be as much of a relief to you as to me. You'd be takin' on a serious liability."

Morris blinked and gazed forlornly into the fire.

Doris hitched up her sleeve to glance at the gold watch Morris had given her on their silver wedding anniversary. "Post office," she said.

"What?" Morris gaped at her, his pale face blank as half a coconut.

"Yesterday. You said somethin' about goin' to the post office."

"Ah, right."

"Well, don't wait for the lunch-time queues. Get goin'."

Morris considered his options. If he reached for the lifeline his wife had thrown him, he could legitimately escape the scene of further potential embarrassment; but in his absence all manner of slurs and accusations might be visited upon him, while he was not there to defend himself. Still, what he didn't hear would surely not hurt him. Yes, what he needed now was a breath of fresh air. He levered himself out of his chair, with the briefest of glances at Alice Farrington.

"Do you want me to go?" Alice asked Doris.

"No, I want you to stay. You an' me, we can 'ave a nice girly chat, get to know each other."

"I'll – uh – be off then," Morris said.

"Take yer coat, it's cold out." Doris adjusted the heating knob on the fire. "An' get me a *People's Friend* while yer out."

Morris took his coat and his blue lambswool scarf from the peg in the hall and peered at his reflection in the mirror. Poor bugger, he thought, you don't stand a chance.

Doris lifted her bottom to pull her chair closer to Alice Farrington, who smiled at her pleasantly and shuffled her feet. "That's got rid of 'im," Doris said. "Now we can relax without 'im gawpin' at us." She pushed a plate across the table. "Thin arrowroot?"

As he passed the bay window, Morris turned and saw Doris leaning over to pour Alice another cup of coffee. He muttered to himself, "They'll soon be thick as thieves. Me, I'm stuffed."

He stood in the post office queue for fifteen minutes. Coming out, he passed a newsagent and went in for Doris' *People's Friend*. He didn't feel like hurrying back. There was a florist across the road and he thought of buying Doris a bunch of flowers, but that would hardly compensate for this momentous infidelity. It would be like an inch of sticking plaster on a broken leg. Instead, he decided to put the money towards a cup of hot, sweet tea and a toasted teacake in Patsy's Pantry. It was warm in there, with just a gentle buzz of conversation. He found a seat by the window and used his sleeve to wipe the condensation off the glass so he could see the people going by and wonder if they had problems like his own. "You could have avoided all this, you daft old sod," he told himself, watching the ambling shoppers out of hooded eyes.

"Sir?"

Turning, he looked up at the waitress' face. She was pretty but looked bored. They mostly did nowadays. On your feet all day, dispensing tea and buns to complete strangers – you couldn't blame the girls. It was a thankless task. This one had even put eyeliner and lipstick on – for what? You didn't get many fit young men in Patsy's Pantry. Beverley, her name was, it said so on her plastic badge. Morris imagined he was the manager and had the responsibility of pinning Beverley's badge on each morning, anxious in case he punctured her bra or gave her the wrong impression as he patted the pale blue rectangle to confirm its security.

"Sir?"

"Oh, sorry, my dear."

Beverley blinked solemnly, signalling that, whoever she might be, she was not Morris Clough's dear, today or any other day.

"I'll 'ave a cup o' tea, nice an' strong, if yer please, an' a toasted teacake wi' butter an' raspberry jam."

Beverley held a notepad but didn't bother to write the order down. In an instant she was gone. Morris resumed his surveillance of the street, his absorption so intense that he didn't notice the waitress return with his snack. Suddenly it was there in front of him, the tea in a small china pot with the string of a teabag dangling from the lid.

He wouldn't see Alice again, he told himself. It was the only way. A married man could have a platonic friendship with another woman, but once they had slept together the rules of engagement became blurred, and it was virtually impossible to return to the safe side of the fence. *Slept together.* The phrase made him smile. Couples conducting an affair hardly ever slept together. It was an absurd euphemism. For either party, marriage made overnight fulfilment impractical, and in any case there could be no point in masterminding a clandestine meeting, only to fall asleep. Still, Mrs Farrington had taught him a thing or two, and for that he was grateful. For a few short days, she had made him feel young again. He had left Cromwell Crescent with a spring in his step.

Butter fingers. He wiped them with a paper napkin, fingered the corners of his mouth for traces of red jam. The teapot remained half full, but he couldn't drink any more; too much tea always made his bladder swell. He pulled his coat about him and approached the till. A plastic dish on the counter bore a cardboard sign: 'Thank You'. There was a layer of assorted coins. Morris thought of the girl with the bored face, paid his bill and ignored the gratuity dish. As he walked to the door, she brushed past him with a loaded tray and an open smile.

"Thank you, sir. Have a lovely day!"

"Yes. You too – Beverley."

Fishing in his pocket as he passed his table, he slid a pound coin under the saucer. Poor girl. Bet she didn't get much. Sweet smile. One pound to make an old man feel good.

It was starting to rain. He should have brought his cap. In the manner of a tortoise retreating into its shell, he hunched down into his coat's upraised collar and walked with his head lowered. A fine drizzle pricked his face.

Apprehension pasted his tongue and quickened his pulse as he turned into Barley Street. He could feel his heart thumping. Against a gathering gloom, Doris had turned the front room light on, and he could see them inside, the pair of them, standing up. Alice had her coat on. Doris was standing next to her. He stopped and stared in disbelief. Doris had one arm around Alice's shoulders and was speaking with a broad grin on her face. Alice nodded, threw back her head and laughed. They moved slightly apart, then leaned into each other and exchanged hugs. Something extraordinary had happened. He stood in the front garden, watching, open-mouthed, not caring about the rain. Alice was saying something to Doris, emphasizing her point with a raised forefinger, whereupon Doris backed away, rocking with laughter, shaking her head vigorously, as if a swarm of bees encircled it. Then Doris saw him, thrust her head towards the window and beckoned him inside.

"Morris, dear, whatever are you doin', standin' in the garden?"

"I'm not standin' in the garden," he said, unwinding his scarf.

"You were, I saw you. You'll be drenched."

"I got your magazine." He held out a rain-spattered copy of *People's Friend.*

"Thanks. Good timin'. Alice was just goin'."

"So I see."

"Yes. We've 'ad such a nice li'l get-together." She clutched Alice's shoulder. "'Aven't we, Alice?"

Alice Farrington nodded, rolling her eyes artfully. Morris peeled off his coat and draped it over the back of Doris' chair.

"Well, thank you for comin' round, Alice, dear. We go back a long way, when you think about it."

Morris thought about it.

"Now show Alice out, dear. Don't let 'er forget 'er brolly. She'll need it, this weather."

Morris escorted Alice Farrington to the front door and handed her the Burberry umbrella. They walked slowly up the path to the gate.

Doris stood in the doorway. "You've got no coat, Morris," she called out.

"Bloody 'ell," Morris said.

Alice went through the gate, turned and hesitated. "Goodbye, Morris. Don't kiss me."

"I wasn't goin' to."

"Just – remember me, in your own way."

Morris remembered her in various positions. She walked away, wiggling her fingers at him. The rain was falling harder. It looked like being a wet night.

Doris stood back to let him in. "You smell o' rain," she said.

He went indoors and picked up his coat. The room was fragrant with Alice's perfume. Doris followed him and ran her fingers through his hair. "You're all wet."

"I'm a bit shivered."

"Well, if you will go standin' about in the rain."

"How – uh – how was Mrs Farrington?" he ventured, cautiously.

"Mrs Farrington was fine, just fine." Her face took on a rosy bloom, a flush of warm satisfaction. "You could say, we set the world to rights."

"Ah, right," Morris said.

"Tell you what."

"What?" said Morris.

"We don't want you catchin' your death. You sit by the fire a minute. There's warm coffee still in the pot. I'm goin' upstairs and run you a nice 'ot bath."

"I had a wash this morning. Did everythin'."

"That's as maybe. Nice 'ot bath, that's what you need."

Morris sat by the fire with a cup of coffee and a jam tart. He picked up *People's Friend* and carefully peeled apart the damp pages. Checking over his shoulder, he reached out to the chair where Alice had sat and felt the seat for her residual warmth. Upstairs he heard water running. He allowed himself a wry smile. The last bath he had been in was with Alice Farrington.

Doris appeared with a pink face and wet hands. "I've put some o' them purple flakes in, the ones as makes the water go all silky."

"Thanks."

"Now you go up an' strip off. Right? Only you don't get in yet. Right?"

Morris frowned.

"You sit on that wicker chair, the one makes your bum go like a waffle."

"Ah, right," said Morris, standing up.

"I'm givin' you two minutes to get your stuff off an' wait."

Hanging his head, Morris climbed slowly up the stairs. In the bathroom he undressed, piled his clothes on the floor and sat on the uncomfortable wicker chair next to the bath.

Doris stood at the foot of the stairs. "You done, Morris?"

"I'm sittin' down."

And Doris grinned and licked her lips. Behind her back she clasped a feather duster, a scrubbing brush and a slotted steel fish slice.

"I'm comin' up!" she called. "'Appy anniversary!"

Doing it for Onslow

Rehearsal weekend. Soon after ten o'clock a silver Lexus drew up at the entrance to Possett Hall. For a moment the doors remained closed, and then the driver got out, reached inside for his tan cord jacket and stepped back to open the adjacent rear door. Slowly, carefully an elderly man with snow-white hair, wearing an immaculately tailored astrakhan coat, eased himself from the back seat, holding on to the doorframe to lever himself upright as his feet touched the ground. The younger man, the driver, stood attentively by the rear door, slipping into his jacket as he waited, head slightly bowed in an attitude of patient concern. Once the white-haired man was standing securely, the driver offered him a supporting hand, but this gesture seemed to irritate the passenger, and he shook his head and pushed forward, raising his head to examine the front aspect of the building. The man in the cord jacket shut both doors with soft thuds and set the car alarm.

"Ah, Mr Ackerman!"

Such was the enthusiasm of his greeting, the man emerging from the doorway, right arm extended, fairly bounded down the stone steps, while the old man's slow advance suggested stiffness from the car seat, rather than the effects of arthritis. At his back, the man in the tan jacket eased him respectfully forward towards the outstretched, welcoming hand, as if shepherding royalty.

"Let's get Mr Ackerman inside," the escort urged, "he feels the cold and it's been a long trip from the United States."

"Nonsense!" Ackerman bellowed irritably over his shoulder. "I'm good, just a little residual jet-lag, nothing more." He appeared embarrassed at the brusque manner in which the introduction had been interrupted, and he reached out, shook hands and offered his host an open smile. "You must excuse my son's impetuosity. Really, I'm fine and happy to be here. Now, you must be Mr Melhuish."

"Indeed. Jeremy Melhuish, Hall Manager. Welcome to Possett Hall."

Undaunted, Ackerman's son was pressing his father's back. "A little chilly out here, Dad."

As if nature had chosen to illuminate the judgment, a sudden gust of wind rushed through the trees bordering the driveway, whipping Ackerman's hair into tendrils of white smoke.

The three men reached the steps, where Ackerman hesitated. "Oh, I'm sorry. Forgetful of me." He turned and clutched his son's arm. "Allow me to introduce this young man. Clyde Ackerman is my son, my guardian and my manager. It's largely thanks to him I made it here."

Melhuish shook Clyde Ackerman's hand and led the Ackermans inside. "Did you have a smooth flight, Mr Ackerman?"

"Could have been better. Two changes of plane between Nebraska and London." He gave a short laugh. "Guess I'm getting a tad old for all this hurtling about."

Melhuish nodded condescendingly. "Might I ask how old you are now, sir?"

"You might. I'm eighty-five."

"Really? Well, if I may say so, you don't look it."

Ackerman pulled a face. "Right, well let's hope I don't play like it, eh?"

"I'm quite sure there's no chance of that," the hall manager said, wondering vaguely if the remark sounded patronizing. "Can we offer you people something to drink — something warm, perhaps?"

"A nice cup of English tea," said the old man, rubbing his hands together.

Jeremy Melhuish ushered the Americans into his office, found them upright chairs and, extending both hands for the astrakhan coat, hung it on a hook behind the door. He picked up the phone. "Ah, Emmett, you're here. Our guests have arrived. Could you organise tea for three, please?"

Clyde Ackerman leaned forward, placing one hand on the desk. "The orchestra, Mr Melhuish. Have they arrived?"

"A small group came early, mainly brass players. The others are coming together by coach. They should be here any minute."

"Very good. And the conductor?"

"Gordon Dakers," the elder Ackerman supplied.

"Yes. Mr Dakers is on his way by car. Please don't worry."

"Oh, I'm not worried, Mr Melhuish. I'm sure you have everything under control."

"It's just, we would like to get started," Clyde said.

"Of course. As soon as we've had our tea, I'll show you to the auditorium."

"Fine, fine." The old man cast his eyes round the room and, finding nothing of interest, focused on Melhuish's face once more. "It's a Bosendorfer, I understand."

"That's right. Wonderful tone. And we also have a small practice room with a Steinway."

Ackerman nodded approvingly. A car drew up outside the window. Doors slammed.

The office door opened and a laden tray, followed by a tall, lean figure, edged into the room. "Tea and biscuits for three," announced the thin man.

"Thank you, Emmett. Just leave it on the desk."

Emmett did so, delivering a tight-lipped smile to each man in turn.

Melhuish began unloading the tray, then stopped. "I think I should introduce this young man. Emmett Carstairs is our – what would I say? – general factotum."

"Pleased to meet you, Emmett," said Ackerman senior.

"Likewise," his son echoed.

"Emmett works here on an ad hoc basis, when his studies allow. He's the kind of man we can't do without. He makes tea, adjusts the heating, tidies up, sells programmes, opens and shuts the hall... You name it, Emmett does it."

"Jack of all trades," the old man commented.

"Good man," Clyde said, looking a little bored.

"Emmett Carstairs," his father repeated. "Hey, sounds like a character out of 'The Great Gatsby'. "So what are you studying, Emmett?"

The young man's face brightened. "Music, sir. At the Royal College in London."

"Oh really? What's your specialty?"

"Piano, sir. I'm looking forward enormously to your concert. The Brahms First is one of my student pieces."

"You don't say?"

Footsteps sounded beyond the door. Melhuish turned aside, ready to get up.

"Some of us have been working on Brahms One since last year, sir. With the college orchestra. I particularly wanted to be here for your rehearsal and performance."

"That's very heartening, Emmett."

"Thank you, sir."

"Oh, I think we can dispense with the 'sir', Emmett. Had enough of that. Why don't you call me Onslow?"

Emmett smiled graciously. "Very well, sir. I mean – Onslow."

Melhuish edged forward as if to abort the conversation. "Mr Ackerman, I believe Gordon Dakers has arrived."

"Oh, right. Better go see him." Standing up, he reached for Emmett's hand. "Pleasure to meet you, young man. See you around?"

"I hope so, sir. Onslow."

As Emmett Carstairs reversed towards the doorway, Melhuish threw him a disdainful glance, from which the younger man inferred that, in the manager's estimation, he had overstepped the mark in his familiarity with this international celebrity. Emmett digested the possibility, but he was not about to relinquish an opportunity. He came to Possett for the job, but his sole inspiration was the music.

Searching for Dakers, Melhuish led the Ackermans into the main hall, where a scattering of instrumentalists were seated at the back, fussing with sheet music and instruments. A trumpeter blew a long, piercing note, then sat back, tugging at his chair. While his son took a front row seat, Ackerman slid on

230

to the piano stool and ran his fingers rapidly, almost soundlessly, over the keys.

Emmett was at the hall steps, watching as a large red coach, air brakes hissing, manoeuvred into the car park. He smiled. The South Forest Symphony Orchestra had arrived. Hooking back the double doors to speed their entry, he nodded curtly to each player as the group passed through, many of them carrying their instruments which they had kept with them on the coach. A green and white Fiat van, with the orchestra's name and logo emblazoned on the sides, pulled up beside the coach, and a huddle of men and women, their instruments too large to travel with them, waited for the driver to help them unload.

"Howling gale with these doors open, Emmett!" Melhuish stamped his feet, scowling.

"Just want to get everyone inside as quickly as possible," Emmett told him, not turning round.

"Oh, right. Make sure you shut them afterwards."

"Everything's under control, Mr Melhuish."

Most of the players filed straight into the auditorium to take their places on the stage. A handful of people asked Emmett to get them a hot drink or make buttered toast, requests which the young man accommodated with his usual unflappable courtesy. Though a casual, lowly-paid employee, Emmett was to all intents and purposes a customer-focused professional who loved his work. He respected everyone and was intimidated by no-one.

The main hall was beginning to come alive. Standing next to the seated Onslow Ackerman, the vaguely aristocratic figure of Gordon Dakers, in dark trousers and white open-necked shirt, his black hair greying at the temples and casually allowed to sweep back thickly over his collar, was talking with his head down, emphasizing a point by puncturing the air with his baton. Some of his words struggled for audibility above the rising clamour of the musicians tuning up: the squawk and whine of bowed strings; animal shrieks from woodwind; raucous blasts from upraised horns and trumpets; an occasional fusillade, like approaching thunder, as the timpanist powered his sticks across the drumskins.

"Whaddya say we press on?" Ackerman checked his watch and tilted his head at Dakers.

"Whenever you're ready," the conductor agreed.

"I'm ready. Are your troops ready?"

"One moment, please, Mr Ackerman." He straightened up, lifting both hands for attention.

"Just call me Onslow. Not so many damned syllables."

The stage fell silent. Dakers stepped to the rostrum and opened his score. He turned his head to left and right, waiting for sixty-five pairs of eyes to look at him. Onslow sat with his hands in his lap, working his lips, as though silently memorising the music.

"No microphone," Dakers called out, "so I hope you can all hear me."

A few people nodded and mumbled assent.

"Okay. Well, unfortunately our orchestra manager, John Stilwell, has met with a minor road accident on the way here – I am assured he is not badly hurt – and so we are unlikely to see him before tomorrow's rehearsal. It therefore falls to me to introduce our most distinguished guest soloist" – Ackerman waved an acknowledging hand above the keyboard – "who, as you know, will perform the Brahms First Piano Concerto with us at next Wednesday's concert, tickets for which are, I am told, selling like the proverbial hot cakes. Onslow Ackerman's 1990 recording of this concerto received worldwide acclaim and won prizes for interpretation and technical excellence in Japan, the USA and Germany, and that same CD remains a mainstay of the catalogue to this day."

Ackerman shifted impatiently on the stool, offering a further, somewhat dismissive, wave.

"Now Mr Ackerman tells me he has all but given up public appearances, so we are doubly honoured to enjoy this rare chance to work alongside him to achieve what I am sure will be a resoundingly successful musical event. Our guest is happily aware that he is – ah – joining forces with an orchestra who have played Brahms One on two previous occasions, I believe with some distinction. We are indeed fortunate that Mr Ackerman's daughter resides in the UK, not far from here, enabling him to stay locally during his visit. Given his disinclination to undertake any more live performances, I think I am right in saying that this family link has encouraged him to agree to do one last concert before he retires – so, please, let's all make sure it's a truly special one."

"Thank you, Gordon." Ackerman nodded his appreciation as Dakers toyed with his baton. "And thank you, ladies and gentlemen."

"All right." Dakers peered over the piano lid. "You want us to go from the beginning?"

"Why not?"

The *forte* outburst in the first bar drew an admiring swing of the head from the poised pianist, timpanist Jolyon Sando reinforcing his opening salvo with two thunderous drum rolls which probably exceeded the decibel rating envisaged by the composer.

Ackerman, awaiting his own quiet introductory statement, shouted over the heads of the strings, "Great timpani!" First violinist and leader Margot Runnicles could not hold back her laughter at the great man's cry of delight.

They rehearsed for a couple of hours, then broke for a late lunch. Onslow Ackerman looked tired, but pleased with the orchestra, and chose to remain at the piano, reflectively going over a number of unaccompanied passages, keeping the volume low, almost as if playing the music in his head. He saw Emmett talking to someone at the back of the stage, and beckoned him to the piano.

"How's it going, Onslow?"

"It's going fine. I'd like another hour. Do you think that's possible?"

"Gordon Dakers has gone for a sandwich. I'll ask him. I'm sure there'll be no problem."

"Okay, Emmett. Good man. Say, do you reckon you could rustle me up a coffee and some buttered toast?"

233

"I could get you some sandwiches."

"Just some toast, Emmett. With some of your beautiful English butter. Oh, and is there any news on your orchestra manager?"

"Mr Stilwell has a cracked elbow, apparently. His car's pretty bad."

"So no show today?"

"No. But I understand he intends to be here tomorrow, come what may."

Ackerman nodded sympathetically. "Well, let's hope so."

"I'll fetch your toast, Onslow."

Sunday's session began at eleven o'clock, and John Stilwell was driven in by his wife, his right arm in a sling. Emmett met him and carried his briefcase to a front-row seat in the hall. The orchestra, Dakers and Ackerman were grouped on stage, all concentrating on their appointed tasks amid the reassuring chaos of tuning recalcitrant instruments. Gazing up at them, Stilwell unwound a red scarf from his neck with his left hand, dropped it on his briefcase and walked to the stage front, where he reached for Ackerman's hand.

"Wrong hand, Mr Ackerman. I'm sorry."

"No, no, I'm sorry. For your accident, I mean."

"Could have been worse." He shrugged. "I hope they're looking after you."

With a shallow smile, Ackerman twisted his hands as though to make them pliable. "I'm easy," he said. "Plenty of seats. Why don't you sit down?"

Gordon Dakers had moved to the piano. Stilwell nodded to him and stepped back to the front seat where he had left his case and scarf. He sat nursing his right arm against the crumpled jacket of his dark suit, the shoulders speckled with dandruff.

The orchestra had fallen silent, watching Ackerman and Dakers expectantly. Ackerman told the conductor he was ready for a complete run-through, which they had not attempted the day before. With extra time at the end for revisions, that would take an hour.

"Your people all set?" he asked Dakers.

234

Dakers nodded, turning to face the rostrum.

"I only want to do this once. Let's go non-stop unless there's a foul-up. Watch that tempo in the last movement. You were ahead of me yesterday, remember. I want a canter, not a gallop."

"You have the lead, Mr Ackerman. We'll follow you."

He tipped his head at the players. "Yeah. Do they know that?"

"Trust me."

They finished the concerto at half past one. Dakers was sweating slightly, but Onslow Ackerman looked grey and a little distracted. His playing had been flawless, dramatically authoritative in the outer movements, sweetly melancholy in the Adagio; but his son Clyde, who had crept into the auditorium at the end of the opening movement, sat staring at his father's face, rather than those eloquent hands, detecting a grainy weariness there, too many years, too many nomadic miles, too many listlessly-acknowledged ovations and encores etched in the furrows of the old man's cheeks.

Half rising from the stool as the orchestra gathered up their scores, Ackerman waved a grateful hand, then sank down again, calling Dakers over. "That's enough. Just one thing."

"Sir?"

"Hell. Please, Onslow."

"Yes, Onslow?"

"Whaddya think about that Adagio ending phrase? The timpani."

"You think...?"

"I think we need *sotto voce*. Mr Sando's leaning on it, kind of telling us he's there. Just because he's had nothing to do for ten minutes. You get me?"

"Of course. I'll have a word."

"Thank you. Otherwise you have a fine orchestra."

It was starting to rain as Clyde drove his father back to his daughter's house. The windscreen wipers squeaked on the glass and Clyde repeatedly fiddled with the interior air to prevent the screen from misting. He seemed gloomily preoccupied.

"You're very quiet, Clyde."

"Am I? Guess I'm just concerned."

"About what?"

"Not what, who. I'm anxious about you, Dad."

"Huh. No need."

"You look tired. Strikes me this is all too much."

"Nonsense."

"You're eighty-five, Dad. You need – "

"Hell, I know how old I am!"

"You ever think maybe this is one escapade too many? You ever think that?"

"No, I never think that. I've still got it, Clyde. I can still do this."

"I'm not talking about the piano. I'm not bothered about the damned piano."

"It's what I do, Clyde. It's paid the bills for sixty years."

Clyde sighed and turned the blower to maximum flow. "Dad, promise me something. Please."

The old man slapped his son on the knee. "I'm ahead of you. All right? I've already promised it. No more concerts, this one's the last." He squirmed uncomfortably in his seat, touched by the filial concern but indignant that his resolve had apparently been challenged. "Satisfied now?"

By Wednesday the rain had returned and a brittle wind strafed the Possett Hall car park as the silver Lexus drew up, its headlights already sweeping the bushes in the gathering gloom. From the back seat emerged the surprisingly lithe and shapely legs of Hannah Harding, Ackerman's daughter, still elegant at sixty-three; while Onslow Ackerman edged himself carefully from the front passenger seat, clutching a brown suede zipped bag with his initials – O.J.A – embossed on the flap. Clyde spared his father and sister the briefest of glances before stepping to the car boot and removing a black suit bag containing Ackerman's change of clothes for the evening's performance. Advancing from the yellowish light of the entrance porch, Jeremy Melhuish shook the elder Ackerman's hand, nodded to his daughter and son and took a light hold of the old man's elbow. A few early patrons, gossiping on the steps, paused to smile at Onslow Ackerman, and one or two seized the rare opportunity for a flash photograph of the approaching party, Hannah Harding walking with her head down, as if ducking under invisible branches, to protect her hairstyle from the worst ravages of the breeze.

Melhuish moved to block Ackerman's way, manoeuvring him to one side. "Some people milling around in there. Come with me, I'll take you to the stage door."

Ackerman pulled a submissive face. "Whatever you say, my friend." He massaged his hands in relief as Melhuish ushered the group into the warmth of the corridor and closed the door behind them.

"Mr Ackerman, we have a small dressing room, if you'd care to rest for a while. Nothing fancy, you understand, but –"

"I don't do fancy, Mr Melhuish. Just lead the way."

Emmett Carstairs had switched on the dressing room light, filled the well-used coffee machine and placed *Kleenex* and a hospitality tray on the knee-hole desk. An upright chair with a red leather backrest and seat was pushed tight to the desk, above which a square mirror hung at a seated artist's head height. In an alcove in the wall opposite the door, a wooden wardrobe offered ample space for clothes and a selection of plastic hangers.

Jeremy Melhuish cast his eyes apologetically round the room. "As I said, it's pretty basic."

"Oh, please. It's really not important. The hall and the piano are just fine, so don't upset yourself."

"Very well." He turned to Clyde and Hannah, waiting behind him. "Er…would you good people like to – I mean, I can get more chairs, or…"

"Thank you, Mr Melhuish," Hannah said, her American accent rounded and softened by the years she had spent in the south of England, "but I think it'll get a little crowded in here." She draped a hand on her brother's shoulder. "Come on, Clyde. Let's you and me get a coffee and give the maestro some space."

Ackerman pulled the chair out and stared at it. "Catch you later," he said absently.

Melhuish looked relieved. He could escort Ackerman's children to the public area and leave them to fend for themselves. It was hot in here. He could feel his shirt sticking to his back. "This way," he told them. "Oh, Mr Ackerman."

"It's Onslow. Always it's Onslow." Ackerman was sitting down, adjusting his windblown hair in the mirror.

"Onslow, good. I'll send Emmett Carstairs to see you."

"You will? What for?"

"In case there's anything you want, anything at all."

Ackerman dismissed him with a tight-lipped smile. "Whatever."

Clyde thrust his father's suit bag past the hovering Melhuish. "You'll need this, Dad."

The old man took the bag and sat with it in his lap. "Now you can go. And thanks for the lift."

Melhuish was as good as his word. Within five minutes Emmett Carstairs tapped on the dressing room door and peeped inside. "Good evening, Mr Ackerman."

"Onslow. Come on – Onslow. Wanna come in, Emmett?"

"Thank you, Onslow." Emmett stood in the doorway, so tall his head almost touched the top of the frame. "We're all looking forward to tonight. It's shaping up for a full house."

"Glad to hear it, Emmett."

"Is there anything I can get you? You've an hour before the concert starts, and there's a harp piece first and then an interval."

"Then me?"

"Then you."

"Okay. Tell you what." He flexed his hands. "I can't get used to your so-called spring weather. These old hands are clammy-cold. Do you have such a thing as a – whaddya call it? – a hot water bottle?"

"Oh, but I can get you an electric heater if you're cold," Emmett said.

"No, it's not the room. The room is fine. It's just my hands, I need to warm them up, make them supple. When I played the Anvil they gave me a hot water bottle – worked a treat."

Emmett chewed his bottom lip. "I'll see what I can do. Could be... leave it with me."

The door clicked shut. Onslow Ackerman munched a biscuit from the tray and sat massaging his cold hands. His face, mobile as he chewed, loomed before him in the mirror. There was a nick on his chin from the new razor blade he'd used that morning, a pink blemish he hadn't noticed until now. Under his jaw some white barbs sparkled in the overhead light, and he ran an exploratory hand down the side of his face, sighing. He found himself confronting the ugly truth; he could play the Brahms First standing on his head, but that didn't make him a young man any longer. Prokofiev Three, Rachmaninov Two, the Totentanz, Scharwenka Four, the Goldberg Variations – the great Onslow Ackerman had surmounted and dismissed them all, and so many others besides, but he could not conquer old age. Clyde was right; this was all too much. Twenty years after most men had taken their pensions and gone smiling into a blue yonder, he was still banging away, clambering on and off aeroplanes, struggling against time barriers across the world, dragging a suitcase in and out of identical plastic hotels. He shook his head at his glowering reflection. *Onslow Ackerman, you're an old fool. You've done the job a hundred times over. You tell them this is the last show, but you said that after Vienna two years ago, and you said it again after Tanglewood. What's the matter with you? Do everyone a favour. Go home, sit on the lawn with a Jack Daniels and a good book. It's called getting a life, for God's sake, or not pissing one away.*

Lost in these reflections, Ackerman didn't hear Emmett knock on the door, but he saw a hand thrust in, a fist around the neck of a yellow hot water bottle. The pianist's eyes travelled up the outstretched arm to meet Emmett's beaming face, radiant with this small triumph.

"What the - ?"

"Sorry for the delay, Onslow. I had to go to the late-night chemist."

"The what?"

"I mean, the drugstore. Be careful, it's hot."

"Oh, Jeez! You went and bought me a hot water bottle?"

"I couldn't find one here. Mind you don't burn your hands."

Ackerman took the bottle, laid it on the desk and flattened his hands on the bulging rubber. "Emmett, you're a marvel."

The young man was pulling a folded leaflet from his pocket. "I got you a programme. You're on page four."

"Just leave it on the desk. Gotta warm these stiff hands. Hey, how much do I owe you?"

"Nothing, Onslow. I'll put it in the store and take the money out of the petty cash."

Ackerman shook his head. "What would we do without you, Emmett?"

"Just doing my job, I reckon." He craned his neck to look over the chair. "That your suit on the floor? Here, I'll hang it up for you."

Ackerman sat quietly warming his waxen, blue-veined hands while Emmett unpacked the collarless black jacket and immaculately pressed trousers and hung them on separate hangers.

"All done."

"Thank you, friend."

"Mr Ackerman, I was thinking."

"Thinking what?"

"Did they tell you there's a practice room?"

"A what?"

"Next door. It's a bit – spartan. But there's an old Steinway you can use. It's not perfect, but it is in tune."

"Well, fancy." Ackerman lifted his hands and made a pedalling motion with his fingers. "Yes, I seem to recall they mentioned it."

"There's just the piano and some chairs. I thought – well, if you wanted to sort of practice."

"Sort of practice?"

"Yes. Then you could."

"Son, I'm not one to brag, but I've played this damned thing a hundred times. Okay, it feels like a hundred times. You understand?"

"I think so, Onslow. It was just a thought."

Ackerman pushed back the chair and stood up, clutching the hot water bottle to his chest. "And, if I may say so, a very kind thought." He ran his tongue ruminatively round the inside of his cheeks. "Say, why aren't you the manager, Emmett?"

"Oh, that's a full-time job. I'm a student, remember."

"I remember. Emmett, would you pick up my bag from the floor there? Then lead the way. Let's you and me play some Brahms."

"What, both of us?"

"As I recall, you said you were studying this concerto."

"That's right." Carrying Ackerman's suede bag, Emmett led him to the practice room and turned on the light. "You've plenty of time," he said.

"On the contrary, Emmett, it's you who has plenty of time. Me, well, I guess I'm pretty well played out. Time is no longer on my side."

"I wouldn't say that, Onslow."

"You don't need to, I've said it for you. I've spared you a very awkward moment."

Emmett propped the lid of the piano and Ackerman flipped up the keyboard lid to reveal a weary row of smoker's teeth. He pressed middle C sharp, cocked his head, nodded and sat down on the shabby stool.

"Pull up a chair, Emmett. You could just be my most appreciative audience."

Ackerman straightened his shoulders, rocking slowly back and forth as he played, his eyes hardly brushing the keys, but gliding around the pale walls, alighting from time to time on Emmett's entranced face, before sweeping on past the darkened window to begin another wave-like circumnavigation of the room. Emmett sat transfixed by the chromatic richness of the sound Onslow Ackerman was drawing out of the old piano,

241

the American's cumbersome grey head tipped back as if seeking the sky, and as the final bars of the concerto's slow movement unfolded, it seemed to Emmett that, in the consummate effortlessness of the delivery, what he was hearing could only be the piano playing Onslow Ackerman, not Ackerman playing the piano, the old man communing with the instrument as a living, breathing vessel, music achieved by osmosis.

"Whaddya think?" Ackerman clasped his hands in front of him as if in prayer.

"I think – I think it's better than perfection, Onslow. When I listen to you, I realise how much I have to learn. But thank you."

"You don't have to thank me. That's not part of the deal."

"What I mean is, I feel privileged."

"You do? Let's hope the paying customers express the same opinion, eh?"

"Oh, I'm sure they will. Don't you worry about it."

"I'm not worried. A little tired, maybe, but not worried." He moulded his hands, stretching the fingers. "Wanna sit here?"

"Me?"

"Of course you. Who else?"

"I – don't you want to practise?"

Ackerman sighed, stroking his hair. "Practice? I don't need any more damned practice. I'm doing this stuff in my sleep, for God's sake. I just wanted to warm up."

"How are your hands now?"

"Better. I have control of them." He pointed at Emmett. "Now, about you, young Mr Carstairs."

"What would you like to know, Onslow?"

Ackerman slid the stool back and stood up. "I'd like to know how you play Brahms, that's what I'd like to know. Come on, swap over."

Emmett made himself comfortable at the piano, placed his hands on the keyboard and lifted them again. "Onslow, I need the music."

"You what? Oh, I see." He picked up his bag, unzipped it and handed Emmett the sheaf of full score. "Sorry, I should have thought."

"What shall I play?"

"Whatever you want. Why don't you play the Adagio ending, same as me, then we can make, let's say, an enlightened comparison."

Emmett flicked through the sheets until he found the closing pages of the wistful slow movement, then he slowly settled his hands over the keys, hitched back his shoulders and began to play. In the corner of his eye he saw Ackerman lean forward with his eyes closed, resting both forearms on his thighs. He remained in that position for several minutes, occasionally moving his head up and down, or from side to side, in time to the music; and when he heard the final bars he sat up and focused on Emmett's face, noting how the young man sometimes moved his lips as he drew out the notes, perhaps in confirmation or self-encouragement, no words, no sound uttered, but his way of touching the heart of the music.

"So – uh – what do you think, Onslow?" He sat rubbing his hands nervously over his thighs.

"What do I think? What do I think?"

"Please. I'd like to know, Onslow."

Ackerman nodded his head, gazing down at the floor. "The truth of it is, Emmett, I'm kind of impressed."

"Oh, really?"

"How many times have you played that?"

"I don't know. Maybe ten times." He shrugged. "But it's all right?"

"All right? Oh no, it's more than all right." He straightened up and offered Emmett a steely smile. "You see, I must have played it...oh, I've lost count, Emmett. You don't wanna know. I suppose it's part of me. What I mean is, I'm in no position to criticise, if you look at it that way. I can make a few constructive comments, of course."

"I'd find that helpful, Onslow."

"You would?"

"That's why I played it. To find out – where I'm going."

"Yeah, I see. Well, for a young man you have a good sense of the spirit of the music. That's encouraging. You're not just playing the printed notes. You read it, but you feel it too. At least, I think so."

"I certainly hope so, Onslow. I understand how important that is."

"Sure. One thing."

"Yes?"

"Be very careful about tempo. Yours tend to be a little – wayward. There's always room for interpretation, of course, but sometimes you can allow yourself to become too liberal, and then it starts to sound presumptuous, not to say irresponsible."

"Like Glenn Gould, sort of?"

"Ah, well, that's another story. Don't let's go there."

"Okay."

"But believe me, you have great promise. And make sure you listen to some benchmark recordings. Of Brahms One, I mean. Maybe Emanuel Ax. Or Curzon, if he's still in the listings, or there's Andsnes, his is a good one. So many in the catalogue. When I say listen, I mean listen, you understand? Listen. *Listen.*" He sighed. "Oh God. Enough."

"Onslow, can I say something?"

"Say anything you like."

"Onslow, you look tired today. Rather pale."

"Do I? Right. Reckon I might take a break – take a nap, even. I see there's a kind of a couch behind the drapes in the dressing room."

"Good idea, Onslow."

Emmett studied the old man's face. A few thin strands of his white hair adhered to his forehead, sealed there by a patina of perspiration. The whites of his eyes were tinted with a pinkish haze, and a creamy spittle had seeped into the corners of his lips. For all that he admired Onslow Ackerman's talent and achievements, he found himself feeling a kind of sympathy for him, an ageing virtuoso driven by circumstance to bring an illustrious international career to an end in a glorified village hall in the back of beyond, half a world away from home.

"Don't stare at me like that, young man, you're making me nervous."

"Am I? Sorry. It's just – you're sweating, Onslow."

"Ah, pay no attention. My body, it's like an old boiler, forever switching itself up and down, trying to work out how to keep up with the thermostat. I'm strong as a bear."

"If you say so."

"I do say so. Look, here's another thing."

"Onslow?"

"You can do me a favour."

"Just name it."

"I seem to have mislaid my wristwatch. Think I must have left it on the bedside table at my daughter's place. So could you knock on the door, either here or the dressing room, about fifteen minutes before I'm due to go on?"

"My pleasure, sir."

"You do that, and I'll step out and wait by the side curtain. Will you do that?"

"I'll do it, Onslow."

Emmett went in search of Jeremy Melhuish in case the manager had any last-minute tasks for him to attend to. People were massing at the entrance now and more packs of programmes needed to be brought from the store room and broken open. Tonight would be a sell-out. Emmett loitered in the foyer, greeting the regular patrons he knew, and shortly he set up an extra stand and occupied himself selling programmes. At Possett Hall he could always find something useful to do. Standing by an open doorway to the auditorium, he could hear the melodic rippling of two harps as the Delgado sisters from Portugal fine-tuned their instruments at the front of the stage. The orchestra, redundant for the first twenty minutes of the concert, would assemble towards the end of the interval, ready to join heroic forces with Onslow Ackerman.

Melhuish approached Emmett's stand, waving one hand vaguely in the air. "You might as well go in and sit down, if you want to," he said. "There's a front row seat or two going spare. Be prepared to shift if anyone comes for it."

"Yes, Mr Melhuish."

He remembered the Delgado sisters, for they had played here before. They were in their fifties, similar in appearance and bearing, though not twins, both pale-skinned and unaccountably swarthy, with muscular, hairy arms. Their gold-glinting harps were elegant under the lights, but the women behind them were unfortunately not an attractive sight. Emmett was, in any case, not moved by the sound of a harp, and as the sisters began to play, he found himself dry-mouthed in anticipation of the Olympian piano concerto that was to follow.

He gave perfunctory contribution to the dutiful applause greeting the Delgados' performance, and immediately left before the public could block his path to the exit. Melhuish, applauding wearily from the wings, asked him if he had seen Ackerman, and Emmett explained their arrangement for a cue call. He walked to the dressing room door, knocked and called Ackerman's name.

"Yeah, okay, I hear you." The voice sounded faint and gravelly. "Be out in five."

Emmett returned to his front row seat and read the tribute to Onslow Ackerman in the concert programme. The Bosendorfer, pushed to one side to make room for the harps, was heaved back into position by stage-hands in jeans. The orchestra filed in. The hall hummed with suppressed excitement as the audience swarmed back from the bar to resume their seats. Margot Runnicles, clutching her violin to her chest, stepped up to the piano and gave the orchestra an A against which to pitch their instruments. Looking to his left, Emmett saw Gordon Dakers' face peering from the shadows, anxiously surveying the scene. Several minutes passed. The orchestra fell silent. Some of the audience coughed expectantly. Emmett glanced at his watch. His mouth was dry again, but this time something other than the normal emotion assailed him.

This didn't seem right. It didn't feel right. Emmett felt his hands beginning to tremble. Dakers had vanished, and now Melhuish's face appeared behind the second violins, his mouth working mutely, seeking Emmett's attention. Emmett sprang from his seat and ran up the steps to the back of the stage.

"I thought you said you had an arrangement." Melhuish was grinding his teeth in apprehension.

"We did. I called him."

"And?"

"He said he was coming in five minutes."

"So where the hell is he?"

Dakers reappeared. "What's up? I can't go out without him."

In Row G of the stalls, Clyde Ackerman stood up, frowned and sat down again.

A frisson of confused concern rustled through the auditorium.

"Emmett, go and find him, for God's sake!" Melhuish snapped.

"I'm going."

Emmett strode to the dressing room and threw open the door. There was no sign of Ackerman. Next door, he entered the practice room, relieved and amazed to see the soloist sitting rigidly at the Steinway, both arms extended over the keyboard.

"Onslow. What are you doing? Everyone's waiting!"

Ackerman made no response and did not turn round.

"Onslow!"

Emmett rushed to the old man's side and grabbed his right arm. With this prop tugged free, Ackerman's body crashed forward, his head striking the music stand, sending the sheets flying to the floor.

"Onslow! Oh my God!"

John Stilwell burst into the room. "Jesus! What happened?"

"Don't know." Emmett lunged for the door. "I'll get Melhuish. Have to get an ambulance."

He ran down the corridor, Stilwell marching briskly behind him. Where the walkway turned towards the stage, they met Gordon Dakers and Clyde Ackerman staring, hollow-faced.

"You find him?" Clyde yelled.

247

Hannah Harding was standing behind her brother, one hand pressed to the side of her face. "What's going on here? Where's Onslow?"

"Ambulance!" Emmett gasped.

"What?" Dakers was screwing up his eyes in a confusion of annoyance and incredulity.

"Just do it! Get an ambulance!"

While Ackerman's son and daughter dashed to the practice room, Emmett and Stilwell left Melhuish to take charge. Gordon Dakers found a metal chair and sat down heavily, one hand supporting his head. At his back, the orchestra could be heard tuning up again, for want of anything better to do. A moment later, leader Margot Runnicles came out to find their conductor. As she bent over him, Dakers whispered in her ear.

"Go back and tell them to stop that noise," Stilwell told her.

"I've dialled 999." Melhuish stood wringing his hands.

"Can I suggest," Emmett said, "you wait at the front and bring them round by the stage door. We don't want greenjackets running through the public area."

"Okay, you're right." Melhuish gripped Emmett's shoulder. "Will you go?"

Emmett turned and hurried outside.

Dakers looked pale, running a forefinger round the inside of his collar. "Jeremy, I think you ought to say something to the audience."

"Me?"

"You're the hall manager."

"Okay. I'll say – I don't know. What shall I say?"

"Just apologise and tell them Ackerman is regrettably indisposed."

"Indisposed?"

"Yes, you know what 'indisposed' means. For Christ's sake don't say he's dead!"

"We don't know he's dead," Melhuish whined. "We're not doctors."

"Well, we'll know soon enough, Jeremy. Go on."

"Should I tell them to go home, do you think?"

"Hmm. We don't want a panic reaction."

"Panic? Why panic? It's not a bomb scare."

John Stilwell had been pacing the entrance hall and now he was back by the side curtain, his right arm dangling out of its sling. "I'll do it if you like," he said. "I'll speak to them."

"Well, somebody has to," Dakers said. "They've paid their money. They want to know what's happening."

"What's happening is, Onslow Ackerman is not about to play the Brahms First Piano Concerto," said Melhuish, testily.

"Then someone go out there and announce that," Dakers urged. "A variation on that theme."

Clyde returned. "Where's that ambulance?"

"On its way," Melhuish said. "Is your father breathing?"

"I don't think so."

Emmett walked back, beckoning to Clyde. "Can you see them in? They'll be here any minute. Take them round the side, it'll be quicker." He raised his hands to forestall any objection. "I want to talk to Mr Dakers and Mr Melhuish."

Clyde left them, brushing people aside as he lurched through the glass doors and into the car park. In the darkness, blue lights glimmered through the trees.

"What are we doing?" Emmett asked no-one in particular.

Melhuish scratched his head. "Not exactly sure. John's going to address the audience."

"And tell them what?"

The manager sighed. "I don't know, Emmett. Do you have any suggestions?"

"As a matter of fact, I do," Emmett said. "We have to go for damage limitation."

"What are you talking about, Emmett?"

"Mr Stilwell."

"Emmett?"

"Tell them not to leave. Tell them... tell them we're carrying on with the programme."

"Oh, right, I get it. We'll prop Ackerman up at the piano and put on the CD. Yeah, that'll do it. No-one'll know the difference."

An ambulance swerved into the car park. Clyde Ackerman met the crew. He told them to douse the flashing lights.

Emmett responded to Stilwell's sarcasm by turning to face Melhuish. Dakers had risen from the chair and was peering on to the stage, shaking his head.

"Mr Melhuish, would you let me help you?"

"In what way, Emmett?"

Emmett licked his lips and took a deep breath. "Mr Melhuish, as you know, I am studying the Brahms First at college. I have played it — after a fashion — with the college orchestra."

"I know that, Emmett."

"Please. Let me finish, Mr Melhuish."

Jeremy Melhuish blinked.

"I have spent some time today with Mr Ackerman, listening to him practise. He also let me play some extracts, which he quite approved of. He brought the piano score with him, although he wouldn't have needed it for the concert, and those pages are on the floor in the practice room. I can rescue them. Now, obviously I can't pretend to reproduce Onslow Ackerman's pianistic skills or his wonderful fluency, but if you'll let me, sir, I will try to salvage the situation, to some small degree, by playing the concerto in his absence. That is, I am prepared to, as it were, give it my best shot."

Dakers stared at Emmett as if he had never seen him before. Melhuish's face creased into a grin and then a stifled laugh. Stilwell eased his arm back into its sling and used his other hand to cover his eyes.

"Emmett, this is patently ridiculous," Melhuish said. "What does John tell the people, eh? Sorry we can't bring you the great Onslow Ackerman, but never mind, the tea boy has agreed to act as substitute."

"It's up to you," Emmett said, sighing. "I've made the offer. That's all I can do." He quickly scanned the faces grouped around him. "Unless anyone else fancies having a go. Or would you rather just send everyone home and give them their money back?"

250

Nobody spoke. Emmett averted his gaze, tugging at his ear. He had thrown them a lifeline. It was their decision whether they took it or not. Like the audience, whose patience was being tested to the limit and beyond, he could go home and try to forget the whole affair. *I can do this, Onslow. You know I can. Make them believe me. Or they'll chicken out of this and all we'll have is a disaster. I can turn this around. I can do it.*

Clyde looked in, breathing heavily, deathly pale. "We're going with him to the hospital. Apparently there's a very slight chance."

Stilwell was staring critically at Emmett. "You think you can do this, boy?"

"I know I can try."

Stilwell nodded. "We can't waste any more time. Some people have walked out already." He turned to Melhuish. "Jeremy, get this young man a tux or something, he can't appear in his pullover."

"John, John, this is absurd!"

"And your alternative proposal is?"

"Jesus Christ Almighty!"

"He won't help us, Jeremy. Get this man equipped – now. I'll pick up the music sheets, brief the orchestra and explain to the audience as best I can what we're going to do. Understood?"

"On your own head be it," Melhuish grumbled. "If you ask me, we're organising madness."

"There are precedents," Stilwell declared. "Previn in London, Carmina Burana, collapsing singer, student substitute. Remember?"

"Yes, and a different scenario, John. We're totally exposed here. But it's your call."

"Absolutely." Stilwell snapped his fingers. "Gordon, follow me on."

Dakers, perplexed, furrowed his brow. "Shouldn't I wait for the pianist? I'd normally trail him on."

"What's normal? Normal's gone. We need to get on with this or there'll be nobody to play to. Come on, you can help me with the announcement."

251

Melhuish sent Emmett to the dressing room, telling him to undress down to his underwear. Scattered, vaguely ironic applause drifted from the auditorium as Dakers and Stilwell confronted the audience. Shaking with a blend of shock and apprehension, Emmett sat on the upright chair, feeling chilled in his socks and underpants. A cup with a lick of cold coffee left in it stood on the desk, Ackerman's lip print drying on the rim. Emmett crossed to the wardrobe and pulled out the old man's jacket, holding it against his chest. Ridiculous. He was six foot-two and rake-thin, whereas Ackerman was some five inches shorter and quite stocky. If he went on dressed like that, the only saving grace would be a chorus of scarcely-smothered laughter.

The door burst open and Melhuish blundered in, holding out an armful of clothing. "Here, one of the stage-hands found these!"

"Where? Whose are they?" Emmett peered at the bundle suspiciously.

"I dunno. Doesn't matter. I think they'll just about fit. Put them on."

"I don't want to look stupid."

"You'll look pretty damned stupid if you go on in your boxers. Get dressed." He backed through the door, then glanced in again. "Oh, I know. Must be Dakers' spare suit. He's near your size. Go to it, Emmett."

It wasn't a bad fit; a little baggy around the shoulders, perhaps, and the trouser cuffs rode up and showed his socks, but that only mattered when he walked, and for the next fifty minutes he would be sitting down. He turned off the light, tugged at the tails of his jacket and strode purposefully on to the stage. Gordon Dakers was already on the rostrum, languidly flicking the pages of his score with the tip of his baton. As he walked into view past the violins, a somewhat condescending applause rippled from the shadowed audience, as though to inform him that they could not find it in themselves to muster the warmth of an unconditional greeting, but were cautiously prepared to acknowledge that a gesture had been made in their interest, whatever the outcome.

The sheet music was on the stand in front of him, the pages slightly buckled from its fall to the floor, and Emmett turned to the first page, relaxed his shoulders and, clutching the sides of the stool, shunted it away from the piano to make room for his long legs. He nervously tweaked the jacket's loose sleeves, ran a hand over his hair, glanced quickly at the audience and raised his head to meet the conductor's downward stare. Dakers, standing motionless, widened his eyes, and Emmett noted the interrogative gesture and responded with a single nod. Now the baton ascended, stabbed the air and, with a force that almost made him jump, the orchestra exploded into life, Jolyon Sando's immense drumbeats reverberating around the platform.

While the orchestral introduction unfolded, Emmett looked to his right and picked out the empty stalls seats which Ackerman's son and daughter would have occupied. There were other vacant seats, too, abandoned by patrons who had, not unreasonably, run out of patience as the clock ticked on. Emmett closed his eyes and flexed his fingers over the keys. This was the point of no return.

You and me, we can do this, Onslow. Inspire me before they fire me. I will have your resolve but not your greatness. Remember, I'm doing this for you. God bless you, Onslow.